Christina Henry

ALICE

CHRISTINA HENRY

TITAN
BOOKS

Christina Henry

Praise for *Alice*

"Hugely creepy and brilliantly inventive."

Heat

"Reads like a Jacobean revenge drama crossed with a slasher movie... A deeply unsettling vision."

The Guardian

"Careful, this white rabbit will lead you on a psychotic journey through the bowels of magic and madness. I, for one, thoroughly enjoyed the ride."

Brom, author of *Slewfoot*

"I loved falling down the rabbit hole with this dark, gritty tale. A unique spin on a classic and one wild ride!"

Gena Showalter, *New York Times* bestselling author of *Alice in Zombieland*

"If you're looking for a book that will make you feel like you were just on a bender with the Blue Caterpillar, I highly recommend *Alice*."

R. S. Belcher, author of *The Shotgun Arcana*

"A dark and deeply disturbing revisit of *Alice's Adventures in Wonderland*. Who wouldn't like it?"

Kirkus Reviews

Also available from Christina Henry and Titan Books

LOST BOY

THE MERMAID

THE GIRL IN RED

THE GHOST TREE

NEAR THE BONE

HORSEMAN

GOOD GIRLS DON'T DIE

THE HOUSE THAT HORROR BUILT

THE CHRONICLES OF ALICE

RED QUEEN

LOOKING GLASS

ALICE

Christina Henry

TITAN BOOKS

Alice
Print edition ISBN: 9781785653308
E-book edition ISBN: 9781785653315
Signed edition ISBN: 9781803366227

Published by Titan Books
A division of Titan Publishing Group Ltd
144 Southwark Street, London SE1 0UP

This hardback edition: September 2024
10 9 8 7 6 5 4 3 2 1

This book is a work of fiction. Any references to historical events, real people, or real places are used fictitiously. Other names, characters, places, and events are products of the author's imagination, and any resemblance to actual events or places or persons, living or dead, is entirely coincidental.

Copyright © 2016 by Tina Raffaele. All rights reserved.

This edition published by arrangement with Ace, an imprint of Penguin, a division of Penguin Random House LLC, in 2016.

No part of this publication may be reproduced, stored in a retrieval system, or transmitted, in any form or by any means without the prior written permission of the publisher, nor be otherwise circulated in any form of binding or cover other than that in which it is published and without a similar condition being imposed on the subsequent purchaser.

A CIP catalogue record for this title is available from the British Library.

Printed and bound in Great Britain by CPI Group (UK) Ltd, Croydon, CR0 4YY

For Danielle Stockley,
because you believed in Maddy and Alice and me

ALICE

If she moved her head all the way up against the wall and tilted it to the left she could just see the edge of the moon through the bars. Just a silver sliver, almost close enough to eat. A sliver of cheese, a sliver of cake, a cup of tea to be polite. Someone had given her a cup of tea once, someone with blue-green eyes and long ears. Funny how she couldn't remember his face, though. All that part was hazy, her memory of him wrapped in smoke but for the eyes and ears. And the ears were long and furry.

When they found her all she would say was, "The Rabbit. The Rabbit. The Rabbit." Over and over. When she acted like that they said she was mad. Alice knew she wasn't mad. Maybe. Not deep down. But the powders they gave her made the world all muzzy and sideways and sometimes she *felt* mad.

Everything had happened just as she said, when she could say something besides "Rabbit." She and Dor went into the Old City for Dor's birthday. Sixteenth birthday. Sixteen candles on your cake, a sliver of cake and a cup of tea for you, my dear. They both went in, but only Alice came out. Two weeks later came Alice, covered in blood, babbling about tea and a rabbit, wearing a dress that wasn't hers. Red running down the insides of her legs and blue marks on her thighs where fingers had been.

Her hand went without thought to her left cheek, touched the long thick scar that followed the line of bone from her hairline to the top of her lip. Her face had been flayed open when they found her, and she couldn't say how or why. It had been open for a long while, the blood oozing from it gone black and brackish, the skin around it tattered at the edges. The doctors told her parents they had done their best, but she would never be beautiful again.

Her sister said it was her own fault. If she had stayed out of the Old City as she was supposed to, this never would have happened. There was a reason why they lived in the New City, the ring of shiny new buildings that kept the Old City at bay. The Old City wasn't for people like them. It was for the filth you threw away. All children were warned about the dangers of straying to the Old City. Alice didn't belong there.

The hospital where Alice had lived for the last ten years was in the Old City, so her sister was wrong. Alice did belong there.

Sometimes her parents came to visit, doing their duty; their noses wrinkled like she was something that smelled bad, even though the attendants always dragged her out and gave her a bath first. She hated the baths. They were icy cold and rough with scrubbing, and she was never permitted to clean herself. If she struggled or cried out they would hit her with the bath brush or pinch hard enough to leave a mark, always somewhere that couldn't be seen, the side of her breast or the soft part of her belly, with a promise of "more where that came from" unless she behaved.

Her parents didn't visit so much anymore. Alice couldn't really remember the last time, but she knew it had been a long time. The days all ran together in her room, no books to read, no things to do. Hatcher said she should exercise so she would be fit when she got out, but somewhere in her heart Alice knew she would never get out. She was a broken thing, and the New City did not like broken things. They liked the new and the whole. Alice hardly recalled when she was new and whole. That girl seemed like someone else she'd known once, long ago and far away.

"Alice?" A voice through the mouse hole.

Many years before, a mouse had gotten into the wall and chewed through the batting between her cell and Hatcher's. Alice didn't know what had happened to the mouse. Probably got caught in a trap in the kitchens, or went out on the riverside and drowned. But the mouse had led her to Hatcher, a rough voice coming through the wall. She had really thought she'd gone round the bend at first, hearing voices coming from nowhere.

"Hey, you," the voice had said.

She'd looked around wildly, afraid, and scuttled into a corner on the far side of the window, opposite the door.

"Hey, you. Down here," the voice said.

Alice resolutely put her fingers in her ears. Everyone knew hearing voices was a sign of madness, and she'd promised herself she would not be mad no matter what they said, no matter how she felt. After several moments of happy silence she released her fingers and looked around the room in relief.

A great sigh exhaled from the walls. "The mouse hole, you nit."

Alice stared in alarm at the small opening in the corner opposite. Somehow a talking mouse was worse than voices in her head. If mice were talking, then there really were men with blue-green eyes and long furry ears. And while she didn't remember his face, she did remember she'd been afraid. She stared at the mouse hole like something horrible might suddenly emerge from it, like the Rabbit might unfold himself from that space and finish whatever he had started.

Another sigh, this one shorter and much more impatient. "You're not hearing bloody voices and a mouse is not speaking to you. I'm in the room next to yours and I can see you through the hole. You're not crazy and there's no magic, so will you please come here and speak with me before I go madder than I already have?"

"If you're not in my head and you're not magic, then how do you know what I'm thinking?" Alice asked, her voice suspicious. She was beginning to wonder whether this wasn't some trick of the doctors, some way to draw her into a trap.

The attendants gave her a powder with her breakfast and dinner, to "keep her calm," they said. But she knew that those powders still allowed her some freedom to be Alice, to think and dream and try to remember the lost bits of her life. When they took her out of her room for a bath or a visit, she sometimes saw other patients, people standing still with dead eyes and drool on their chins, people who were alive and didn't know it. Those people were "difficult to deal with." They got injections instead of powders. Alice didn't want injections, so she wasn't going to say or do anything that would alarm the doctors. Doctors who might be trying to trick her with voices in the wall.

"I know what you're thinking, because that's what I'd be thinking if I were you," the voice said. "We're in the loony bin, aren't we? Now, come over and have a look through the hole and you'll see."

She stood cautiously, still unsure it was not a trick, whether of her mind or the doctors. She crossed under the window and crouched by the mouse hole.

"All I can see are your knees," the voice complained. "Come all the way down, won't you?"

Alice lowered to her stomach, keeping her head well away from the opening. She had a vague fear that a needle might flash through the hole and plunge into her eye.

Once her cheek was on the ground she could see through the small, tight opening. On the other side was an iron grey eye and part of a nose. There was a bulge just where the rest of the nose disappeared from view, like it might have been broken once. It didn't look like any doctor she knew, but Alice wasn't taking any chances. "Let me see your whole face," she said.

"Good," the grey eye said. "You're thinking. That's good. Not just a pretty face, then."

Alice's hand moved automatically to cover her scar; then she remembered she was lying on that side of her face and he couldn't really see it anyway. Let him think she was pretty if he wanted. It would be nice to be pretty to someone even with her fair hair all snarled and nothing to wear but a woolen shift. She heard the *swish-swish* of wool on batting as the grey eye moved away from the hole and became two grey eyes, a long broken nose and a bushy black beard with flecks of white in it.

"All right, then?" the voice asked. "I'm Hatcher."

And that was how they met. Hatcher was ten years older than Alice, and nobody ever came to see him.

"Why are you here?" she asked one day, long after they were friends, or at least friends who never really saw each other.

"I killed a lot of people with an axe," he said. "That's how I got my name. Hatcher."

"What was your name before?" Alice asked. She was surprisingly undisturbed by the knowledge that her new friend was an axe murderer. It seemed unrelated to who he was now, the rough voice and grey eyes through the hole in the wall.

"I don't remember," he said. "I don't remember anything from before, really. They found me with a bloodied axe in my hand and five people dead around me all slashed to pieces. I tried to do the same for the police when they came for me, so I must have killed those people."

"Why *did* you do it?"

"Don't remember," he said, and his voice changed a little, became hard. "It's like there's this haze over my eyes, black smoke filling everything up. I remember the weight of the axe in my hand, and the hot blood on my face, in my mouth. I remember the sound of the blade in soft flesh."

"I remember that too," Alice said, although she didn't know why she said that. For a moment it had been true, though. She could hear the sound of a knife piercing skin, that sliding slicing noise, and someone screaming.

"Did you kill a lot of people too?" Hatcher asked.

"I don't know," Alice said. "I might have."

"It's all right if you did," Hatcher said. "I would understand."

"I really don't know," Alice said. "I remember before and I remember after, but that fortnight is gone, save for a few flashes."

"The man with the long ears."

"Yes," Alice said. The man who hunted her, faceless, through her nightmares.

"When we get out we'll find him, and then you'll know what happened to you," Hatcher said.

That had been eight years before, and they were both still there, rooms side by side in a hospital that had no intention of ever letting them go.

"Alice?" Hatcher said again. "I can't sleep."

She blinked away the memory, brought on by the moon and the sound of his voice.

"I can't sleep either, Hatch," she said, crawling along the floor to the mouse hole. It was much darker down here. There was no light in their rooms save that of the silver moon through the bars, and the occasional passage of a lamp by the attendant walking the halls. She could not see the color of his eyes, only the wet gleam of them.

"The Jabberwock's awake, Alice," Hatcher said.

It was then she noticed his voice was thin and reedy. Hatcher wasn't often afraid. Mostly he seemed strong, almost relentlessly so. All day long she heard him in his room, grunting with effort as he went through his exercises. When the attendants came to take Hatcher to his bath, there was always a lot of noise, punching and kicking and yelling. More than once Alice heard the crunch of bone, the angry curse of an attendant.

She asked once how come he didn't get injections like all the other troublemakers. He'd grinned, his grey eyes crinkling at the corners, and said the injection had made him wild, wilder than before, so after that they left him alone. He didn't even get powders in his food.

Hatcher was never scared, except when he talked about the Jabberwock.

"There's no Jabberwock, Hatch," Alice said, her voice low and soothing. She'd heard tales of the monster before. Not often, although lately it seemed to be on his mind more.

"I know you don't believe in him. But he's here, Alice. They keep him downstairs, in the basement. And when he's awake I can feel him," Hatcher said.

There was a pleading note under the fear, and Alice relented. After all, she believed in a man with rabbit ears, and Hatcher accepted that without question.

"What can you feel?" she asked.

"I feel the night crawling up all around, blotting out the moon. I feel blood running down the walls, rivers of it in the streets below. And I feel his teeth closing around me. That's what he'll do, Alice, if he's ever set free. He's been imprisoned here a long time, longer than you or me."

"How could anyone trap such a beast?" Alice wondered aloud.

Hatcher shifted restlessly on the floor. She could hear him moving around. "I don't know for sure," he said, and his voice was quieter now, so that she had to strain to hear him. "I think a Magician must have done it."

"A Magician?" Alice asked. This was more far-fetched that anything Hatcher had said before. "All the Magicians are gone. They were driven out or killed centuries ago, during the Purge. This place is not that old. How could a Magician have captured the Jabberwock and imprisoned it here?"

"Only a Magician would have the skill," Hatcher insisted. "No ordinary man would survive the encounter."

Alice was willing to indulge his fantasy of a monster in the basement, but she couldn't countenance this myth about a Magician. It didn't seem wise to argue, though. Hatcher took no powders and had no injections, and sometimes he could get agitated. If he got agitated he might howl for hours, or beat his hands against the wall until they were bloody despite the padding.

So she said nothing, only listened to his shallow breath, and the cries of the other inmates echoing through the building.

"I wish I could hold your hand," Hatcher said. "I've never seen you altogether, you know. Just bits through the hole. I try to put all the bits together in my head so I can see all of you, but it doesn't look quite right."

"In my head you're just grey eyes and a beard," Alice said.

Hatcher laughed softly, but there was no mirth in it. "Like the Rabbit, just eyes and fur. What would have happened if we met on the street, Alice? Would we have said hello?"

She hesitated for a moment. She didn't want to hurt his feelings, but neither did she want to lie. Her parents lied. They said things like, "You're looking well," and, "We're sure you'll be home soon"—things Alice knew were not true.

"Alice?" Hatcher asked again, and brought her back to him.

"I don't know if we would have seen each other to say hello," she said carefully. "I lived in the New City, and I think . . . You seem like you were from the Old City."

"Well, la-di-da," Hatcher said, and his voice was hard. "Fancy girl wouldn't soil her dainty hem in the Old City. Except you did. You got good and soiled. And now you're here, just like me."

His words were like knotted fists to her gut, and all the breath seemed to leave her for a moment. But they were true words, and she would not pretend otherwise. The truth was all she had left. The truth, and Hatcher.

"Yes," she said. "We are both here."

There was a long silence between them. Alice waited in the darkness, the moonlight shifting on the floor. Hatcher seemed to be walking the knife's edge tonight, and she would not be the one to knock him off.

"I am sorry, Alice," he said finally, and he sounded more like the Hatch she knew.

"Don't—" she started, but he cut her off.

"I should not say such things," he said. "You're my only light, Alice. Without you I would have succumbed to this place long ago. But the Jabberwock is awake, and he makes me think of things I should not."

"The sound of a blade in flesh," she said, echoing the memory of his words.

"And warm blood on my hands," Hatcher said. "I feel most like myself when I think those thoughts. As if that is who I really am."

"At least you have some idea," Alice said. "I never had the chance to find out. I lost my way first."

She heard him shifting again on the floor.

"I feel like I've got bugs inside my skin," he said. "Sing me a song."

"I don't know any songs," she said, surprised by this request.

"Yes, you do," he said. "You sing it all day long, and when you're not singing it you're humming. Something about a butterfly."

"A butterfly?" she asked, but as soon as she said this, it came back to her, and she heard her mother's voice in her head. This sound was so painful, piercing her heart, this remembrance of love that was lost to her forever. She began to sing aloud, to cover the memory with her own voice.

Sleep little butterfly
Sleep little butterfly
Now the day has gone

Sleep little butterfly
Sleep little butterfly
Soon the morning will come
Close your eyes and let the night go 'round you
He'll keep you safe and warm
Sleep little butterfly
Sleep little butterfly
Soon the morning will come.

Her voice trailed off, her throat full of love and loss and pain. Hatcher said nothing, but she heard his breath go deep and even, and she let her eyes fall shut. She matched her breath to his, and it was almost like holding his hand as the night closed in.

Alice dreamed of blood. Blood on her hands and under her feet, blood in her mouth and pouring from her eyes. The room was filled with it. Outside the door Hatcher stood hand in hand with something dark and hideous, a thing crafted of shadow with flashing silver teeth.

"Don't take him from me," she said, or tried to say, but she could not speak through the blood in her mouth, choking her. Her eyes were covered with smoke then, and she couldn't see Hatch or the monster anymore. Heat enfolded her body, and then there was nothing but fire.

Fire. Fire.

"Alice, wake up! The hospital is on fire."

Alice opened her eyes. Hatcher's grey one was pressed to the mouse hole, and it was wild with fear and anticipation.

"At last!" he said. "Stay low, away from the smoke, and get near the door but not in front of it."

Alice blinked as he disappeared. The dream still clung to her brain, and her mouth was dry. Her shift clung to her body, and her face was wet with sweat. The odor of smoke finally permeated her nostrils and her fuzzy head, and there was another smell too—like cooking meat. She didn't want to think what that might be.

Alice turned so she was flat on her back, and saw a thick blanket of smoke just a few inches from her face. The heat beneath made the floor an agony to lie upon, but there was no way to escape it.

The sounds filtered in then. The crack of flame, of heavy objects crashing to the ground. Horrible, horrible screams. And close by, the repeated grunts and pounding of someone slamming his body into the wall. Hatch was trying to break the door down in his room.

The noise was terrible. Alice did not think it was possible. The walls might be soft, but the doors were iron. He would kill himself.

"Hatcher, no!" she cried, but he could not hear her.

There was a sound of something crunching, but Hatcher did not cry out, and then there was no more noise.

"Hatcher," she said, and her voice was soft and sad. Two tears leaked from the corner of each eye. There was no point in getting up then, if Hatcher was gone. The smoke and the noise told Alice that the fire was well under way. The attendants and the doctors would not bother to free the patients, especially when most families would be thrilled to be free of the burden of their mad relatives. So they would all burn.

Alice found she was not as distressed about this as she ought to be. Perhaps it was the powder in last night's dinner, or the smoke that filled her lungs in place of air. She felt very calm. She would just lie there and wait until the fire came.

Her eyes closed again, and she drifted away, away to a place she had never been in real life, a silver lake tucked in a green valley, wildflowers dotting the shore. There was no smell of medicine there, or harsh burning soap. There was no smoke and no pain, no heartache and no blood. It was the place she always went, the place where her mind hid when the doctors asked questions she did not want to answer, or her parents sighed in disappointment.

Something grabbed her around the shoulders, and her eyes flew open in shock. It had been years since anyone touched her except to drag her to the bath. Hatcher's face was close to hers, twisted in anger, and blood ran from a cut on the side of his head.

"I told you to get near the door, you silly nit," he said, dragging her up to sitting and then immediately pushing her down to her belly.

"Follow me," he said, crawling toward the door.

The open door.

She followed automatically, keeping his filthy bare heels in sight. She wanted to ask how he had gotten out, how he wasn't battered and dead. But he was moving along with surprising quickness into the hall. He paused after a few moments so she could catch up to him. There was no one except the two of them, and the frantic pounding of other patients still trapped in their boxes.

It was then she noticed that his right arm hung at an odd angle and he was using only his left to pull his body along. "Hatch, what happened?" she asked. She was out of breath from just that short period of exertion.

"It came out when I broke the doorframe," he said. "I'll fix it later. We have to go. The floor is getting hotter, and he's almost out."

"Who?" Alice asked.

He started along again. "The Jabberwock."

"Hatch," she said, trying to keep up with him. Her lungs and throat were burning. "We're going the wrong way. The stairs are behind us."

"The stairs are on fire," Hatch said. "I've already checked. We've got to go out this way."

"But, Hatch," Alice said, shaking her head from side to side to clear it. The smoke was getting to her. "We're on the third floor."

"We'll go out the back to the river. Just keep up, Alice."

"The river?" she said, and a faint alarm sounded in her head. There was something about the river, but she couldn't recall exactly what it was.

Just then they passed the door of a patient who was repeatedly throwing himself against the iron and screaming. The cloud of smoke above them blocked the small viewing window, so Alice was fairly certain the man could not see them escaping. She felt a tinge of guilt all the same as they went by.

"What about the others?" Alice asked. "Shouldn't we let them out?"

"There is no time," Hatcher said. "And they would only be millstones in any case. They've no sense. We'd have to lead them from here like children. And then what? Would we take them with us? No, Alice, it's best to leave them as they are. We must get away before he's free."

It was a cold thing he said, but true. Not the bit about the Jabberwock getting free, but the other part. She and Hatcher would not be able to safely lead the others to freedom without endangering their own lives.

Hatcher reached the end of the hallway before Alice did. He came to his knees, and she noticed he held a small ring of keys in his left hand.

"Where did you get those?" she asked.

"From the attendant at the top of the stairs. How do you think I opened your door?" he asked as he methodically fitted first one key, then another, then another.

"There was nobody in the corridor when we came out," she said.

"I took his keys and threw him down the stairs. That's how I knew the steps were on fire," he said.

The fifth key clicked, and Hatcher pushed the door open, waving her inside the room.

A cloud of smoke followed them in before Hatcher was able to close the door behind them, but it dissipated quickly as the far window was open. The heavy, seething air of the City, hardly fresh, poured into the room. Still, it had been years since Alice had smelled anything but the rank asylum—unwashed bodies, laudanum, chloroform, vomit and blood and burning soap over it all. By contrast the soot and refuse outside seemed like a burst of clean country breeze.

Suddenly a head appeared in the window from outside. It was one of the attendants, a ginger-haired man with only half a nose. His eyes widened when he saw Hatcher and Alice in the room, and he started to climb back inside.

Before the man could get any further than throwing one leg over the sill, Hatcher was upon him. He punched the man in the face hard with his left hand, twice, three times. Then he kicked the man in the side so hard Alice heard ribs break. Finally he pushed the now-unconscious attendant out the window, looking out after the falling man to follow his progress to the river below.

He nodded in satisfaction before turning back to Alice. "I was the one who bit half his nose off. He was coming back to make sure we couldn't get out—do you see? He would never have let us leave."

Alice nodded. She did see. The smoke must have gone up in her brain because everything seemed soft at the edges.

"There's a ledge out here," Hatcher said.

He went to the wall next to the window, grabbed his right wrist with his left hand, pushed his hanging right arm against the wall and did some kind of maneuver while Alice watched. When he turned back to her, his right arm appeared normal again. He flexed his fingers as if to ensure they were still functional. Throughout all of this he never made a sound, not even a hint that the process was painful, though Alice was certain it must have been. He held his hand out so she could join him by the window.

She approached him, and gasped in shock when his hand closed around hers. It seemed like an electric current ran from their joined hands up into her heart, which hammered in her chest. His grey eyes sparked, and he squeezed her hand tighter for a moment. When you are in an asylum, no one ever touches you in kindness, and Alice knew the shock was as great for him.

He said nothing as he released her. He climbed through the window and onto the ledge, and Alice followed him, because that was what she was supposed to do.

She swung her left leg over the sill. Her shift rode up, exposing her skin to the morning chill, and she shivered. She supposed it wasn't so terribly cold out, but after the furnace of the burning hospital, the outdoors seemed frigid.

Alice ducked her head under the sash and saw the ledge Hatcher wanted her to reach. Below it, too far below for comfort, was the river, grey and putrid. Now that she saw it she remembered what she had forgotten before.

Hatcher moved on the ledge behind her, and his hands were at her waist, guiding her out until they stood side by side, their backs pasted against the brick exterior of the hospital. The ledge was barely wide enough to admit the length of Alice's feet. Hatcher's toes curled around the edge as if that grip could save him from falling.

His expression was fierce and exultant. "We're outside, Alice. We're *out*."

"Yes," she said, and her thrill at this prospect was much tempered by the sight of the river. Now that she was away from the smoke, her mind was clearer, and this plan seemed riskier than trying to climb down a set of burning stairs. The stench of the water reached her then, and she gagged.

Hatcher grabbed her hand to keep her from stumbling forward into the empty air. "We jump into the river," he said, "and swim across to the opposite bank. We can disappear into the Old City after that. No one will look for us in there. They will think we're dead."

"Yes," she agreed again. "But we're not supposed to go into the river. It will kill us. All the factories dump their waste there. I remember Father speaking of it. He said it was an outrage."

"Neither can we stay here," Hatcher said. "If the fire does not consume us, then they will catch us in their nets and put us back in our cages. I cannot go back, Alice. I cannot spend the remainder of my life as a moth beating its wings against a jar. I would rather perish in the mouth of the Jabberwock than that."

Alice saw the truth of this, and felt it in her heart as well. She did not want to go back inside the box they had made for her. But the river was so far below, churning with poison. What if their skin was seared from their bodies? What if they swallowed the river water and died writhing on the shore as the foul substance coursed in their blood?

As these thoughts occurred, a burst of flame caused a nearby window to explode outward, startling a huddle of soot-coated pigeons that had taken foolish refuge on the same ledge Alice and Hatcher perched on. The birds took flight, squawking in protest, and Alice looked at Hatcher, knowing he saw the fear in her eyes.

"Now we must fly," he said. "Trust me."

She did. She always had, though she didn't know why. He squeezed her hand, and the next thing Alice knew she was falling, falling away into a rabbit's hole.

"Don't let go," Hatcher shouted just before they hit the water.

His grip on her fingers tightened painfully, and she cried out, but he didn't let go. Which was a very good thing, because as soon as the horrible muck coated her head, she reflexively loosed her hold, and if Hatcher hadn't been holding her that way, she would have drowned.

He yanked her, coughing and gagging, to the surface, scooped an arm under her ribs and began paddling toward the shore. "Kick your feet."

She fluttered her ankles weakly in the water. It felt thick and strange, with none of the fluid slipperiness water was supposed to possess. It moved sluggishly, the current hardly enough to push them a few inches off course. A noxious vapor rose from the surface, making her eyes and nose burn.

Because of the way Hatcher held her, she couldn't see his face or the opposite shore that they approached. His breath was smooth and even, like he was unaffected by the miasma floating above the surface of the river. He pulled them both along with smooth, sure strokes as Alice floundered in the water, trying not to cause them both to go under.

She saw the asylum burning behind them, as tongues of flame emerged from newly opened windows. The distance and roar of the fire drowned out the sound of the inmates screaming. There were people running around the sides of the building, trying to stop the spread to the adjacent structures. She had never given much thought to the places around the hospital before.

On one side was a long, low building crouched against the bank of the river like a squat turtle. That must have been on the side that Alice's room had been; else she wouldn't have been able to see the moon. The edifice on the opposite side was huge, much bigger than the hospital, and the smoke belching from its chimneys seemed as thick and dangerous as that pouring from her former home.

"Put your feet down," Hatcher said suddenly, and Alice realized he was walking now, not swimming.

Her toes sank into the muck, and the water was still up to her neck, but they were nearly there. A small knot of people was gathered a little ways down the bank on a jetty, pointing and exclaiming over the collapsing asylum.

"I see them," Hatcher said in a low voice. "Over here."

He guided her toward a place where the shadows lay thick despite the rising sun, away from the flickering exposure of the gas lamps set at intervals to alleviate the fog from the river and the factories. Alice fell to her hands and knees just out of the water, taking great gasps of air. Even a few feet from the river, the air was noticeably cleaner, though hardly what one would call "clean," she thought.

Everywhere was the stench of the water, the reek of smoke and flame, the chemical burn of factory exhaust. Underneath it all was the smell of the morning's cooking coming from the warren of flats just before them.

Hatcher had done much more than Alice to get them out of the burning hospital and through the disgusting river, yet he had not collapsed like she had when they emerged from the water. He stood beside her, still and calm. Alice rolled to her seat and looked up at him. He stared, transfixed, at the fiery structure across the water. He stood so still that she began to worry, and she struggled to her feet.

"Hatcher?" she asked, and touched his arm.

His hair and clothes were steaming now that they were onshore, and he was coated in the filth they had just crossed. His grey eyes glowed in the reflection of the fire, like the coals of hell, and when he turned those eyes on her she felt, for the first time, a little afraid of him. This was not Hatch, her constant companion through the mouse hole. Nor was this the man who had methodically rescued her from a burning building. This was Hatcher, the murderer with the axe, the man who had been found covered in blood and surrounded by bodies.

But he would never hurt you, Alice told herself. *He's still Hatch, somewhere in there. He's just lost himself for a moment.*

She put her hands on his shoulders, tentatively, and said his name again, for he stared at her but did not seem to see. Then his hands were at her wrists, his grip bruising the thin skin, and his iron eyes were wild.

"He's out, he's out, he's out," he chanted. "Now the world will break and burn and bleed . . . Everyone will bleed."

"The Jabberwock?" Alice said.

"His mouth will open wide and we will all fall in, fall in and be devoured," Hatcher said. "We must get away, away before he finds me. He knows I can hear him. He knows that I know what evil he will do."

Suddenly there was a tremendous noise from the asylum, a sound like the very heart of the building crashing in on itself. Alice and Hatcher turned to watch, and all the walls collapsed like a melting sand castle. There seemed to be nothing but fire now, and the fire shot impossibly upward into the sky, well past the point where there was anything to burn. It filled the horizon, the wings of a monster outstretched.

Behind the flame was a darkness, a gigantic shadow that spread, as if something that was trapped was now free, reaching its arms toward the sun.

"Is that . . . him?" Alice asked. She'd never believed in the Jabberwock, not really. And perhaps there was no shadow at all. She was exhausted, and had spent some time breathing smoke and poison. Her brain might tell her there was a shadow when in fact there was none. That was the trouble with not being right in the head. You couldn't always tell if your eyes were telling the truth.

Hatcher did not reply to her question. He stared for a moment at the tower of flame, and then grabbed Alice's right wrist, tugging her up the bank. The mud inhibited fast progress, but they finally managed to clamber onto the narrow cobbled path that ran around and between the warrens of tilting structures stacked crazily against one another.

The Old City seemed to have no beginning and no end, a circling maze of stairways and narrow alleys connecting buildings that had been patched and rebuilt on top of crumbling ruins for centuries. There was nothing gleaming and new there, not even the children, who seemed to be birthed with haunted eyes.

Hatcher ducked into the nearest alley, pulling Alice after him. The rough stones scraped her bare feet, but she understood the need to disappear quickly. Aside from the question of the Jabberwock, Alice had recognized the distinctive brass-buttoned gleam of a copper's uniform. Never mind if the asylum was naught but a cinder now. If they were caught out in their hospital whites, the police would drag them away. And Alice had a feeling Hatcher would not go quietly.

So they dipped and darted between the girls with their customers pressed up against the alley walls, or old men gathered in clusters around a shell game or a cockfight.

Hatcher led them deeper into the Old City, to a place where the rising sun was blocked by the closeness of the buildings and the air was blanketed in fog from the factories. Mist rose from the cobblestones, hiding approaching figures until they were nearly upon you.

Which was how the men surrounded them.

Hatcher paused for a moment, seeing Alice out of breath and suffering. He did not pat or comfort her, but waited. In that moment that they were still, an enormous ogre loomed out of the darkness and swung a club at Hatcher. Alice opened her mouth to scream, but a filthy hand covered it and another hand latched on her breast, squeezing it so hard tears sprang to her eyes.

"What have we here?" a rough voice cooed in her ear. "A little lost lamb?"

She kicked out, tried to slip out of his clutch as Hatcher and the ogre—whom she now saw was a man, the largest man she had ever seen—disappeared into the fog. Her struggles were useless against her captor's strength as he dragged her away.

His free hand moved from her breast to the hem of her shift, pulling it to her waist, his fingers on her thighs, and she went wild then, biting down on the hand that covered her mouth because she remembered—remembered a man over her in the flickering light, pushing between her legs, and it hurt, she screamed because it hurt, but he kept at it until she bled.

The man who held her now swore as he felt her teeth but he did not let go. "Little hellion," he snarled, and slammed her forehead against the brick wall.

She went limp and dazed then for a moment, and something wet and sticky covered her eyes. Then she was on the ground on her belly, her bare thighs scraping against the stones, and his hands were on her bottom, pulling her legs apart.

Just go away, she thought. *You're not here; you're in a green field in a valley, and the sun is shining down, and here comes someone smiling at you, someone who loves you.*

Then the hands on her were gone and she heard the sound of flesh meeting flesh. She rolled to one side, her shift still up around her waist, and wiped the stickiness from her eyes.

Hatcher was pounding her attacker repeatedly with his fists. He had pushed the man's back against the wall and was methodically reducing the man's face to an unrecognizable blob of jelly. After several moments, Hatcher released the man, who fell limp to the ground. He did not appear to be breathing.

Hatcher turned to Alice, his chest heaving. He was covered in blood, his hands and his chest and his face. His eyes went from the cut on her head to her bare waist, and lingered there for a moment. Then he said, "Cover yourself," and turned away to search the man's pockets.

Alice pulled the shift down to her knees again and used the wall to help her stand. She leaned there for a moment and her body began to shake all over. When Hatcher turned back, her teeth were chattering. He held a small pouch in one hand.

"Full of gold," he said, nudging the limp body with his toe. "Probably a slave trader. He would have used you and then sold you."

"I th-th-think I w-w-was sold before," she said. She had a memory of money changing hands, of seeing a smaller hand being filled with gold from a larger one.

"By the man with the long ears, or to him?" Hatcher asked.

She shook her head. There had only been that flash of terror, of memory best forgotten. There had been a man, but she couldn't remember his face. Then her mind reasserted itself, keeping her safe.

He paused in front of her, a savage splattered with the blood of her attacker, and there was something about his face that was oddly vulnerable.

"May I . . . ?" he asked, and he mimed putting his arm around her shoulder.

Everything inside her clenched and cried *no*. Then the moment passed, and she remembered how he had stared at her bare legs but turned away instead of falling on her like a ravening wolf. She nodded, and saw relief on his face.

His arm went around and pulled her tight to his body for a moment, so she could feel the coiled strength in him. Then he loosened enough so she could walk, but did not let go.

They returned to the place where the ogre had attacked. Alice saw the body of the larger man there. He still breathed shallowly through the broken mess where his teeth used to be. Nearby on the ground was the club he had used on Hatcher. It was actually just a thick rod of wood with a slightly oversized end. It was broken in two pieces.

"We must get inside somewhere," Hatcher said.

"Where can we go that's safe?" Alice asked. "Does this place seem familiar to you?"

"It does," he admitted. "Though I don't know why. From the moment we stepped inside the Old City, my feet have been leading us someplace."

"Someplace safe?" she asked. The cold was in her bones now, making her tremble all over despite the warmth of Hatcher holding her close. She was hungry and tired and more scared than she could ever remember being. For a brief moment she longed for the certainty of the hospital, the security of four walls around her.

"I don't know," he said. "It's been many years since I've been here. Some places look the same. More the same than you'd think. And others seem much different, though I can't put my finger on why."

"I don't think your memory is as gone as you think it is," Alice said. "You remember things like the time of Magicians. And that men like that sell girls like me. And you know the City. You've only forgotten who you are."

"No," Hatcher said. "I know who I am now. I've forgotten who I was before. Probably for the best. You might not like who I was then. I might not either."

Alice remembered who she was before. She just couldn't recall what had happened to that girl to make her this girl. And given the flashes she'd just seen, that was probably for the best. Hatcher was right. Maybe not remembering was better.

She shook under his arm. He rubbed his shoulder with his hand, fruitlessly trying to impart heat.

"I can't get warm," she said.

"We're nearly there."

"Nearly where?"

"I don't know. It's where my feet are leading us. It's someplace safe."

Alice noticed they'd emerged from the maze of alleys into a thoroughfare. It wasn't packed, but there were plenty of people going about their morning's business. Women with their heads wrapped in scarves against the chill, carrying baskets of eggs and cabbage and fish wrapped in paper. Men leading donkeys laden with coal or firewood, or making quiet trades on the sly. Boys in ragged caps and bare feet pinching apples from carts when the proprietor wasn't looking.

Everyone who saw Alice and Hatcher averted their eyes and veered away, but the two of them did not seem to cause sufficient alarm that the police were called, for which Alice was grateful. None of these folk would want the authorities sniffing around, for she was certain that more than fruit and coal were being sold off those carts. Every person made it clear that no help was to be found there, but no hindrance either.

"When we arrive," Hatcher said, "there will be an old woman, and she will know me, and she will let us in."

Alice wondered who this old woman was, and why Hatcher was so sure she would help. She wanted to ask, but Hatcher probably would not know the answer anyway. And her stomach was starting to churn, even though there was nothing in it. If they'd still been in their rooms, the morning porridge would have come hours ago. Alice coughed, and tasted something foul in the back of her throat.

"I feel sick," she moaned.

"Nearly there," Hatcher said, steering her around the corner of a storefront selling healing potions and down another alley.

"I won't make it," Alice said, and broke away from Hatcher to heave against the wall.

Her stomach wrenched upward, her throat burning, but all that came out were a few thin drools of bile. Alice leaned her aching forehead against the cool brick and winced when the rough surface scraped against the scabbed knot given her by the man who would have raped her. The nausea had not passed. Instead the outburst had only made her feel worse.

"Just a little farther," Hatcher said, tugging at her hand, her shoulder. "It's the powder making you sick."

"I haven't had my powder today," Alice said.

"Precisely," Hatcher said. "How many years have you had a powder with breakfast and supper?"

"Ever since I went to the hospital," she said.

It was a terrible struggle to put one foot in front of the other. She could barely lift her leg from the ground. Her toes curled under and scraped along the stone, the skin there peeling away and leaving it raw.

Hatcher badgered and dragged her the last few feet. When finally they reached the plain wooden door tucked in a notch halfway down the alley, Alice was on the verge of collapse.

Hatcher pounded on the door with his fist, his other arm keeping Alice from folding up in a heap on the ground. The door opened and a very small woman, knotted and ancient, appeared in the opening. She wore a blue dress covered by a faded red shawl. Her hair was white, and her eyes were as grey as Hatcher's. She took one long look at him, and Alice thought she heard a little sigh.

Then the woman said, "Nicholas. I've been waiting for you for three days."

She moved aside so they could enter. Hatcher showed no sign of recognition at being called by this name, but he crossed the threshold as though he belonged there nonetheless.

"What happened to the girl?" the woman said, crossing to stoke the fire at the edge of the room.

Alice shook off Hatcher's arm, staggering toward the flame, that lovely warmth, and fell facedown on the rug. She never heard Hatcher's answer, for after that there was blessed darkness.

When she woke again she was in a soft bed on a feather pillow, covered by a blanket of scratchy wool. It had been years since she'd slept in a bed or had a blanket, and for a moment she just luxuriated in the feeling of being comfortable for a change.

A candle guttered on a small table across the room. There were no windows. There was a pitcher and bowl beside the candle. Alice felt sore all over, but clean, and her head was strangely light. She put her hand there and found her hair was gone, and gasped. Her fingers went from the nape of her neck to her crown. The knotted tangle had been neatly sheared away, leaving silky straight strands barely the width of two of her fingers.

She touched her forehead, the place where her head ached, where pain radiated through her skull. Someone had cleaned the wound and tied it together with thread. She could feel the neat little stitches going up in a line. Alice was glad she had slept through that.

She lifted the blanket, and saw a clean but worn muslin nightgown. The muck and blood had been washed away. She pulled back the sleeves of her gown and saw purple bruises at her wrists.

"The boy said he did that, though he did not mean to," a voice said.

Alice looked over her right shoulder and saw the old woman had pulled aside the curtain at the entryway. She held a plate in one hand, as though she had known Alice would wake at that moment and be hungry.

She walked slowly, like she was hobbled by stiffness, to Alice's side and handed her the plate. There was brown bread and a hunk of crumbly yellow cheese. Alice took the plate and murmured, "Thank you."

"Eat slow," the old woman advised. "Nicholas said you've been ill."

Alice laughed, a short barking sound that surprised her. She could not recall the last time she'd laughed.

"Yes, you could say I've been ill," she said, and suddenly she was weeping, weeping in a way she had not since she was a child.

All the years of walking only the square walls of her cell, of being pushed and pulled by attendants who saw her only as a task to be completed. All the nights she'd woken in terror from a nightmare that would not leave her, all the nights no one had been there to soothe or comfort away that fear. All that had happened since the hospital had begun to burn—the smoke and the terror and the man's hand pushing between her legs. All these things had been stopped up inside her, blanketed by the comforting haze of the powders they dumped in her food every morning and night. The world was abruptly sharp and clear, too clear, and too alive. It was terrible beyond words.

The old woman did not hold her or offer false words of comfort. She waited, with patient and compassionate eyes, until Alice had cried herself dry. Then she offered a worn handkerchief, which Alice used to dry her face. Her hands stopped on her left cheek, realizing with horror that her scar was now completely exposed by her shorn hair.

"Why did you cut my hair?" Alice asked. It wasn't what she meant to say. She meant to say, *Thank you for washing and feeding me and binding up my wounds*, but it had come out differently than she'd intended.

"You were crawling with vermin," the old woman said matter-of-factly. "You and the boy. It's likely been years since you noticed it. 'Twas easiest to cut off as much as we could and scrub the rest out. Besides, Nicholas seemed to think you might be safer dressed as a boy. Considering what he told me happened along the way here, that might be true. You're thin enough to pass for one, and tall too, for a girl. Though your face is a mite too pretty, even with that scar you're so concerned about. And in certain places boys are just as much at risk as girls. Still, Nicholas will be with you."

"Who are you?" Alice asked. "To Hatcher, I mean?"

She couldn't bring herself to call him by the name this woman called him. It didn't fit with the man she knew.

"My name is Bess, and he's my grandson, though he doesn't remember it," she said. "His mother was my daughter. She left me when she was nineteen, and then came back three years later with him, and left him with me, still wrapped in his swaddling clothes. Considering the way her eyes looked, that was likely the best thing."

"How did her eyes look?"

"Like she was soaring somewhere above the City, like those flying machines the New City folk ride about it. She was not tied to the same earth as the rest of us anymore."

"So you know what happened to Hatcher, then? Why he was in the asylum?"

Bess shook her head slowly. "Until yesterday I had not seen Nicholas' face for twenty-three years. When he was seventeen, he took to running with a bad lot. I told him I'd have none of that nonsense beneath my roof, and he left. 'Twas like his mother all over again, and it seemed I'd made the same mistakes twice, though I'd tried my best both times."

She paused here, and Alice saw her regrets as clear as if she'd spoken them aloud.

"I did not hear word of him after he left here," Bess continued. "Then four nights ago I had a dream, a dream that he would return. There's a bit of Seeing in our blood, enough to know that our visions are true things. Nicholas has it too. That's why he speaks of the Jabberwock."

"I thought it was some dream of Hatcher's," Alice said.

The old woman looked at her sharply. "Did you not see the creature in the fire? Do you not believe the truth of your own eyes?"

"No, I don't," Alice said. "Once, I saw a Rabbit, who was also a man, and everyone said I was a liar."

Bess hissed at the mention of the Rabbit. "Oh, aye, he's real enough, and as bad as they come. You stay away from him, girl, you hear? If you were lucky enough to crawl out of his hole once, you won't be so lucky a second time."

Alice was taken aback by the old lady's vehemence, and also by her words. "You know of the Rabbit?"

"I told you to stay away from him," she repeated. "Don't let your curiosity lead you down the garden path. That, I imagine, was what got you into trouble in the first place."

"Yes," Alice said quietly.

Bess was right, of course. Nothing good would come of being curious about the figure that had haunted her nightmares for years. But there was a small place inside her that glowed with triumph, for they had all said she was mad, talking of a rabbit-man, but she'd been *right*. She was right.

"Heed me," Bess said. "Do not go seeking the Rabbit, else you wish for more death and madness."

Alice shook her head. "I won't. I promise."

The old woman looked at her closely, peering into Alice's eyes. She nodded her head, as if satisfied by what she saw there.

"Good," she said. "You'll have no time in any event. You and the boy must find the Jabberwock."

"Us? But why?" She'd hardly believed in the monster in the first place, but if it was real she didn't think it any wiser to go seeking it than the Rabbit.

"You are the only ones who saw him loosed—saw and knew what you were looking at, that is. He's already begun hunting again, and the blood he drinks only makes him crave more."

"Surely the police will catch it, if it is that bad," Alice said. "Or soldiers from the New City."

"No ordinary human could catch the Jabberwock," Bess said. "The police would not even know rightly what they were looking at. He can pretend he's a man if he wishes, and often does, for it allows him ease of passage. And soldiers, as you well know, do not come into the Old City for anything. If the Old City were nothing but monsters and riots, the soldiers would not come. Their task is to keep the filth of the Old City out of the New, to keep the New City clean so the fine ladies there don't trail their hems in the dirt."

This was so like what Hatcher had said to Alice the night before that she flushed in shame. The old woman, sharp-eyed even in the meager light, noted this and cackled.

"Not from around here, are you, dearie? Still, you survived the Rabbit, so you must not be as dainty as your kin. And my dream told me the two of you must find the Jabberwock. There must be something inside you, something you haven't shown yet."

The old woman peered at Alice closely, and Alice turned her face away from the other's scrutiny. She felt a sudden burning resentment against this woman, this woman who had cared for her though she had no obligation to do so.

Who was she to say Alice must do this or that? For ten years she'd been told what to do—ten years and more, for when she'd been her parents' daughter they had always been commanding, always correcting, always, *No, Alice, you must not do that. It is unseemly. You must not keep that friend. She is not appropriate.*

She had never had freedom, freedom to be whom she liked and do as she chose. And now here was this strange person telling her that she still had no freedom. She did not have to seek out a murdering nightmare if she did not wish it, and no grandmother—seer or not—would tell her otherwise.

The old woman put her fingers on Alice's chin and turned the girl's face toward her. "Nay," she said. "Do not think you can turn away from your fate. I have Seen it, and once foretold, it cannot be undone. If you go chasing your freedom your fate will only follow you there, and drag you back."

Alice's cheeks were wet again. "It's not fair."

"Fair or not, it is what it is," Bess said, standing. "You'll go and see Cheshire, up in Rose Way. He'll help you, point you where you ought to be. Nicholas will be back soon. You should dress."

She pointed to a bundle of clothes hanging from a peg just next to Alice's bed.

"Where did Hatcher go?"

"To fetch some things for me that I usually have to pay a boy to carry. He needed busyness, Nicholas did. Near lost his mind when you fainted like that, and sat staring at you sleeping until I chased him out."

Bess left, and Alice sat staring at her hands. She held the plate of bread and cheese, having taken only a bite of each. The old woman's words still rang in her ears.

If you go chasing your freedom your fate will only follow you there, and force you back.

Why was she, Alice, the one who must find the Jabberwock? There was nothing special about her. And what were she and Hatcher to do when they did find him? Hatcher might have a gift of Seeing, but he was no Magician, and neither was Alice.

She took another bite of bread as she thought. The bread was good, far better than any food she'd eaten at the hospital. Her hunger was abruptly overwhelming, and she jammed the rest of the bread in her mouth, unable to chew fast enough.

She was so hungry. She had never been so hungry. The bread disappeared in the blink of an eye. When she looked at the cheese, her stomach suddenly heaved like the day before. She dropped the cheese to the plate, threw off the blanket and ran to the table.

The bare floor was cold against her bare feet. The pitcher was half-filled with water, as she'd hoped, and she lifted it to her lips, guzzling down as much as she could swallow. The water was so icy that it burned her parched throat, made her chest cramp from the cold. She stood, leaning on the table with her hands, breathing hard through her nose until the cramping and nausea passed and her body seemed normal again.

Alice shivered, for now that she was out of the cocoon of the blankets, she was aware of how chilly it was. She thought of the fire, which she could smell crackling away in the next room, and hurried to dress so she could go out and put her whole self as close to it as possible.

The bundle of clothes was revealed to be a man's wool pants, a rough white pullover shirt and a grey jacket and cap. Alice spread all these things on the bed and tried not to think of the fine dresses she used to wear before, when she lived in the New City.

That life is gone. And anyhow this is better than what you wore at the hospital.

She pulled the nightgown over her head, and paused, getting a good look at the state of herself. There was a large purple bruise around the slight curve of her right breast, and abrasions down her stomach and thighs. There were matching purple finger marks on the sides of her legs, and the tops of her feet were scraped raw.

Her ribs and hip bones showed through the skin, so pale as to be nearly translucent, and everything hurt from the exertions of the day before, even if you could not see that on the surface. It had been years since she had walked so far, and she had certainly never jumped out of a third-story window into the river.

She looked up, her eye attracted by some movement, and found a strange man had pulled aside the curtain and was staring at her. Her heart seemed to stop beating for a moment, and she opened her mouth to scream, but no sound came out.

His hair was black, sprinkled with white, and cut very close to his head. His face was clean-shaven, revealing hollow cheekbones and a sharp chin. He was dressed in the same sort of rough pants and shirt that Alice had just unbundled. Her voice worked its way up to her throat, and then she remembered his eyes. His iron grey eyes, burning like she had never seen them before.

He approached her, pulling the curtain shut behind him, pinning her in place with his eyes. Her heart fluttered in her chest, a moth captured in a net. He stopped before her and his hand moved to her cheek, the one that had been flayed open so many years before.

He cupped her face, and she had never noticed before how large his hands were, or how tall he was, much taller than she. At this distance she could see a multitude of faded white scars all over his face that had been hidden by his beard.

His hand left her face, and he sank to his knees, laying his cheek against her stomach so gently that she wanted to weep. His arms went around her hips, not so tight as to hurt, but just enough so she knew he would not let her go. His skin seemed to melt into hers, like he was trying to crawl inside her.

Her hands went to his hair, the strands even shorter than her own, and much thicker and coarser. They stayed there for a while, each breathing in the other until that breath moved in the same rhythm.

Then Hatcher stood, and Alice saw that the fire in his eyes was banked. He touched her hair, smoothing it down, then left the room without a word.

Alice dressed quickly then. Her legs trembled as she tried to pull on the pants, and she did not know whether it was from cold or what had just happened. The pants would not stay up on her bony hips. She clutched the waist with her hands as she hobbled in her cold bare feet to the main room.

Bess and Hatcher were in conference, standing side by side over a variety of articles spread on the floor. The old woman noticed Alice struggling.

"I'll get some rope for those," she said, moving down the hallway toward the back of the flat. She disappeared into one of the two doorways Alice could see.

"Sorry about that," Hatcher said, pointing to the pants, which also dragged on the floor a bit by Alice's heels. "I was in a hurry when I got them and was mostly thinking this way"—here he gestured with his hand up and down—"and not this way," he finished, moving his hand side to side.

Alice moved around beside him, partially because the fire was there and she desperately wanted the warmth, and partially because she was curious about the objects on the floor.

"Why were you in a hurry?" Alice asked.

"Hmmm?" Hatcher said. He'd gone back to studying the assorted items.

"Why were you in a hurry when you got the clothes?"

"Oh." He grinned, and that grin went straight to her heart and lodged there. She'd never properly seen his smile before. "I was stealing them off a wash line."

"Hatch," Alice said, her voice chiding. "You didn't need to steal clothes. You got a fistful of gold off that trader."

"It's less than a fistful now that I've bought these things," he said. "Besides, we'll need some of that gold where we're going. Bess says her name will be enough to get us in to see Cheshire, but I remember plenty of palms needed crossing before you got there."

"You remember," Alice said.

Hatcher looked at her, surprise in his eyes. "I do. I do remember that."

"Just that, or other things?"

"Just that for now," he said. "It's like I can only recall what I need to at that moment."

"What are all these things?" Alice asked.

"Supplies," Hatcher said.

Alice thought their ideas of "supplies" were very different. If Alice had been the one who'd gone out she would have come back with food and clothing and blankets, things necessary to survive. The spread before her looked more like an armory.

There were two knives—one a standard-looking dagger with a leather grip, and the other thinner one with a straight side and a curved side, almost like the kinds of knives butchers used. There were several coils of rope of different thicknesses and lengths. There was a small hand axe, and Alice gave Hatcher a sideways glance when she saw it. He followed her eyes back to that wicked-looking blade, and shook his head.

"It doesn't make me remember, not as you'd think it should," he said. "Though when it was in my hand it felt the most natural thing in the world, like it was part of me."

There was one more object on the floor, and it was so strange to see that Alice stared at it.

"Is that . . . ?" she asked, pointing. She didn't even know how to say the word. She'd only ever seen pictures in books, never the real thing.

Hatcher grinned again, and she realized deep down, underneath all the blood and madness, Hatcher was a rogue. Somewhere inside him was still the boy who liked to cause trouble.

"It's a gun, yes," he said.

"A gun," Alice repeated. Nothing could have shocked her more, not even if he'd said he was a secret Magician. "Only the Royal Guard is allowed to carry guns. Not even the soldiers who protect the New City have them."

Hatcher tilted his head to one side, like he was seeing her for the first time. "Do you always believe what you're told?"

The way he asked the question made her feel foolish, and she flushed under his attention. "No. I suppose I used to. I don't know if I do now."

"Don't believe anything the coppers or the soldiers or the government tells you, Alice," Hatcher said. "They're not interested in your happiness. They just don't want you to cause trouble for the swells in the New City. Those soldiers have guns, Alice, sure as your eyes are blue. You just don't see them."

She didn't care so much about the guns the soldiers carried as the one Hatcher was proposing to carry. "It's illegal. Taking that gun will draw attention in a way a knife won't."

"Because they expect the rabble to have knives and use them on each other, so that's not questioned." Hatcher nodded. "I know. Don't trouble yourself. It will be well hidden. It's a last resort."

Alice gave him a doubtful look, but said nothing more. He started collecting all the things on the ground. The knives and axe and gun all disappeared under his coat, so smooth that you would never know they were there. The ropes went into a small pack, along with some bundles of cloth she hadn't noticed before.

"What are those?" she asked.

"Cloaks," he said. "Better than blankets when night falls. You won't lose it if we have to leave in a rush, see? And though during daylight you stand out a mile, they make you one of the shadows after dark."

So he had considered something besides the violent defense of their lives, Alice thought. She was so warm by this fire she never wanted to leave. She didn't want to think about what was going to happen when they walked out that door.

It was true that if they were discovered to have escaped from the hospital, they would be in plenty of trouble to begin with. But if Hatcher were caught with a gun, he would be executed. No trial, no semblance of justice. Likely they would shoot him with his own weapon.

Her head jerked up then from her contemplation and she stared.

"What is it?" he asked.

"You bought that gun so you wouldn't have to go back to the hospital," she said, and she was a little surprised to hear the anger, the accusation, in her voice. "You know if you're captured with it they'll kill you on the spot."

Hatcher nodded. "Yes. I told you, I can't go back there. I can't abide the thought of four walls closing around me again. And they would separate us, Alice. No more comfort through the mouse hole. They would keep us apart, and I can't bear the thought of that any more than being trapped. So I'll make sure, if there is no other way out, that I still *have* a way out. And I can do it for you too."

She knew what he offered. He would kill her first, with the gun or the knife or his fists if he had to, and make certain she was never trapped in that cage again. From another man this might be terrifying, that he would so blithely consider murdering his companion. But she understood that from Hatcher this was tantamount to an offer of marriage. This was what he could do for her, how he showed he cared.

The thought of returning to her prison made bile rise up in her throat. At the same time, she found something inside her would not let her accept Hatcher's offer. She'd never lived properly, and could not so willingly agree to the promise of death. Not yet.

"Thank you. I will consider it," Alice said.

Hatcher nodded, and returned to his task. Bess returned to the room carrying a leather belt in one hand and something red that sparkled on a silver chain in the other.

"I almost thought I'd lost this," she said by way of apology for the long wait. "Took more time than I expected to find it."

Alice took the belt Bess handed her, absently wrapping it around her waist and pulling the pants tight. The sparkly thing glittered in the firelight, fascinating her.

"This is for you," Bess said. "It was from my great-great-great-great-grandmother, who was a true Magician, long ago before the Purge. It will keep you safe."

She held it out to Alice, who hesitated. "I should not take a family heirloom."

Bess snorted. "I've no family left, save Nicholas here, and you're the closest thing to a bride he's ever brought home. If you don't take it, it will only be stolen when they find me dead here, and that day is coming soon."

Alice thought that Seeing must be a terrible gift if you could see the hour of your own death. She saw Hatcher's hands still in his task as the old woman spoke so casually of her passing. So he was not entirely unaffected, then. Perhaps a small part of Hatcher did remember Nicholas, and the grandmother who had done her best by him.

Bess offered the chain to Alice again, a little impatiently, and Alice took it, peering closely at the jewel that sparkled in her palm.

"It's a rose," she said, and suddenly she felt like she was drowning, drowning in memory, rows of scarlet roses marching through the garden, rows of roses on the dress she wore the day she snuck away with Dor.

"My mother . . ." she began, and for a moment felt she might swoon again. "My mother loved roses. She grew them like magic. No one's roses were as lovely as hers, and she would hardly permit the gardener to help her."

She did not say the other thing, the other memory that had leapt to the fore, but kept it in her secret heart. Her hand, very small and fat, in her mother's slim and elegant one, the sun behind her mother's head lighting up her golden hair so she looked like an angel, and her face smiling down at Alice, cooing, *My little rose Alice, my blooming rose.*

What had happened to that woman, that loving mother? Why had she not loved Alice when she was hurt and scared? Why had she sent Alice away, away to the most horrible place in the world?

She thought she'd cried out the past already, but here it was again, rising up in her chest, making it hurt, making tears prick in her eyes.

Bess watched her with the same patient gaze, and after a moment Alice scrubbed at her eyes with her knuckles.

"Thank you," she said, and lifted the chain over her head.

As the rose settled on her chest it began to glow, as if lit by candle fire from within. Bess gasped, and grabbed Alice's chin, turning her face so the smaller woman could look into her eyes.

"You. You," she said.

Then Hatcher stood suddenly, his face white to the lips.

"He's near," he said, and his eyes rolled back in his head before he collapsed to the floor.

CHAPTER

4

"The two of you," Bess tutted as Alice wrenched away from her. "Falling all over the place, both of you. I don't know how you'll get by if you're fainting all the time."

Alice rolled Hatcher to his back. His lids were closed, but she could see his eyes darting back and forth underneath.

"Hatcher," she said, shaking his shoulders. "Hatcher."

Bess shook her head. "There's no use in that. He's in the grip of the Jabberwock, and won't wake up until that one finishes his work."

"I don't want him there," Alice said, remembering the dream she'd had just before she woke up to the hospital on fire. "I don't want the Jabberwock to take him from me."

"Then you'll have to get rid of the monster, won't you?" Bess said, a little gleam in her eye. "A stronger reason than fate, I imagine."

Alice stared helplessly at Hatcher's bloodless face, his twitching eyes. "What power do I have?"

Bess looked at the rose around Alice's neck and said, "More than you think. You needn't flutter over him so. The boy will come out of it soon. The Jabberwock is almost finished feeding."

"How do you know?" Alice asked.

"I can feel him too," Bess said, and her voice had a singsong quality. "He's close, and he's nearly sated. He spent the night hungry, anticipating the taste of blood. He knows folk expect horror in the night, so he waited till day. Till it was so terrible that he could swallow the fear whole."

"Why don't you have a fit, like Hatcher?" Alice asked.

"The boy lived close to the Jabberwock for years, listening to him whisper. His power was blocked then by whatever prison held him, but Nicholas knew he was there. That connection is not broken though both have been loosed from their cages. Now the Jabberwock's power courses through that link with nothing to halt it. And every drop of blood, every ounce of fear sustains it, makes it stronger, makes the shadow deep and wide."

Alice felt the task before them must be impossible, that they—two broken children that they were—could not overcome such a thing. If every murder only made the Jabberwock stronger, he only had to kill until he could devour the world.

"Don't despair," Bess said. "There is still time. He is seeking something, and until he finds it he will not reach his final form."

"What does he seek?"

"Something a Magician stole from him," Hatcher croaked.

Alice put her hand to his cheek. There was no color there, and his eyes were a little wild. "Be still."

He shook his head, rising until he was seated. He exchanged a glance with Bess. "He's looking for something. Could you See it?"

The old woman shook her head. "But I felt his desire for it."

Hatcher shivered. "As did I."

Alice looked from one to the other. "The Jabberwock—he can be stopped? Unless he finds this object?"

Hatcher nodded. "But it will not be easy, and we need some things ourselves. That's why you're sending us to see Cheshire."

"Yes," Bess said. "He's forgotten more than you or I will ever know. He knows of the history of magic and Magicians. He may be able to tell who trapped the Jabberwock before, and how. You should leave when night falls, so darkness will cover you."

"What about the Jabberwock? What if we encounter him before we're prepared?" Alice asked. She wasn't ready to leave. She wanted to feel safe and warm awhile longer.

"He's moving away now," Hatcher said. "He came near here, but now he's searching for the thing he needs. I can feel him approaching. We will be able to avoid him."

Hatcher was up now, finishing the work he'd begun before he'd fainted. Bess moved into the kitchen and returned with a wrapped loaf of bread and some apples. Hatcher tucked them in the bag with his other things.

Alice watched all this helplessly, twisting her fingers together for lack of anything else to do. Bess beckoned for her to follow into the kitchen. Alice expected the other woman to give her more food to pack, but was surprised when she was instead presented with a little dagger, no longer than her hand. It was sheathed in worn leather.

"What am I to do with this?" Alice asked, although as she said that, she had another flash of memory—a knife slicing through flesh, and hot blood on her hand. She had used a knife once to save herself.

"Protect yourself," Bess said. "The boy is tied to the Jabberwock. He may not always be able to keep watch over you."

It was a terrifying thought. Hatcher might fall to the ground in the middle of the street, helpless against any attack, leaving her helpless as well. Or worse, he might not faint at all. He might be overwhelmed by the spirit of the Jabberwock, and turn on her.

Bess watched her as she thought these things, and nodded, and Alice knew her worries were plain upon her face.

"That's why you must keep that, and be prepared to use it."

Unspoken between them was the truth that Alice did not want to face—that she might have to use it on Hatcher.

"Put it in your pocket now," Bess urged.

Alice reluctantly tucked the little knife in her jacket. If the time came, she hoped she'd have courage enough to use it.

Once all the preparations were made, there was nothing to do but wait. Bess settled in a chair by the fire, and set about knitting a shawl.

His task completed, Hatcher paced back and forth through the flat like a tiger in a zoo. Alice had seen a tiger only once, for her mother thought zoos were common.

There was a governess, when Alice was six or seven, whose ignorance of this dictum had resulted in a forbidden outing. Alice recalled the pushing crowds, pointing and gasping at gorillas and snakes from the deepest jungle, the musty smell of animal fur, the sweetness of a lemon ice on her tongue. The ice was another forbidden treat, but Alice was not about to correct her governess, not when she so willingly provided things Alice was not to have.

The novelty wore off by midday when the beating sun and pressing throngs conspired to give the governess a headache, which resulted in her being much more short and cross than at the outset. She was dragging Alice along by the wrist toward the exit when Alice caught a glimpse of stripes and pulled her arm away from her minder.

She'd darted between grown-up legs, trees made of wool and muslin, smelling of tobacco and perfume. She squeezed up to the bars that kept the people separated from the animals.

The great beast stalked from one side to another, paws as large as her face, the claws sharp and cruel-looking. Its eyes captured her, green and full of mystery and malice and the wild heart the zookeepers tried to beat out of him. As she watched she felt her own wild heart pounding in her chest, thrumming like a rabbit caught in a hunter's gaze. Then she heard "Alice!"— a sharp admonition there in her name—and her governess' tight grip was on her shoulder, dragging her away.

Alice drowsed in front of the fire, lured into a half sleep by the rhythmic *click-clack* of knitting needles and the methodical footsteps moving back and forth across the floor.

A rabbit caught in a hunter's gaze. And cake. There was a rabbit and there was cake.

Cake. She was thinking of cake, the soft crumbly sweetness of it on her tongue. She had not eaten cake for years. There certainly was no cake at the hospital, only thin grey gruel, thin as the faces that delivered it morning and night.

There used to be cake with tea, before the hospital. A plate piled high with fat wedges of yellow cake with different icings—pink and blue and violet. Her mother would pour out the tea and then Alice would be permitted to choose one small slice, only one, for her mother did not approve of sweets.

It wasn't like that other tea party, the one where the Rabbit told her she could have all the cake she liked. Alice had tried not to be too greedy, but she had been unable to disguise her pleasure. She sat at the table with Dor and the Rabbit and . . . another. There was someone else there, some shadow.

Alice could not see his face as she crammed cake in her mouth, and the Rabbit laughed and stroked her braid with his white hands, saying, *Pretty little Alice. We'll make you fine and plump, won't we, pretty girl? Pretty Alice.*

Alice. Alice.

His hand on her braid, wrapping around it, pulling her head back so she could look into his eyes, his blue-green eyes so angry (*though they really ought to be pink, you know, like a proper rabbit's*), eyes snapping, hand pulling her hair until she cried, his voice cracking like a whip, *Where do you think you're off to, pretty Alice?*

Alice. Alice.

"Alice, wake up."

Hatcher's voice, impatient, his hands at her shoulders, shaking her, but not hard enough to hurt. Not cruel. Hatcher was never cruel to her. Not like the Rabbit. She opened her eyes and sat up a little, her hand automatically going to the back of her neck to touch her braid and feeling her bare nape instead.

"We have to go, Alice," Hatcher said.

He'd already stood, adjusted the placement of all the weapons in his coat, slung the pack of supplies over his shoulder.

"You shouldn't call me Alice," she said, trying to shake the dream away, standing carefully until she was sure of where she was. "I'm supposed to be a boy."

The cap that completed her disguise was in her pocket, and she pulled it on. She felt the weight of the little dagger in her jacket as she tucked the rose charm beneath her shirt.

"What shall I call you, then?" Hatcher asked, frowning.

"Alex," said the old woman. "'Tis close to her real name, and if you call her the wrong one, folk might simply think they misheard."

"Alex," Hatcher said, like he was trying out how it felt in his mouth. His nose wrinkled slightly. "It doesn't suit you, even with the cap and the short hair."

"It doesn't suit her to be taken by a trader just because you don't like the idea of her as a boy," Bess said tartly. "Now, put those cloaks on. It's time."

The cloak was thick and scratchy, but when it settled over her, Alice felt she was someone else, someone who could disappear into the shadows.

Bess came to Alice and took her hands. "There is more to you than you know. Remember that."

She leaned forward and kissed Alice's cheek. Alice wanted to thank her, but tears were choking her, tears of gratitude and of fear. Bess moved away before she could speak.

The old woman stopped in front of Hatcher. He stared down at his grandmother, the woman who'd done her best by him, and as Alice watched, something passed between them without a word spoken. Bess put her arms around his neck, and Hatcher let her, though he did not return the embrace. After a long moment Bess stepped back and away, wiping her face with her apron.

"Mind the Jabberwock," she said.

Hatcher nodded, and moved toward the door. Alice was frozen in place. Her heart pulled her toward Hatcher; her brain told her to stay, stay here where it was safe. Hatcher pulled open the door and looked back over his shoulder, his face a question.

"Alice?"

She glanced at Bess, who stood where Hatcher left her, tears flowing freely down her face. She seemed smaller and frailer than a moment ago. She did not return Alice's gaze, nor turn to see Hatcher go, but stood with her back to him so he could not see her tears.

"Alice?" he asked again.

She lifted her hood so her face would be hidden in shadow. "It's Alex," she said, and followed him into the night, closing the door behind her.

"Stay close to me," Hatcher said.

"How far is it, to Rose Way?" Alice asked.

"A day's walk, likely two," Hatcher said. "We're going into the heart of the Old City, and we can't walk there in a straight line."

Alice had already noted the meandering crooked paths that stood in for streets, and the maze of alleys that connected them. She mentioned this to Hatcher and he gave a little laugh.

"It's not the streets that are the problem, love. It's who owns them."

"You mean—like bands of ruffians?" Alice asked.

This was not a world she was familiar with, even before the hospital, although she recalled her father complaining of gangs of thieves roving the edges of the Old City. They would dart into the New City, past the patrols, rob the rich folk, and slip back into the Old City before an alarm could be raised.

But that was long ago, Alice thought. Ten years ago. The world had changed even if Alice herself had stood still.

Thinking of this, she said, "Will things be as you remember them? It's been a long time."

Hatcher shrugged, the motion barely visible under the cloak. "I *don't* remember, not really. But Bess told me a bit of what to expect, and it seemed to remind me."

He fell silent then, and Alice knew him well enough to know he was brooding on something. He was unpredictable in this mood, so she let him be. The night was cold, and were it not for the cloak, Alice would be shivering. Even with the cold, the air felt close and still, like everything in the City was hushed and waiting.

Alice thought she knew what that was about. The Jabberwocky had struck, and no one knew when he would strike again. Even if nobody except her and Hatcher and Bess knew what the Jabberwocky was, even if nobody knew he was a monster from nightmares, he had obviously done something terrible. It wasn't difficult to draw that conclusion, based on the things Bess said and on the state of Hatcher when it was happening. Still, most folk in the Old City would know something was out there, something unusual, something horrifying.

Even with that the streets were hardly empty. There was plenty of business of a furtive nature being conducted, and more than one gaze followed Alice and Hatcher, assessing.

The first time they passed a couple of tough-looking characters, Alice tucked her head and hurried past them, afraid that if they saw her face they might take her for a girl, and then what happened before would happen again. The bruises on her body seemed to throb in fear, anticipating more pain to come. But nothing happened, except that once they were out of sight Hatcher grabbed her elbow and made her look at him.

"Don't scurry like a mouse," Hatcher said, his voice harsh. "You'll draw them to you quick as flame if you do."

"I thought—" Alice said.

"I know what you thought, and you could hardly be blamed for thinking it. But if you go on like that you'll attract every trader we pass. And while I can defend you—and I will—I'd rather save my energy for what lies ahead."

Alice nodded, feeling chastened. "I need to defend myself."

"Start by holding your head high," Hatcher said. "You're only a mouse if you let them make you one."

After that Alice tried to copy the way Hatcher walked—his long legs taking long strides, his upper body still, coiled and ready to spring. His head hardly moved, but his eyes were always on the lookout, taking in everything. If any threat lurked in the shadows and fog, Hatcher would see it.

They walked for a few hours. Alice knew they moved deeper into the City because the scent of the river had become very faint, though its reek was so strong it had not disappeared entirely.

Sometimes they moved through the alleys, and sometimes they walked in the thoroughfares. Hatcher seemed to know where to go, for he moved with a purpose, never hesitating or contemplating where to next. Alice tried her best to keep up, to not be a burden, but despite the sleep she'd gotten, her body was worn-out. It wasn't long before her breath came in audible pants and her head began to spin.

For the first time she felt frustration at her weakness, and shame. All those years in the hospital Hatcher believed they would get out. He'd trained, prepared for the day that would happen, even though he'd no reason for that belief. He had no family that he knew of, no one to tell the doctors it was all right for him to come home.

Alice had a family, one she knew would be no help to her. But Hatcher was certain one day they would fly from their cage, and now he was strong and capable and she was about to fall down—again. She could almost hear Bess tutting in her ear.

Alice pushed on a little longer, but after a while she couldn't keep up, and lagged farther and farther behind.

"Hatcher," she said, and her voice was so reedy she was surprised he heard it.

He turned around then, as she leaned against a building, the world tilting to one side.

"Sorry, sorry," he muttered, returning to her. "Let's have some of that bread, then."

They sat on the ground where they stopped, their cloaks billowing around their feet, and Hatcher broke off a large chunk of Bess' bread, giving half to Alice.

"I was following the map and not thinking of much else," he said by way of explanation.

"What map?" she asked around a mouthful of bread. Her tongue was dry and it made the bread hard to swallow.

Hatcher tapped his temple. "Trying to remember all the whos and wheres, all the lines drawn. I figure even if the bosses have changed, the territory is likely the same. If one goes down, another will always be there to scoop up the goods."

"Goods?" Alice asked.

"The area and the business in it," Hatcher said.

"Oh." Sometimes Alice felt there was more than one person inside Hatcher, pushing to get out. She'd never noticed so much when they were in the hospital, but now he would talk one way and then another, like the street tough he used to be was nudging aside the man he was now, and both of them tangled with the madness inside.

A pair of rats the size of cats scuttled near them, sniffing the air, attracted to the smell of bread. Alice stilled in the act of chewing, hoping they would go away. She'd never liked rats, having been bitten by one as a child. A particularly large rodent had gotten into their house and bit her face in her sleep.

She'd woken screaming, and the whole household had chased the creature until it was cornered. The parlormaid, whose name was also Alice, later told her "the master beat the wretched animal with a stick till there was naught left but bones and blood."

Alice had trouble picturing her very proper father, with his starched cravat and polished spectacles, as the author of such heroics. But the other Alice assured her it was so.

Dr. Horner came to treat the bite, and he said it wasn't unusual for rats to do what this one had done, for the face smelled of food and that's what rats were interested in. There had been a little scar on Alice's cheek from the teeth, but that scar was gone now, covered up by the long ridge that went from her mouth to the top of her cheekbone.

Hatcher continued eating, seemingly unconcerned about the presence of the rats. The vermin grew bolder, approaching Alice's and Hatcher's feet. Alice tensed, huddled in her cloak.

As the first rat drew within range of his boot, Hatcher casually kicked out his leg so hard the creature flew into the opposite wall with a sickening *crunch*.

The second rat scurried away as soon as Hatcher's leg moved. The other one lay motionless in the faint circle of light emitted by the gas lamp just outside the alley. Alice released the breath she'd been holding and finished her bread, though the sight of the broken corpse left the food tasteless in her mouth.

"All right, then?" Hatcher asked. "I'll try to walk slower."

Alice nodded and they got to their feet, moving out into the maze of the City. She had no inkling how he was able to tell where they were in relation to anyplace else. All the streets appeared the same to Alice—foggy and sooty and smelling of sweat and frying food.

In the New City the avenues were lined up neat and straight, at orderly angles to one another, and all the streets were marked with pretty names like Daisy Lane and Geranium Street. Bess said that Cheshire lived up in Rose Way. Alice doubted very much that roses grew there. The sun barely penetrated the haze that blanketed the Old City. And how could anyone tell which street was Rose Way at any rate? Nothing was marked.

"We'll go until sunrise, then find somewhere to sleep for a few hours."

"Not in the street?" Alice asked hopefully.

Hatcher shook his head. "I changed some of that gold for small coin, so we won't attract attention if we take a room."

"At an inn," Alice said, picturing downy soft beds and maids with tea trays and breakfast buns.

"There are no inns hereabouts—leastways, not any where I would take you," Hatcher said, his face grim.

"They're not really inns," Alice said, understanding at once.

"No," Hatcher said, and left it at that.

Alice wondered how many girls went missing every day in the Old City, how many mothers cried because their daughters never came home.

Her mother had cried, the day they found her. She'd thrown her arms around Alice and wept and said everything would be all right now, she was home.

Except it wasn't all right, and soon her mother stopped weeping with gratitude and instead spoke sharply, telling Alice to stop talking nonsense about a Rabbit. In the end there was no trace of the woman who'd loved her, only an impatient mask, eager to send away the person who no longer fit neatly in the little jigsaw puzzle of their house.

Alice dragged alongside Hatcher, desperate for rest, squinting hopefully at the sky for any pink-and-orange ray of light. She was looking up instead of around, which was why she didn't see the sentries.

Hatcher did. He touched her shoulder and pulled her into a little alcove next to a cobbler's shop.

"There's two guards ahead," Hatcher said. "We're passing into the red streets now, and every captain will have soldiers patrolling to keep the enemy out."

"The red streets?" Alice asked.

"Aye. This is a part of the City where the bosses don't simply sit back and collect tithes from the shopkeepers. They fight each other tooth and claw for every penny and every square inch of ground." Hatcher put his hands on Alice's shoulders. "If you go missing from me here, or if they find out you're a girl, I'll never see you again."

She nodded, trying to look brave though everything inside her quaked. "I understand."

"You'll wish you were dead," he said.

"I remember," she said, her voice faint. "I remember wishing that. I'll stay close, and I won't be a mouse. I'll be your brother."

Hatcher nodded. "Let's pack up the cloaks. They're noticeable, and we don't want the guards to pay us too much mind."

Alice took off the cloak with no small amount of regret, and shivered. She tugged her jacket close around her and felt the weight of the little knife in her pocket.

Hatcher spent a moment arranging things in the pack and then said, "I'll do the talking if there's any to be done."

She followed him back into the street, her cap pulled low over her eyes, and stuck her hands in her pockets. Her fingers went around the handle of the knife and gripped it hard. The street ahead of them appeared deserted. She didn't see any sentries. Perhaps Hatcher imagined them in the fog.

Then, as suddenly as if they'd crossed some trip wire, two men appeared out of the darkness, one from each side.

"Just where do you think you're going, lads?" one asked. He was a little shorter than Hatcher, and had a blaze of white just above one eyebrow. It stood out in stark relief against the darkness of his hair and the night.

The two men formed a wall in front of Alice and Hatcher, their bodies saying quite clearly that nobody was going around without their say-so. Alice felt a quick burst of relief that the man referred to her as a "lad."

"Just passing through," Hatcher said. His head was up, staring directly into the face of the man in front of him, not insolent, not daring, just . . . not afraid.

Alice thought it best to copy him. She lifted her chin and faced the man in front of her. He was around her age, or maybe even younger. His face was crusted with dirt and some rusty stains that might have been from splattered blood. Two of his bottom teeth were missing, and he held a long knife in his right hand. Alice thought that in a duel with her own blade, he would win. He had the advantage of size.

But then, you don't have to duel, do you? she thought. *Just find somewhere soft and push it in as hard as you can, like you did before.*

The thought startled her. Before? When she'd escaped from the Rabbit?

She'd gotten lost in the tangle of memory for a moment, so she missed some of what passed between Hatcher and the man with the blaze, who seemed to be in charge. When she came back to where she was supposed to be, everything seemed more fraught than it had been a moment before, like the air around them was a balloon slowly filling up with tension.

The man in front of Alice—*Toothless,* she thought—took a firmer grip on his knife. In her pocket, Alice did the same.

The other man—Blaze, she thought of him—took two fingers and pushed at Hatcher's shoulder. "I asked what you were doing here. No one passes through Mr. Carpenter's streets without his permission, and I'm the one gives permission when he's not about. If you know what's good for you, you'll tell up and then pay up, and mayhap we'll let you through without too much damage."

Hatcher did not speak. Alice darted a quick look at him. His face was blank, and she thought with a flare of terror that the Jabberwock might be near, possessing him.

Blaze pushed Hatcher's shoulder again. "What's the problem, my lad? Are you daft?"

Hatcher's head moved slowly, like an automaton Alice had seen once on an outing with her governess. He looked from Blaze's hand on his shoulder to the other man's face.

Alice sucked in her breath. "Hatch, no," she said, but it was too late.

The blade of the axe flashed in the dim light, before anyone even knew it was there. Hatcher buried it in Blaze's throat, the force of the blow so great that the head tipped back, almost but not quite severed.

Blood spurted in a wild spray, splashing Alice's face. There was one motionless second where they all watched Blaze's body falling backward, the head lolling in an unnatural curve.

Then Toothless opened his mouth, and Alice thought, *He'll raise the alarm.*

Before she had time to consider it, Hatcher was in front of her, his blade sliding into the other man's belly. *The belly is soft,* she thought, as he pulled the knife across quick as a wink, under the ribs, making a red gaping mouth there.

Toothless stared at them in shock, his hands going to his stomach. His lips separated, but no noise came out. He fell to the ground like his friend, writhing and panting.

Hatcher moved beside her, the bloody axe in one hand, his knife in the other. "You can't leave them like that," he said, as if he were instructing a student. "You have to do the job properly or they come back for you."

The axe flashed again, and Toothless stilled. Hatcher wiped the blade on the inside of his coat, where the blood would not be so obvious. She uncurled the fingers that gripped the knife in her pocket. Her hand shook badly so she fisted it at her side, willing it to be still.

"Let's go, before someone else comes around," he said, leading her past the two bodies, his hand around her upper arm, guiding her.

"I th-thought the second man might raise an alarm."

Hatcher looked at her sharply when she stuttered. "And he would have, too. Don't regret what's done, Alice. We would have had to fight those two and more if I hadn't killed them both."

"I don't," she said. "Not really. I know they weren't good men. It's only . . ."

"Only what?"

"Why did you kill that other man, anyway? The second man wouldn't have yelled out if you'd left the first one alone."

Alice was shocked to realize she was angry—terribly, terribly angry. She could not recall the last time she'd been angry, when she'd felt something other than fear and confusion and cold.

"I don't know," Hatcher admitted. "He touched me and then there was red in my eyes. I didn't really think about what I was doing."

"You were the one who told me not to draw attention," Alice hissed. Her voice was low, as was his. They both instinctively did so, unwilling to attract any more notice than they already might have done. Hatcher had moved quickly away from the thoroughfare, darting into a nearby alley and continuing on wherever his mind said they should go.

"Aye, I did," Hatcher said. "You're right. It was a foolish thing to do. But it's done, and it's nearly dawn, so let's find a place to rest."

A half hour earlier Alice would have given anything for food and a warm bed. Now her blood ran so hot and busy she wasn't sure she would ever be able to sleep again.

"Where are you taking me?" she asked.

Hatcher gave her a sideways glance. "I've never seen you mad before, Alice. It's brought some color to your cheeks."

She grabbed his wrist then, though a small part of her knew it was dangerous to do so, dangerous to do anything so unpredictable around a man who'd just murdered someone for no particular reason.

"Stop treating me like a child," Alice said, yanking him around to look at her.

There was a momentary flare in his eyes; then it was banked, and she knew he would not hurt her.

"I know I've acted like a child. I know I've been helpless. But you just killed two men for no reason that I can see. You might have attracted more attention than I ever could, and I would be the one to pay for it."

They stared at each other, Alice breathing hard. Her hand latched on his wrist, and Hatcher was still as the sea before a storm.

Finally he moved, and his hand went to her cheek, the scarred one. "You're like me, deep down," he said, his eyes drawing her near, like a snake charmer from the East. "You'll do what you must. I see that now. But me, Alice—I'll do what *I* must, and I'll do anything for you. No one would have taken you. I would never let you pay for my mistake."

His hand dropped, and he turned away. Alice's fingers loosened of their own accord, letting him go. She wasn't entirely sure what had happened, but she knew her anger had run out of her, leaving her feeling deflated.

She walked beside him, sensing something had shifted between them, but uncertain as to what that "something" was. The sun was coming up now, so far away, its light piercing the fog but not bringing any heat to pierce the cold and damp.

Hatcher paused as they reached the thoroughfare, busy with morning activity, carts and sellers setting up for their trade. He pulled a handkerchief from his pocket and wet it with his tongue.

"You've blood on your face," he said, wiping her face with the same attention as a mother preparing her child for Sunday worship.

"You also," she said, and took the handkerchief from him.

It was the first time she'd really *looked* at him since he'd shaved off his madman's beard, really took in the hollowness of his face, the shadows under his eyes. He was haunted, same as she was, except he didn't know the name of his ghost. Was there comfort in that? she wondered. Did it make it better or worse to know who or what chased you through your dreams?

Hatcher indicated the pub across the way, and they crossed the street. The folk going about their morning business paid them no mind. A few bleary-eyed fellows staggered out of the pub in question. Hatcher slipped around them and Alice followed, blinking in the dim light as they entered.

A middle-aged man wiped long wooden tables with a grey rag, and a woman of about the same age collected plates and glasses in a bucket. Both of them had the worn faces and knotted fingers that showed a lifetime of hard work. A much younger woman, younger than Alice, mopped the floor in lazy circles.

The man looked up, frowning as the door shut behind Alice and Hatcher. "We're closed," he said, straightening. "Just chivvied the last of the stragglers out."

Hatcher didn't speak. He approached the man, who appeared to swell a little. Alice saw that despite his age, the forearms exposed by rolled sleeves were thick and muscled.

"I said we're closed," he repeated.

Hatcher put two shiny silver coins on the table. The girl paused in her pretense of mopping and watched the proceedings with avid eyes.

"We're looking for a room for the day," Hatcher said, his voice quiet, nonthreatening, but Alice noticed he let his jacket fall open a little.

The tavern keeper's eyes flickered from the axe at Hatcher's waist and back to his face.

"Dolly!" he shouted.

The girl with the mop started, nudging the bucket and sloshing grey water on the floor.

"Take yourself back to the kitchen and get yourself a pie for breakfast before you leave," he said.

Dolly eagerly picked up the bucket, obviously pleased to be released before her task was complete. She stopped halfway to the kitchen, looking from Hatcher to Alice to the keeper. "What about me wages?"

The older woman huffed, putting the dishes on a table. She hurried to the girl's side, muttering, "Come along, you ninny."

They disappeared into the box, leaving the other three around the table. The keeper looked at the scar on Alice's cheek, and then back at Hatcher. "I don't want no trouble with Mr. Carpenter."

Hatcher reached into his pocket and doubled the number of coins on the table. "We don't know Mr. Carpenter. We just need a bed until nightfall, and perhaps some food."

The man looked at the coins on the table, and back at Hatcher, who added two more. "You'll never even know we were here," he said, and Alice understood this to mean that the keeper was to forget them entirely after they left.

The keeper nodded, scooping up the coins. "Up those stairs," he said, jerking his thumb over his shoulder. His eyes moved to Alice's shirtsleeve.

She saw the blood there, coating the cuff, which she hadn't noticed before. Hatcher's right hand, his axe hand, had it too, and along the back of the wrist. Alice supposed they should have done a better job of cleaning up, but then, the blood seemed to help the tavern keeper take them more seriously than he otherwise would have.

"My wife will bring you up some pies in a moment. Second room on the left. I can't vouch for the mattress. Some of the lads who come in take it for an hour."

Alice paused on the steps behind Hatcher.

"Don't worry," he said, not looking back.

At the top of the stairs there was a little turn and then a hallway that stretched back above the tavern floor. Hatcher opened the door to the room and waved Alice in ahead of him.

She exhaled a breath she hadn't realized she'd been holding. For a moment she'd been afraid that they would come upon a man and a woman in the act. But the room was empty.

There was a dirty mattress on the floor, straw leaking from a hole in one side. A filthy wool blanket was tossed at the foot. Alice had spent ten years sleeping on the floor in the asylum, but she shuddered when she saw the foul bed.

"You don't have to sleep there," Hatcher said solicitously.

"I'm not certain I can sleep at all," she said.

"You have to try and get some rest," he said. "Mayhap after you eat something you'll feel calmer."

A small dusty window let in the faint sunlight. Alice went and looked out at the alley below. Hatcher joined her.

"Useful," he said. "You can see the back entrance from here, and right down onto the tavern floor from the door."

"Do you think someone will come looking for us?"

Hatcher shook his head. "Who's to know we're the ones killed those two guards? It was dark."

"Someone could have seen," Alice said, thinking of the buildings all around, with their windows that hid watchful eyes.

"They would have followed us, then," he said. "Any soldier of Mr. Carpenter would have raised the alarm on us right away. And any looking to curry favor with him would have tracked us here."

"How do you know nobody did?" Alice asked.

She felt restless, and strangely trapped. She wasn't certain she could fit through that dirty little window, skinny as she was, if they needed to get away. And the stairs could be blocked.

"Don't worry, Alice," he said. He lay on the bare floor, away from the mattress, and tucked the pack behind his head. He held out one arm to her. "Come and sleep."

"Not yet," she said, watching the activity under the window. A grubby-looking girl of twelve or thirteen approached a young man smoking a cigarette. They talked for a moment; then the girl took the man's hand and led him away to the shadows. Alice turned away, feeling sick to her stomach.

The tavern keeper and his wife seemed all right, but she couldn't get rid of the feeling that they weren't safe here. "Hatch, don't you think there's something wrong?"

"No," he said, pulling his cap low over his eyes. A moment later his breathing was deep and even.

He always slept like that, Alice thought. He would be wide-awake and talking to her through the mouse hole, and then suddenly the talking would cease and she'd hear the sound of his breath, smooth and regular. Except when the Jabberwock was awake. When the Jabberwock was awake he couldn't sleep at all.

There was a soft knock at the door, and Alice remembered the landlady was going to bring them some pies. *But it might not be her,* she thought. She pulled the knife from her pocket and kept it low against her thigh as she opened the door a small crack.

The tavern keeper's wife stood there, holding a tray covered with a piece of flour sacking. She expressed no surprise at Alice's caution. "Pies," she said.

Alice nodded, tucking the knife back in her jacket before opening the door further. She took the tray from the lady, murmuring, "Thanks."

The woman peered over Alice's shoulder at the sleeping Hatcher. "That your man?"

"Yes," Alice said without thinking. Then her eyes widened in terror, because she was supposed to be a boy.

The woman shook her head. "Don't worry. I won't tell."

"How did you know?" Alice asked, her voice low.

She was worried that Hatcher might not be completely asleep, that he may have overheard. If he had, there was no telling what he might do. He could decide to pay the keeper and his wife to keep their mouths shut. Or he might think killing them was easiest. Hatcher was not easy to predict. That fact was clear after his actions with the guards. Alice didn't want to leave a trail of bodies behind them all the way to Cheshire's place. If anyone *were* following them, the bodies would be better than bread crumbs.

"I was like you, once," she said, her eyes full of understanding. "My Harry saved me, and kept me safe all these years. You can trust us."

There was a history in those few sentences, the story of a girl who'd been taken and used, like Alice. Only Alice didn't remember who had saved her from her captor. She might have had help. She might have saved herself. The feeling of a knife in flesh had felt so familiar. Still, Hatcher had rescued her from the asylum, and from the traders who would have taken her the moment she was free from there.

"I don't think others will know what you are, unless they're looking for a girl," the woman went on. "But they won't find a girl here."

Alice met her eyes, and a shared understanding passed between them. "Thank you . . ." she said, her voice trailing off into a question.

"Nell," the woman said.

"Thank you, Nell," Alice said.

"Now, you eat up those pies," Nell said. "I've got the sense you have some traveling ahead of you. Are you running from Mr. Carpenter?"

Alice shook her head. "He told your husband true. We don't know Mr. Carpenter."

Nell wisely did not ask whom they had escaped or where they were heading. She nodded and went away down the stairs.

Alice sat on the floor with the tray in her lap and pulled off the sacking. She'd half expected something greasy and half-cooked, automatically assuming that the quality of food would not be so remarkable in this part of the City.

But the pies she uncovered smelled heavenly, and the pastry that wrapped them was golden brown and flaking, which meant Nell used lots of butter in them. Alice knew that because as a child she'd spent many an afternoon in the kitchen, watching Cook magically turning flour and water and butter and a little sugar and salt into delicious pies.

She bit into the crust, savoring the melting buttery taste on her tongue. The pie was stuffed with meat and gravy and potatoes, the smell of it taking her back again, until she was just four or five years old, perched on a chair eating a bun while Cook stirred the pot at the stove.

She finished the pie before she knew it, and looked longingly at the second one on the tray before wrapping it in the piece of sacking and tucking it in her jacket pocket. Hatcher would want it when he woke.

Alice knew she should sleep, knew that Hatcher would push the pace when night fell. She was eager to escape Mr. Carpenter's territory. The uneasy feeling stayed with her, growing despite Nell's assurances that they were safe. Something was coming. Alice was sure of it.

But Hatch is a Seer, and he doesn't think anything is wrong, she thought. It was just nerves. There had been nothing except stress and danger since they'd emerged from the poisoned river, and now that they were a few moments away from that danger she couldn't shake it.

"Sleep, little butterfly," she whispered, pulling her jacket close around her and crossing her arms. The cap tilted low over her eyes, like Hatcher's, but she did not lie down. She was under the window and across from the door, feeling that if something came through either opening she would know immediately.

And what's coming through the window, you nit? she thought. She'd noted herself that it was too small for any but a child to fit through.

"Sleep, little butterfly," she repeated, and closed her eyes, humming the tune softly.

She did not expect to fall asleep, but she must have, for she woke later with Hatcher's hand on her arm, his face close to hers in the darkness. The darkness had a different quality, the dark of falling night. They must have slept all day, or at least Alice had, and Hatcher allowed it. She could just make out the finger over his lips, silently telling her to stay quiet. Alice shook off the dream that clung to the edges of her brain, something about cake. She'd eaten the cake and gotten very tall, so tall she'd filled up the room.

Hatcher moved away from her, tiptoeing to the door. The pack was already slung over his shoulder and the axe in his hand. Alice slowly came to her feet and followed him, stepping carefully so the floor would not creak, until she was at his shoulder. Now she could hear the sounds of struggle downstairs, glass breaking, benches falling over. Hatcher turned the knob on the door and eased it open a tiny crack, just enough to peer over the balcony and down into the tavern room.

There were five men there, all of them wiry with muscle and wielding knives. There were two other men near their feet, who looked like they might have been customers. They would not be customers any longer. Both of the men had slashed throats.

The attackers appeared to be untouched. They also seemed to be better kept than the sentries Alice and Hatcher killed earlier. Their faces were clean, as were their clothes. They were all dressed in a kind of uniform, blue coats and grey pants and black bowler hats.

The intruders formed a loose half circle around Harry, who stood in front of Nell and Dolly, his hands curled in fists. Nell had her arm around the girl, who was shaking with terror, her mouth open in a silent scream. There was no one else visible. Alice assumed that the other patrons had fled.

She put her mouth close to Hatcher's ear, speaking so low only a mouse could hear. "Do you think they're from Mr. Carpenter? Looking for us?"

Hatcher shook his head once—*No*—and then cupped his hand over his ear to indicate they should listen.

The man in the middle of the group spoke. He didn't look different from the rest of the men, but he had clearly been designated the leader.

"The Walrus is taking over this street, and as you can see," the man said, nudging one of the bloody corpses with the toe of his boot, "the terms of your agreement may be different from your terms with Mr. Carpenter."

Alice took an instant dislike to this man. It wasn't the posturing and bullying—she'd seen that already, and would see it again—but the oily *smugness* of his tone made her back teeth grind.

Someone should teach him a lesson, she thought, and she felt the handle of her knife under her hand.

"I pay Mr. Carpenter thirty percent of the takings, plus the rent," Harry said. "Anything more and we won't be able to eat, nor pay the girl wages."

"Thirty percent," the man said, his tone musing. "Well, that is quite generous of Mr. Carpenter. Unfortunately the Walrus is not quite so generous. Forty percent is where he starts, and your books will be checked by Allan here every week."

He gestured toward the man next to him, who did not look like he knew very much about figures, in Alice's opinion. But perhaps that blank snake's look was what the Walrus wanted in a number-checker.

"Forty percent?" Harry said, his voice hoarse with outrage. "I might as well close up shop and leave. We've barely enough to get by as it is."

The leader of the little gang sidled forward, touching the tip of his knife with a finger. He looked at Harry, the position of the knife suddenly more purposeful, and Alice thought that blade would slide right between Harry's ribs smooth as a spoon through jam.

"I don't think it will be so difficult for you to make forty percent," the man said, and pointed the knife toward Nell and Dolly. "Especially since the two of them will be coming with us, and that will be two less mouths for you to concern yourself with."

Dolly did scream then, a howl of fear that chilled Alice to the marrow of her bones. "No! No! I won't go to the Walrus, I won't! He'll eat me!"

"That'll do," Hatcher said, and threw the door open.

Alice watched in astonishment as he leapt over the rail, his axe in his hand. By the time she collected her wits he had already killed the two men closest to the stairs.

Harry took advantage of Hatcher's surprise appearance and swung a meaty fist at the leader. The man was likely too fast for Harry under normal circumstances, but the tavern keeper managed to land a blow hard enough to make the man's nose crack.

The leader snarled as blood gushed over his mouth, slashing at Harry with the wicked-looking blade. Alice wouldn't have credited the big man with speed but he avoided the slash easily, punching at the leader again. The smaller man avoided Harry's blows. The two of them settled into a kind of dance, each one striking, missing, settling back to try again.

Alice hurried down the stairs, her knife out. Hatcher appeared to have the other two under control. These men were considerably more skilled than the thugs that Hatcher dispatched the night before, but a glance told her that Hatcher could manage them. One of the attackers already sported a large gash in his left shoulder from Hatcher's axe. His face was white and Alice didn't think he would last much longer.

Nell and Dolly had scampered away from the fighting, toward the stairs. Dolly still screamed, though Nell shook and shushed her, trying to keep the attention of their attackers away. Alice pushed around them, one goal in mind, and Harry made that goal much easier by keeping the leader's attention on him and his back to Alice.

She jammed the knife into the leader's back with so much conviction that the blade disappeared up to the hilt. It wasn't quite the same as pressing a knife into a soft and squishy part

(*like eyes*)

but her anger gave her strength she didn't know she had. *Eyes? Where had that come from?*

He stilled for a moment; then his arms flailed out, clawing for the thing that was stuck inside him. Harry stepped in and punched the man one last time. He caromed backward into Alice and she fell over an upturned bench. She scrambled to her feet again, hands curled and ready to fight, though she had no idea how she would defend herself without the knife. The leader crashed against the bench as well and spun to the floor, landing on his stomach, his legs kicking unnaturally.

Harry and Alice stared down at the twitching body of the leader for a moment. Dolly was still screaming.

Alice had missed Hatcher's final blows but the other two men were also on the floor now. He wiped the blade of his axe on his coat—where, Alice noted, there was quite a stain building up—and crossed the room to Dolly and Nell. Nell backed away from him, her arm around Dolly, pulling the girl with her. Alice couldn't blame her. Hatcher was splattered in blood and his grey eyes were fierce and wild.

"Don't you hurt her," Nell said, and though the tavern keeper's wife was putting on a brave face she didn't seem very sure of Hatcher at the moment.

"I won't," Hatcher said, his voice impatient. He put his hand under Dolly's chin and made her look at him. "That's enough, now."

Dolly's mouth clapped shut and she gave him a small, frightened nod.

Hatcher looked around the room at the bodies—two the result of the attackers' actions, the rest due to himself and Alice. "Do you know these lads?" he asked Harry.

Harry shook his head. He seemed somewhat deflated now that the fight was over. He and Nell shared a frightened glance. "They said they were from the Walrus."

"And who is the Walrus?" Hatcher asked. Alice could tell by his tone that he was walking on the thin edge of patience.

"He eats them," Dolly said, and her voice was small now, scared to be heard.

"Eats who?" Alice asked.

"The girls he likes best," Dolly said. "He's monstrous, they say, bigger than four men put together. And when a girl catches his eye his men bring her to him, and she's never seen again. 'Cos he takes them and eats them while he's doing it. Eats them alive."

The vision these words presented made Alice shudder. As if rape were not enough of a horrifying specter for those girls, now there was this—a man so hideous and evil that he ate his victims even as he defiled them. Could this be a true thing? Could the world really be this terrible? Every step Alice took made her long again for the safety of the hospital, a place where the only nightmares to burden her were familiar ones.

"That's only a story, girl, and one you shouldn't be repeating," Nell said, though her eyes told Alice a different story.

"No, it's true," Dolly said, shaking her head. "Everyone knows."

They all fell silent then, looking at one another, wondering whether it was real, that such a monster could exist. The specter of the Walrus seemed to fill the room, an enormous shadow casting a pall over their seeming victory.

Hatcher, ever practical, said, "No sense troubling ourselves over him now. We need to clean up this mess before any of his other men come looking for their friends."

"We'll have to wait a bit before we take them out," Harry said. "It sounds as though the rest are having a bit of fun outside."

Now that it was mentioned Alice heard the sounds of trouble in the streets—breaking glass and wood, rough shouting, the horrified screams of women. She started toward the door, but Hatcher grabbed her arm, shaking his head.

"We can't just leave them out there," she said. The screaming was hurting her brain, hurting her heart. Those girls were going to be taken to the Walrus.

"We're not an army, Alice," Hatcher said. "You and I, we can manage a few tough boys, but we can't stop them all."

"I don't want to leave them," Alice said. "All those girls. All those screaming girls."

She remembered screaming herself, screaming until she was hoarse, screaming until blood ran and her scream mingled with his, a knife pushing into soft flesh

(*into his eye, his blue-green eye*)

and she ran, and she couldn't scream anymore because she needed her breath to run.

Hatcher shook his head again, and his thumb wiped away the tears on her cheek. "We can't save them all."

"This place is terrible," Alice whispered. "So terrible. Why did you take me away from the hospital? I was safe there, safe from all this."

Hatcher pulled her close, put his arms around her. Her head rested against his chest and she heard the steady, reassuring thump of his heart. Harry and Nell and Dolly seemed to fall away, to disappear outside the little circle of Alice and Hatcher. "How could I ever love you properly with a wall between us for all time? I won't let anything happen to you, Alice. I will kill you before I let the Walrus or anyone else take you away from me."

She gave a choked laugh through her tears, a grim and not-so-merry sound. "Most men give a girl a ring, you know, not threaten them with murder."

Hatcher put his hands on her face so he could look in her eyes. "A ring won't save you from the men who would use you and break you. I don't want you to suffer, Alice, not one moment. I won't let them take you."

She was staring in his eyes, so she saw when it happened. Saw the love and the fierce will disappear, and his eyes go blank. His arms fell away from her, limp at his side.

"No," she said. "Not now. No."

"He's coming," Hatcher said, and his voice was not like Hatcher's at all. It was low, full of menace and glee. "The blood is like honey to him. He's coming."

Hatcher slumped to the floor on his knees like a marionette with cut strings.

"What's happening to him?" Dolly asked. "Who's coming? The Walrus?"

Alice barely heard her. She crouched at Hatcher's side, shaking him, tugging at his hand. "Not now, Hatch. Don't let him in. Hatch, stay with me. Stay with me."

He hadn't fainted, but this frozen blankness was far worse. It was as if Hatcher could only feel the Jabberwocky, see what he was seeing.

The noise in the street stopped abruptly. Harry crossed the room to Dolly and Nell and put his arms around them both. Alice could see her breath in the air. The shadow of the Walrus had been replaced by something else, something infinitely more terrible.

There was a footstep on the walk outside, a deliberate ring of heels. The shape of a tall, thin man in a topcoat and hat drifted underneath the door, and as it passed they all exhaled the breath they'd been holding.

The footsteps stopped. The shadow under the door inched into view again. The knob began to turn.

Hatcher clutched Alice's hand with a sudden bruising force, and she saw blood and fire in his eyes.

"No," she said again, and felt something rising inside her. She wrenched her hand from Hatcher's and faced the door, her body filled with fury. She would not lose Hatcher to this thing. She would not. "No, you can't have him. You *can't have him*!"

The room was lit by light then, a light that was as red as Alice's burning, bleeding heart. There was a hideous sound from outside, the sound of all the monsters beneath the bed howling as one, the sound of all the lurking nightmares that clung to the darkness, the sound of something terrifying realizing that it could be frightened itself, frightened by a power it had long considered gone and vanquished.

The shadow under the door disappeared. Alice was rooted in place, her heart galloping in her chest, sweat running down her face and in the small of her back.

"Alice?" Hatcher's voice, small and confused.

She turned back to him slowly, feeling like she wasn't entirely herself in her own body, feeling like something inside her had woken up and she didn't really want that something there.

"He was here," Hatcher said. His eyes were clouded, waking up from a dream. "But he went away."

"Yes," Alice said, helping him to his feet. "Thank goodness, he went away."

"Not goodness," Nell said.

Alice and Hatcher looked at her. The tavern keeper's wife loosed herself from Harry and Dolly, approaching Alice with shining eyes.

"Not thank goodness," Nell repeated. "Thank *you*."

"Thank Alice what?" Hatcher asked.

Nell gestured at Alice with a trembling hand. "She sent . . . whatever that was at the door. No, don't say its name. I don't want to know. When you know the name of a thing, it can find you. She sent it away. She's a Magician."

"A Magician? No. There are no more Magicians. Not really," Alice amended, thinking of Bess and Hatcher and their Seer's blood.

Hatcher glanced from Nell to Alice. He shook his head like a dog with a flea in its ear, and the dazed expression cleared away. He peered closely at Alice, his eyes focused on her but also on something else, as if he were listening to a voice in his head.

"Yes, you are," Nell said, taking Alice's hands in hers. She was crying now, even as she smiled up at Alice. "Now that you are here, everything will be better. The other Magicians will return. All of this darkness and grief will go away."

Alice tugged her hands away from Nell's, panic rising up inside her. "I'm not a Magician. You're mistaken. I'm just a perfectly ordinary girl."

Hatcher shook his head. "There's nothing ordinary about you, Alice. Nothing could have sent the—"

"Please, don't say his name," Nell repeated.

"Him," Hatcher said. "Nothing could have sent him away except magic, real magic. He's not afraid of people or weapons. But he is afraid of Magicians, for a Magician put him in his prison, and could do so again. Bess said you had a fate, that only you and I could defeat him. Now we know why."

"I'm not a Magician!" Alice said again. She felt that if she could just go on saying it, if she could say it often enough, then it would be true.

"Leave the girl be," Harry said. He watched Alice with troubled eyes.

"But she is a Magician," Nell insisted.

"I said to leave her be," Harry said. "We've enough troubles here with this lot to clean up."

Yes, a lot to clean up, Alice thought. Seven bodies, and so much blood her boots were sticky with it.

The leader had long since stopped twitching. Alice reached for the hilt of her knife, protruding from his back. As the blade slid wetly from the flesh she again had that flash of (*memory? dream?*) blue-green eyes, and a man's voice howling in pain and fury.

Outside in the street was the sound of movement again, although the screaming and shouting and breaking had ceased. Instead it seemed that everyone drifted aimlessly, just awakened from a terrible dream. Alice hoped that some of the girls would come to their senses and escape before the Walrus' men could take them away.

I wish I were a Magician, she thought. *I'd find all those lost girls and bring them home. I'd take all those men who hurt those girls and make* them *cry.*

But she wasn't a Magician, whatever Nell or Hatcher liked to believe. She was born to an ordinary family in an ordinary part of the New City. There had never been a hint of anything out of the way in their blood, not on her mother's side or her father's. They were quiet and perfect and eminently respectable.

Except you, Alice thought. *You were not any of those things.*

That did not mean she was a Magician, though. It just meant that she didn't belong.

"You shouldn't bother with the cleaning," Hatcher said. "If what you say is true and the Walrus will take a cut too large for you to handle, then you need to leave. And if he finds out his men were killed here your life won't be worth a tin coin."

"I thought you didn't know who the Walrus was," Harry said.

"I don't," Hatcher said. "But I know how these bosses are. If they let you get away with killing their soldiers, then others will think they can do the same. That's how these fellows lose their power, and they don't like to lose power once they've got hold of it. So once it's discovered that these boys went missing after visiting you, the Walrus will come back to you, swift and hard. You'll wake up one night in a burning bed and find there's no way to escape."

Dolly whimpered. "If they leave what'll happen to me and me mam? I need this work. She can't walk. And I don't want to be taken by the Walrus if he's moving in."

Alice looked at Hatcher, who only shrugged. She felt helplessness rising up inside her, the inability to solve problems for all of them. It was just as it was when they left the hospital. They could save everyone, and they all could die. Or she and Hatcher could jump out of a window and leave the others to their own lookout.

"Give her some money, Hatch," Alice said.

"Why?" he asked. "We need that money for ourselves."

"Give her some, and Harry and Nell too," Alice said. "We can't watch over them, and we can't help them get away."

"You needn't worry about us, girl," Harry said. "You've done enough keeping them from taking my Nell."

"I need it," Dolly said. "I can't move me mam on me own."

"Hatcher," Alice said.

He frowned at her, but didn't protest any further. He drew several coins out of his pocket and passed them to Harry. The tavern keeper tried to refuse them.

"Take them," Hatcher said. "Alice will feel better about it if you do."

Harry looked between them, and Alice nodded. He took the coins from Hatcher with obvious reluctance.

"We must leave now," Hatcher said. "I don't want to tangle with any more of the Walrus' men unless it's unavoidable."

He jogged up the stairs to collect their things from the room. Nell went into the kitchen to gather some food, and Harry passed a few coins to Dolly.

"Go on home and get your mother, girl," he said. "And leave as soon as you can."

Dolly nodded. Harry followed Hatcher up the stairs, presumably to collect things for his own journey. Alice and Dolly were left alone with the bodies and the mess in the serving room.

"What was it your man called you? Alice?" Dolly asked.

"Mm," Alice said.

She wasn't really paying attention to the girl. She was thinking about a blade and a blue-green eye. Did she dream that? Or had she taken out the Rabbit's eye when she escaped? If she had, then maybe he was dead. Maybe the face that had haunted her for ten years was moldering away under the earth, never to worry her again.

"Alice," Dolly repeated, like she was trying to remember it. "Alice. And Nell says you're a Magician."

Something in Dolly's voice drew Alice back from her reverie. There was a flash of cunning in the girl's eyes that Alice didn't care for.

"I'm not a Magician," Alice said, her voice harsh.

"But I seen you," Dolly said, all innocence now. "We all seen that light come out of you and that scary thing under the door went away. So that makes you a Magician, to my way of thinking."

Could Alice have imagined that look in Dolly's eyes? The girl seemed as dim as ever now, amazed by what she thought Alice had done.

I should show her my knife, make sure she understands not to repeat what she saw, Alice thought. But then she hesitated. Firstly she didn't want to get in the habit of flashing her blade around. She wasn't a street tough, even if she was dressed like one. Secondly she didn't want to draw any more attention to herself than she already had. Dolly would likely be more concerned with getting away from the Walrus. Once Alice and Hatcher left, she would forget about what she saw, or perhaps her mother would tell her she imagined it. And that would be that.

Then Hatcher came down the stairs, carrying his sack, and Nell came out of the kitchen, carrying armfuls of pies. She pressed several on Alice and Hatcher, who took them gratefully. After a few more moments of farewells and wish-thee-wells, Alice and Hatcher managed to extract themselves from Nell and slipped into the alley behind the tavern.

There was nobody in the alley, no working girls at their trade.

Already scooped up by the Walrus, Alice thought. She could hear the occasional scuffle out in the street, a scream cut short, the wet slap of boots on stone. Hatcher leaned close to her ear.

"We get out of Carpenter's streets quick as we can," he said. "We don't want to get mixed up in a territory war."

"But how will we know when we're out?" Alice whispered.

She was conscious of the silence in the alley, and the shadows that lurked farther on. Anyone could be hiding there. Anyone could be waiting.

Hatcher wouldn't let her be taken. She wouldn't allow herself to be taken, come to that. But she was weary of blood and fighting and running, which seemed to be all they had done since they left the hospital.

"There will be sentries at all the borders," Hatcher said. "When we cross them, we cross out of Carpenter's streets."

"And what do we cross into?" she asked. "We could be heading straight for the Walrus."

"If the Walrus is moving on Carpenter's streets, then his attention will be here, not in his own space. And every territory has four sides, Alice. Walrus could be on the north, and we're heading west."

That was certainly news to Alice. It seemed they'd wandered willy-nilly through the Old City, despite Hatcher's claims of following a map in his head.

"How far to Rose Way?" she asked.

Hatcher moved through the alley, quiet and cautious. "We should be there by morning."

If nothing else happens, Alice thought. She wanted to ask about Cheshire, but it was wiser to stay silent while they knew there was still a chance of being discovered by Carpenter's men.

She deliberately ignored any thoughts of magic, or Magicians, or the Jabberwocky. Bess said they had to find him and capture him again, and to do that they needed to find the thing the Jabberwocky was looking for, the thing that a Magician had taken from him long ago. Alice would do her best there, because she didn't want Hatcher in the Jabberwocky's grip any longer. But she didn't have to dwell on why the Jabberwocky had run from the door of Harry's tavern. She didn't have to think about that if she didn't want to.

It was another long night of darting through dark places and avoiding the street soldiers who seemed to be everywhere. Alice convinced Hatcher that climbing over a roof near a checkpoint was more efficient than killing off the sentries again, and once they were above the streets they decided it was nicer to stay there. It wasn't precisely easy to clamber up and over roofs, and several of the spaces between buildings were a little too far apart for Alice's liking. But there was no fear of blades and blood, for anyone with sense kept both their feet on the ground.

It was even more impossible for Alice to track their path through the City from this height. Above, all the streets underneath faded into a disturbing sameness, their mazelike quality ever more pronounced. But the air was a bit clearer. The heavy fog and the entire surrounding stench tended to settle in the canyons of the City, seeping into the layers of wood and stone. On the rooftops Alice could see the faint hint of stars through the haze.

They stopped once to stuff their mouths with Nell's pies, now cold but still delicious. Alice's flagging strength revived then, and she was better able to keep up with Hatcher's silent-footed bounding.

Really, he is like a cat, she thought. His boot heels never seemed to ring on roof tile like hers, his weight barely touching down before he sprang forward again. She had yet to see Hatcher confounded by any circumstance. Alice felt as though she had been teetering on the edge of a black hole (*a rabbit hole*) since they'd escaped, and one more strange or frightening event might tip her into that hole. Yet Hatcher never seemed permanently affected by their circumstances. Even the possession of the Jabberwocky fell away from him as soon as it was over.

The sun was pushing faint orange rays through the fog when Hatcher suddenly raised a hand to indicate they should stop. Alice crab-walked to his side—they were on a slightly steeped roof, and Hatcher was perched like a pigeon on the crux of it—and peered at what he was staring at.

Almost directly below and across from their perch was a little house nestled between the larger, multistoried buildings that occupied the street. It was so small compared to its neighbors that it seemed like a toy. Alice half expected to see a little girl's hand pushing a doll through the front door to water the roses.

And there were roses—masses of them, so many Alice could scarcely credit it. They twined over the door and the window, up the walls, and covered the roof so thoroughly that the tiles were not even visible. The roses seemed to glow with an unearthly light, pink and red and white and yellow wrapped together in an impossible bouquet. The scent of sweet flowers drifted up to them.

Alice inhaled deeply. The smell made her head feel like it was drifting away from her body. For a moment everything spun in a circle.

She didn't realize she'd tipped forward until Hatcher grabbed her shoulder, keeping her from tumbling off the roof.

"What . . . ?" she asked, her voice faint. She tried again, shaking her head to clear away the scent of roses. "What is that?"

"That's Cheshire's place," Hatcher said, and there was a note of pride in his voice. "I knew I could find it again, even if I couldn't remember properly why."

"But the roses," Alice said. "How can those roses be there, like that, in the middle of all this filth and fog?"

Hatcher gave her a crooked half smile, his grey eyes glinting in the morning light. "Magic."

Alice sucked in her breath, astonished. "You mean Cheshire's a Magician? How can that be? Why wasn't he driven out with all the other Magicians?"

It seemed incredible that such a blatant display of magic would go unnoticed by the City officials.

"No, he's not a Magician," Hatcher said. "But his house was built by one, and Cheshire moved in when the Magician left."

"How has he managed to keep it?" Alice asked. Given the fighting she'd already seen over money, territory and girls, how was it that Cheshire's house hadn't been snatched up by the local boss?

Hatcher gave her a slightly sneaky sideways look, as if he knew she was not going to pleased. "Cheshire's the head of this area."

"He's a boss?" Alice asked. "You're taking me into the house of one of those—those people?"

"No, no," Hatcher said hastily. "Cheshire doesn't deal in girls. He'll have no interest in you—leastways, not like that. He deals in information. So be careful what you say to him, or around him. No matter how he seems, Cheshire is not your friend. He'll sell you out in an instant if he thinks it will benefit him."

"Hatch, that does not comfort me in the least," Alice said.

"Just talk as little as you can," Hatcher said, walking to the edge of the roof and peering down. "And it may be a good idea for you to keep being Alex."

"Right," Alice said.

She'd half forgotten the clothes she wore were meant to be a disguise. Nell had seen through the fiction so easily that Alice hadn't practiced being a boy in actual company yet.

"There's a balcony just below here," Hatcher said, indicating with his hand.

"Don't people live there?" Alice asked in a whisper.

"Likely," Hatcher said. "But we'll only be there for a moment and then we'll be on the ground."

"And what if someone sees us and starts screaming?"

"We need to get to Cheshire's house. We can't land on his roof from here. Well, come to think of it, we can't land on his roof at all."

"Why not?"

"I told you, those roses have magic," Hatcher said. "They keep intruders away."

"And how do they do that?" Alice asked. The roses appeared less beautiful to her now, the gleaming petals less obvious than the pointed thorns and malicious vines.

"Just don't get close to those flowers until Cheshire has approved you," Hatcher said. "I'll swing you down here. As soon as your boots touch that landing, you climb over the side and drop to the street. I can't go down there until you move; there's not enough room. Hurry it up, Alice. The sun's coming up and folk will be about their business soon. We'll be seen."

Hatcher grabbed Alice under the shoulders and swung her over the edge of the roof before she had a chance to look the situation over properly. She had a terrible moment of fear that the landing was not below her, that Hatcher would release her and her feet would kick wildly in the air and find no purchase. But then his hands slid away from her and the balcony was there a second later, just as he said it would be, and she made less noise than she expected.

Washing hung out to dry on a line—a woman's underthings, and a couple of men's shirts. There was a grimy window and a wooden door that wouldn't have kept out a curious cat. Inside, the occupants stirred, the slow shuffle of morning feet on bare floor.

Alice swung her leg over the side and made a concerted effort not to think about what she was doing. Going up on the roof had seemed like such a smart idea when it was dark and she couldn't really see how high she was. She glanced down just long enough to make sure she wasn't about to land in a coal cart or on top of someone's head. The ground looked very far away.

"Alice!" Hatcher hissed.

She closed her eyes and pushed away from the side and hoped she would not break her legs. Or her nose.

Somehow a miracle occurred and the ground did not take a bite out of her. A moment later she stood in the street in front of Cheshire's house, on her own two feet and nothing broken. There was a faint warmth at her chest, and she lifted the shirt a little to see the rose pendant that Bess gave her glowing with a faint light, though it faded so quickly that she wondered whether she'd imagined it.

Then Hatcher was at her side, light-footed and sure. She rearranged her clothing so the pendant was well hidden and followed him to Cheshire's doorstep.

The roses' perfume was stifling at this distance. It permeated the air around them, pushed away the usual stink of sweat and food and offal that hung in the air. But it wasn't necessarily a *better* smell, Alice thought. There was something not right about that sweet, twining scent, something that snuck up in between her eyes and made her head ache.

The cottage—for that was what it was, really—was covered so completely in roses that not a sliver of the outside wall was revealed. Only the door—painted white like a gleaming tooth—and a scrupulously clean four-paned window escaped the pervasive touch of the flowers.

Hatcher knocked three times on the door, his hand dark and filthy against the shimmering white paint. Only after Hatcher knocked did something occur to Alice.

"Perhaps it's a little early to come calling?" she asked. "The sun has barely risen. Won't Cheshire be angry at being woken?"

Hatcher shook his head, not chagrined in the least. "He won't be angry if he thinks we've brought him something interesting."

"What do we have that's interesting?" Alice asked, but she never found out the answer.

The door opened then, smooth and silent on oiled hinges. A very large man stood there, about as tall as Hatcher but much better fed. He was dressed in unrelieved black and held a short coil of silver wire in one hand. There was a tattoo of a smiling cat on the back of that hand, between the last knuckle of his thumb and the thick bone of his wrist.

His eyes were as black as his clothes, and they took in Alice and Hatcher's ragged appearance in one glance.

"Get off with you," he said, and started closing the door.

Hatcher reached to stall him, his hand stopping the door halfway. The man looked from Hatcher's hand to his face, those black eyes calm and endless and unyielding. Hatcher returned the gaze with the same calm, though Alice fought the impulse to tug at Hatcher's arm and pull him away.

"We're here to see Cheshire. Tell him Bess sent us," Hatcher said.

"Mr. Cheshire don't have time for the likes of you," the man said. "Now, I'm telling you for the last time, get off and stay off."

"Cheshire will be very unhappy if you don't tell him we're here," Hatcher said. "And if I remember right it's not a pretty sight when Cheshire isn't happy."

Fear flared in those black depths, a flash so quick that Alice thought she imagined it. The guard's expression never changed. He and Hatcher continued to stare at each other for a moment longer.

"Wait here," the guard said, and shut the door.

"Hatch, what is it we have that Cheshire will find interesting?" she asked again.

"Us, of course," Hatcher said.

"But I thought you said not to say anything in front of him," Alice said.

"I said to *watch* what you say," Hatcher said. "Cheshire likes information, and you don't want him to have any information that you don't want him to have."

Alice shook her head, not sure whether the conversation was actually going in circles or whether the roses were making her feel like it was.

"But he likes new things, and new people. And he likes Bess, or he did. He helped her once," Hatcher said.

"Are you remembering more?" Alice asked. Hatcher seemed a wealth of information all of a sudden.

He tilted his head to one side, thinking. "No. Just what I need to remember. There are still black spots where other things were."

Alice wondered about the black spots in her own memory, and whether Cheshire could tell her if the Rabbit was dead. If he was such a fountain of information, then he was sure to know. But Bess had told her to stay away from the Rabbit and anything to do with him. And Hatcher said not to tell Cheshire anything. If Cheshire did know about the Rabbit's fate, then he would wonder why Alice wanted to know. And that might lead to other questions. No, it was better not to bring up the Rabbit at all.

Behind them on the street people were going about the business of their day. Alice heard a noise above them and glanced behind and up. A careworn woman of indeterminate age was removing the washing from the landing that Alice and Hatcher had used to climb down from the roof.

The door swung open again, and the guard stood there. Alice thought he appeared sourer than before, as if he'd eaten something that didn't taste very pleasant.

"Mr. Cheshire will see you now," he said. His grip tightened on the silver wire he held, as if he were itching to use it.

They were led through a very tiny foyer with a marbled floor into a small parlor, with the most exquisitely carved furniture Alice had ever seen, all of it white and spotless like the front door. A beautiful little round table with elegant curved legs sat in the middle of the room, four matching chairs arranged around it. The chairs had plump embroidered cushions on the seat and the backs were carved filigree.

All around the walls were smaller tables and fat cushioned ottomans, and everywhere there were roses. Roses in vases on the tables and roses painted in pictures and hung in frames. Roses were sewn into the chair cushions and multiplied in patterns on the wallpaper. The same heavy scent that hung outside the house was even more pronounced here, despite the presence of fewer flowers. The windows were shut, keeping the perfume contained in the small space.

On the table were several cakes shaped like roses, and small sugar candies carved in the same likeness. There was a pot of tea, steam curling from the spout, and three cups set out for pouring. Alice wondered that all of this was put together so quickly, while they stood at the door and waited. It was almost as if Cheshire had known they were coming. But that couldn't be. They'd discussed their plans with no one but Bess.

In the midst of all this petaled splendor was a man, standing near the center table and grinning an oversized grin. Everything about this man was unexpected. The huge guard had appeared scared of Cheshire's anger. Alice thought a man who wielded so much power and frightened such a large man would be large himself, that he would appear a strong man not to be crossed. But Cheshire was nothing like that.

He was as small and neat as the parlor he stood in. His head would come to just above Alice's elbow if he was close by her. That head was covered all over with golden brown hair carefully curled in ringlets. His eyes were bright and green and curious and he wore a velvet suit of rose red. It seemed so soft that Alice longed to stroke it with her fingers.

Cheshire's grin widened as he looked them over, a glint of recognition in his eyes when he saw Hatcher. Alice decided she didn't like that grin. It wasn't happy. It was more like a predatory animal baring its teeth.

Cheshire waved at the guard. "Thank you, Theodore."

Alice glanced behind her as the guard left. He did not appear pleased at being sent from the room.

"Well, well. Bess Carbey's grandson. What are you doing out of your cage, little bird? I heard a long while ago that you did very bad things and they sent you away, away where all the mad little birds are kept."

Hatcher started in surprise. "How do you know that? Bess didn't even know where I'd been."

"Oh, I know many things. Many things," Cheshire said, pulling out a chair and seating himself. "Please join me."

It was not a request. It was spoken in the same cheery tone as everything else, but Alice heard the steel underneath it. She and Hatcher maneuvered into the little chairs, both of them so tall that their knees knocked against the table.

Cheshire poured out the tea, his eyes roving over them all the while. "Yes, I know about Nicholas. But I don't know you, my lad. And quite big and dangerous-looking you are with that scar. That scar. Hmmm."

Alice didn't like the thoughtful look on his face. In fact, she was quickly realizing that she did not like anything about Cheshire at all—not his rose-covered house or the heavy perfume of roses that made her feel sick, not his knowing smile or the speculative way he peered at her scar. She didn't want to have tea with this man. She wanted to find out what they needed to know and then leave.

"This is Alex," Hatcher said, before Alice could speak.

"Alex," Cheshire said, rolling the name around in his mouth like he was tasting it. Then he shook his head. "No. That is not your name." The grin was gone now. The merry eyes were flat as a snake's. "It is not polite to tell lies, especially when you are my guests. I do not care for lies."

He had not threatened them, and the idea of this little man physically overpowering them both was absurd. Yet Alice felt a distinct chill in the air, a threat of menace that had not been there before. This man was dangerous, more dangerous than she'd thought.

She took the cap from her head, thinking quickly. "It's not Alex. It's Alice. And I hope you'll forgive us for the deception, sir. It's only for my own safety."

Hatcher gave her a quick, annoyed look, as if to say, *Why pretend to be a boy if everyone you meet knows you're a girl?* And Alice didn't disagree. But it seemed far more dangerous to lie to Cheshire.

The hard glint in Cheshire's eyes softened a bit as he considered. "Alice, is it? Alice. And that scar . . ."

He drifted off, his eyes dreamy now as he sifted through the vast stores of knowledge in his head. Then he suddenly snapped his fingers and sat up straighter, that horrible grin returned.

"Alice! Yes, of course. Another naughty little bird. You ran away, Alice, yes, you did. And you made the Rabbit so distressed, and he couldn't find you."

Her body went stiff with fear. Cheshire knew who she was. It didn't sound as though the Rabbit was dead. It sounded as though he was alive. And this man knew who she was, and who she was to the Rabbit. If Cheshire wanted, he could have his guard put her in a gunnysack and carry her straight to the Rabbit again.

"But he marked you, didn't he?" he continued.

At these words Cheshire reached across the tiny table, the first two fingers of his hand extended. Alice knew what would happen and steeled herself not to show any emotion.

Cheshire's fingers, cold and slightly damp, stroked down the scar on her cheek. She swallowed the shudder of revulsion at his touch.

"Yes," Cheshire said. "He marked you so that he would know you again, and know that you belong to him."

"I belong to no one," Alice said, her voice harsher than she intended. She would fight if she must, and so would Hatcher. Whatever power Cheshire wielded, he could not make her go back to the Rabbit.

Cheshire giggled. "Oh, yes, there's that spirit that the Rabbit liked, before you spirited away, that is. Then he was not so fond of your energy, particularly after what you did to him."

(*a blade in a blue-green eye*)

Cheshire watched her carefully, and Alice feared he could read the thought that had gone across her face. She must be careful now, very careful.

"Yes," Cheshire said, taking a bite of rose-shaped cake. "I think the Rabbit would be very interested to know you're in the Old City."

Alice didn't know what to do. Should she threaten Cheshire? Should she tell Hatch to pay him so that he wouldn't talk? He seemed the sort of person who might like knowing something another didn't. He might like lording it over them in his own mind. Then, suddenly, she knew what to do.

"The Rabbit and me is hardly news, is it?" Alice said lightly. "A very old affair."

"But one, I assure you, that the Rabbit thinks of every day. You made quite sure of that, my dear," Cheshire said.

Yes, if I did take his eye, I imagine he would think of me every day, Alice thought. She plunged on, aware that Hatcher watched the proceedings with a curious gaze. They were doing the precise opposite of what they'd intended—that Hatcher should talk and Alice should listen. But Hatcher was wise enough not to muddy the waters, and to wait until Alice was finished.

"I think the more interesting news is the return of the Jabberwocky. Do you not agree?" Alice asked.

It hadn't seemed possible, but Cheshire sat up even straighter then. Alice thought he was surprised, but she couldn't tell for certain. Cheshire was very difficult to read.

"And what does the Rabbit's lost toy know of the Jabberwocky?" Cheshire asked.

Something in her heart burned when he called her a "lost toy." She did not show it.

"We have seen him," Alice said, indicating Hatcher and herself.

"Seen him and survived?" Cheshire asked, and now it was clear that he was surprised. "How can that be?"

"Good fortune," Alice said. She did not want Cheshire to know about the pendant or how Nell claimed she sent the Jabberwocky away.

"Good fortune indeed," Cheshire said, and he narrowed

his eyes and looked between the two of them. "Of a kind not usually found in his presence."

"It is because of the Jabberwocky that we are here," Alice said. "Bess told us that you could tell us how to trap him again."

The little man chortled. "Trap the Jabberwock? You are ambitious, aren't you, little toy?"

Alice said nothing. He was baiting her, hoping she would lose her temper and reveal something she did not want him to know.

"Bess said the Jabberwock was searching for something," Hatcher said. Alice noted that Hatcher did not mention his own connection to the monster. "And that you would know what that something was."

"Oh, yes, he searches," Cheshire said. "Snicker-snack, snicker-snack. He must have it before anyone else does, before anyone realizes what it does."

"What is 'it'?" Alice asked, unable to hide her impatience.

Cheshire sat forward, his eyes eager. "Would you like to hear a story, my little ones? For I have a story I could tell. I like to tell my stories, sometimes."

Alice thought he would like such a thing. It would be a way for him to show off what he knew, but only as much as he wanted to tell.

He looked at them expectantly, waiting for them to acknowledge the treat.

"I would like very much to hear a story," Alice said, and tried to sound properly grateful (instead of resentful, which was what she actually felt) when she said it.

"A long time ago," Cheshire said, his voice dreamy again, "there was a Magician. Well, to tell it properly, there were two Magicians. And these two were friends, close as brothers. Both had an insatiable hunger for knowledge, to find the furthest reaches of their power, to discover how deep magic could take them. But one line they swore never to cross, and that was into dark magic, for they knew that once tasted, the darkness would overcome even the purest of intent. And so they went on, day after day, experimenting and growing ever more powerful, until no other Magician could possibly defeat them. They were the strongest, most magnificent Magicians the world had ever seen. And for one of them, it was enough. He used his magic to help the common folk, to make their crops grow, to heal their sick, to do good with the gifts he had been given. But the other . . . Well, there are some who will never be content. He grew restless, and saw the giving of magic to simple folk as unworthy of his power. And so, in secret, he went to the dark places, and learned all the dark things there were to know."

As Alice listened to Cheshire's dreamy remembering voice she heard another, laid over the voice of the man. It was light and soft and full of love, and it sounded like her mother. She could see her mother's face there, just above her in the flickering candlelight, as she snuggled under the coverlet.

"His friend, once so close as a brother, saw the changes in him and protested, tried to stop him. But the other had drunk deep in the well of shadows, and for him there was no returning. The good Magician knew then what he must do, for such a threat could not be allowed to exist in the world. He went to the blacksmith, and asked him to make a blade, a special blade that curved like the moon at its crescent. Before the last strike of the blacksmith's hammer the good Magician took the blade in his palm and closed his hand around it. His blood seeped into the blade, and so did a little of his magic, and his intent.

"Then the blacksmith struck the blade once more, and declared his work complete. The good Magician took the weapon with a heavy heart, for he mourned the friend and brother he once had.

"He went to the place where the other Magician was learning the ways of darkness. His friend had become a monster, hideous and twisted, and the good Magician was repulsed by this creature. The monster that had once been a Magician laughed as his old friend stood before him, and said nothing could defeat him.

"But the good Magician had right on his side, and his pure heart, and though the two battled for many days, in the end the good Magician prevailed. He pinned the monster to the ground with his blade, and that blade drew away some of the monster's magic, so that he could no longer defend himself. The monster told the Magician to kill him, for if not, he would rise up again, and destroy the Magician and all of his line. But the Magician could not kill his friend, though he knew it was necessary. In the end he took the monster and put him in a box, a tiny prison without a key, and buried the box deep in the soil. Then he went away from that place, taking the blade with him."

Her voice faded away, and it was only then that Alice realized she spoke in time with Cheshire, and that he and Hatcher both stared at her.

"You know the story of how the Jabberwock was formed, then?" Cheshire asked, and his eyes were more speculative than before.

"My . . ." Alice began, and then thought it wise not to mention her mother. "Someone told me once, when I was young. But I'd forgotten until you told it again."

"It is interesting that you know that tale," Cheshire said. "Yes, you are very interesting, Alice. I can see why the Rabbit prized you so."

Each time Cheshire mentioned the Rabbit so casually she felt like ice was pricking her all over her skin. Memories surfaced, one by one, and she was afraid to see all of them at once, and afraid that if Cheshire continued to mention it, all of her lost thoughts would return in a rush, and destroy her.

"So the Jabberwock was a Magician, and another Magician took some of his power in the blade that defeated him," Hatcher said. Alice knew he tried to steer Cheshire away from the topic of the Rabbit, and she was grateful.

"Snicker-snack," Cheshire said again. "The Jabberwock seeks that blade, for he is crippled without the magic inside it. He cannot fully become until that power is returned to him. And the blade is also the only way to defeat him, for the good Magician put his power inside it also."

"Then we simply need to find it," Alice said. "And the Jabberwocky."

"Oh, don't fret, my dear. I am certain he will find *you*. You are very interesting," Cheshire said again.

Alice did not wish to be interesting to Cheshire, or to the Jabberwock. It was true that the Jabberwock would be drawn to them, but that was because of Hatcher's connection to the creature, not because of her. In Alice's mind, therefore, the wisest thing would be to find this sword as soon as possible, before the creature drew near them again.

"Do you know where the blade is?" Hatcher asked.

His feet moved restlessly under the table. Hatcher never liked to be still for long. Even in the hospital he was constantly moving, pacing, twitching, rolling. The uncomfortable chairs and low table essentially penned him in place, and Alice sensed he was on the verge of having enough.

"I know many things, Nicholas, grandson of Bess Carbey. I know things you yourself do not know. I know where Jenny is. Far away, over the forest and over the mountains she's gone." Cheshire sat back a little, apparently to appreciate the effects of his news.

But these words apparently meant nothing to Hatcher, who only frowned slightly. "Do you know where the sword is?" he repeated.

Cheshire looked put out, as though he were expecting to enjoy an explosion that didn't occur. "I don't know where the blade is now," Cheshire said, his tone short.

Alice and Hatcher looked at each other, their feelings plain. *This was a wasted trip.*

"However," Cheshire said, and the crafty tone was back in his voice. "I know someone who may know."

"And who is that?" Alice asked, though she did not relish the thought of another goose chase across the Old City only to find someone who may or may not have what they were looking for.

"I shall tell you," Cheshire said. "First, you must give me something in return."

Alice wanted to say he had already gotten plenty, more than they had intended to give, but she did not want to remind him of the Rabbit again. It was too much to hope that he would forget who she was, but perhaps the Jabberwocky would distract him.

"What is it you want?" Alice asked.

"Why, your memory, of course," Cheshire said. "Your memory of taking the Rabbit's eye."

Alice blinked in astonishment. "But I don't remember. I don't remember that at all." *But thank you for telling me. Thank you for letting me know I didn't imagine it.*

Cheshire seemed disappointed. "At all? Not a spick? Not a speck? Not a shadow?"

Something sharp sinking into something soft, and a man screaming.

"No," she said, with as much guile as she possessed.

Cheshire peered at her very closely. She had the uncomfortable feeling that he was trying to look past her eyes and into her brain, trying to search and find that fragment of memory so he could snatch it away. Good or bad or broken, her memories were her own, and Cheshire had no right to them.

After a long moment Cheshire grinned. "Just because there is nothing there now doesn't mean there won't be in the future. What if we agree that you owe me that memory, when it returns to you?"

Hatcher shook his head once, short and sharp. "No. I won't have Alice owing you anything."

Cheshire smiled wider, very well pleased now and showing it. "Oh you won't have it, will you, Nicholas? Perhaps the Rabbit's little toy now belongs to the Hatcher of Heathtown?"

"She told you she belongs to nobody, and she told you true," Hatcher said, though his eyes flickered a little when Cheshire called him that name.

"The Rabbit doesn't think so. The Rabbit says he marked her, and she is his," Cheshire said.

"That's more than enough," Hatcher said, pushing away from the table. "You don't know where the sword is, so you're of no use to us."

"Your manners did not improve in your cage, Nicholas," Cheshire said. "You are my guest, and a very poor one. You didn't even eat any of my cakes."

He raised a finger, almost as if he were testing the wind. Then the scent of roses was abruptly stronger, overpowering. Alice coughed as thick perfume filled her throat like fog.

Two things happened at once. The roses set in vases around the room shot from their containers like spider's silk, impossibly long, as if their stems had not been cut at all.

At the same time Hatcher pulled something from his coat. It was not the axe, as Alice expected. It was the gun, the forbidden weapon. She had nearly forgotten he carried it.

Cheshire crooked his finger down in the shape of a hook.

The roses halted midair in their flight. For the first time since their arrival, Cheshire did not seem smug or in control. His left eye twitched as Hatcher pushed the gun very close to Cheshire's face.

The very idea of the gun made Alice nervous. Hatcher wasn't supposed to have it, and it was too easy for an accident to happen. When you used a knife or an axe, you had to think; you had to be deliberate. If Hatcher's finger twitched, then it wouldn't matter if he meant to kill Cheshire or just frighten him. The little man would still be dead.

"Your manners most definitely did not improve," Cheshire said. "I could have Theodore run to a copper. You would be hanged on the spot just for holding that."

"You would be dead whether the copper came or not," Hatcher said.

Alice did not like this. This was not going as it was supposed to at all. Cheshire liked Bess, and so was to be disposed to help her grandson. They were not supposed to be threatening the person who was to provide them help. Hatcher's temper was short, and if he "saw red" as he had when they met Carpenter's sentries, then there was sure to be a tragedy.

If Cheshire were killed, then who would move in to take over his territory? A monster like the Walrus? Certainly whoever moved in would think nothing of selling girls. The women of Cheshire's district were likely safer here than they would be elsewhere.

Finally, despite all their bravado, they had no clue where to look for the sword, and Cheshire did. They needed him, like it or not.

Alice reached for Hatcher's hand, not the one that held the gun but the other, and gave it a very soft squeeze. "That's quite enough, Hatch."

He stared at Cheshire a moment longer, and Alice was certain he would pull the trigger. Instead, he exhaled slowly as he hid the weapon under his coat.

Cheshire grinned again, his default expression. Alice felt a nearly overwhelming urge to slap at that smile, to break the perfect line of too-white teeth.

"That will be enough to be getting on with," he said. "The two of you have given me a lovely morning's entertainment. I'm so pleased I told Theodore to let you in."

Alice and Hatcher glanced at each other, baffled. Cheshire appeared unaffected by the events that had just occurred. The roses slid slowly back inside their vases, harmless flowers once more.

He reached for another cake and stuffed it in his mouth, talking through the crumbs. "Oh, yes, a lovely morning's entertainment. And now I know something the Rabbit does not know."

"Will you tell him?" Alice asked. She disliked the hesitant tone in her voice, the tiny little hiccup of fear.

Cheshire waved his hand. "Oh, no. Why would I do that?

Then he would know too, and it's so much more fun when I have something he doesn't. His streets press right up against mine. Just to the west. And sometimes his lads come in at night and take my girls from their beds, though it's hard to prove with ruffians on all sides. I don't know why they're all so crude. So I will enjoy knowing that his girl Alice is walking free and he's ignorant."

"For the last time, she's not his girl. She's mine," Hatcher said.

"Of course, of course," Cheshire said soothingly. His manner was completely different from before. He was friendlier, and apparently took no offense at Hatcher's waving a gun in his face. "Though I wouldn't mind being there when you tell him that. Oh, yes. I would enjoy that indeed."

His green eyes gleamed just like a cat's in the dark, Alice thought.

"Now, as to your question," Cheshire continued. "My knowledge of the sword ceases with the story of the Magician and the formation of the Jabberwocky. However, there are many collectors in the City."

"Collectors?" Alice asked.

"Yes, they collect things that are interesting or precious. The Rabbit is one, you know. He collects many things, pretty things and rare things, and you are one of those pretty and rare things, my girl. So you keep out of his sights, for he wants you back in his collection, and he won't let you get away again."

It's strange, Alice thought. *It's almost as if he's warning me, like he cares what happens.*

"I don't like these men that scoop up girls and use them for their own purpose," Cheshire said. "I try to keep the girls in my district safe. I keep them safe by knowing more about these men than they know of themselves. But I am, alas, a rare breed."

"Do you know of the Walrus?" Alice asked, thinking of what Dolly said.

"Whatever you have heard is not only story," Cheshire said, and there was no hint of playfulness now. "He eats them as he defiles them, and I cannot imagine a worse fate. You would be better off in the Rabbit's collection than taken by the Walrus."

"I won't let him take her," Hatcher said.

"You are very much a man, Nicholas." Cheshire sighed. "But you were not able to protect Jenny. Though you were younger then, it is true. And there was deceit."

This time a spasm went across Hatcher's face at the mention of Jenny. Alice wanted to ask who Jenny was, if he remembered, but she did not want to do so in front of Cheshire. He was too unpredictable.

"But that is old business. We are concerned with this moment, and at this moment the Jabberwocky is walking the streets. Now, the craftiest collector of all is the Caterpillar. If the blade is in the Old City, then he will know. He may even have it, which would certainly make your task much simpler. Although if he does have it, he may not want to give it up."

"Everyone has a price," Hatcher said.

"Yes, but can you pay it?" Cheshire asked. "The Caterpillar is not as interested in simple coin as some might be."

"Where will we find him?" Hatcher asked.

"His streets are north of mine. Most nights he can be found at an establishment he calls Butterflies. You may imagine what kind of establishment that is," Cheshire said. "And now, while this has been very amusing, you must run along. I have much business and you are delaying me."

His attitude was again different from what it had been a moment before. Now he was brisk, waving them out of the parlor and back into the small foyer before they realized what had happened. The door to the parlor closed behind them with a firm *click*.

Alice and Hatcher looked at each other, and Alice saw the confusion she felt reflected on Hatcher's face. What had just happened? Had Cheshire helped them or harmed them? It certainly seemed that he had obtained more information from them than they had from him. He appeared genuinely concerned for Alice's safety from the Rabbit and other predators about the Old City, yet at the same time he was not a friend. He could not be relied upon to assist them unless he could gain by it.

The guard Theodore waited there, and Alice thought he seemed pleased about something.

"This way," Theodore said, leading them through an extraordinary hallway.

It was patterned all over in black and white tiles, ceiling and floor and walls. Looking at it made Alice sick and dizzy, and she already felt a bit ill from the heavy blanket of roses in the parlor air.

"Why are you taking us this way instead of the way we entered?" Alice asked.

"Mr. Cheshire has important visitors coming and doesn't want rabble like you crossing them on the step," Theodore said.

Alice wanted to take offense at the "rabble" designation, but it didn't seem important enough to bother with. Besides, they hardly appeared presentable in their dirty and bloodstained clothing. She had a feeling Theodore would enjoy using that silver wire he carried on them, and she wasn't interested in providing him motivation to do so. She glanced over her shoulder at Hatcher. He frowned fiercely, like he was trying very hard to remember something. He likely had not heard what Theodore said.

The hallway went on and on, much longer than should be possible for such a small house. Far at the end there was another white door—*like a house full of teeth,* Alice thought. *Teeth in every doorway, waiting to bite.* Theodore stepped to one side and indicated they should exit that way.

Alice turned the doorknob and opened the door. Outside, the glare of the sun was surprisingly strong, and for a moment she was blinded. Then Hatcher pushed into her back and she tumbled to the ground. The door closed very firmly behind them, and Alice heard the lock turn.

She rolled to her back, ready to snap at him for pushing her, but stopped when she saw large rosebushes, taller than Hatcher, rising up from the ground on either side of her.

Hatcher reached down to help her. "He pushed me out the door. That guard. I think he didn't want us to get a good look at what was out here."

"Where are we?" Alice asked, staring around in wonder. "This can't be Cheshire's garden."

The bushes grew above them and stretched on in the distance, much farther than should have been possible. There was an intersection in distance, turnings going left and right.

There was no sign of the City, the buildings that surrounded the cottage, the noise of the street. It didn't even smell the same. The air was clean and fresh and the roses here lightly perfumed the air instead of clawing at Alice's nose and throat. The sun was so bright compared to the dreary Old City that it hardly seemed to shine on the same world.

"This is Cheshire's idea of fun," Hatcher said.

Alice studied the passage before them for a moment. "It's a maze."

"Yes, and I'll wager anything we're trapped in here until we solve it," Hatcher said.

He turned back to the white door and gave it a hearty kick, strong enough to rattle the panes of glass in the windows.

"We haven't the time for this, Cheshire!" Hatcher shouted. "Have you forgotten the Jabberwocky?"

There was no answer, although Alice thought she heard the faint sound of laughter in the wind.

"This is the price for what he told us," Alice said. "He must be a Magician himself, Hatch. How else could this be? And we saw what he did with the roses inside."

Hatcher shook his head. "He is not a Magician. I told you a Magician built Rose Way. Whoever built it must have added this maze, and Cheshire is simply taking advantage."

"But doesn't he need magic to manipulate the space?" Alice asked.

"I don't know that much about magic, Alice," Hatcher said. "You would likely know more than me."

"Don't repeat that nonsense Nell said," she said, irritated.

"Why not? You did something in that tavern. They all saw you. I felt the Jabberwocky leave, and he wouldn't leave unless he was forced."

"What if he simply found better prey elsewhere?" Alice asked. She did not want to believe that she had the power to send something so horrible away. She did not wish to be any more "interesting," as Cheshire had said, than she already was.

Hatcher did not say anything more. That wasn't his way. He walked away and into the maze, expecting her to follow. He would not stand and argue with Alice when they did not agree, even if she wished to.

And she did wish to. They had left the hospital, and since then she had felt as though she were buffeted in a rushing river, pulled along by the force of the water and knocking up against everything in her path. There had hardly been a moment when she felt her fate was in her own hands.

She did not wish to be a Magician, and to draw attention from those who would seek to exploit her. Alice was no fool, even if she had been muddled for a time. If anyone thought she as a Magician (and Alice did not believe she was), then even Hatcher's skills would not keep her safe. She would be scooped up by a boss and presented as a curiosity to the discerning men who frequented the Old City looking for excitement. If a boss did not kidnap her, then the government would. It was illegal to practice magic in the City, to be a Magician. Alice did not know how Cheshire managed to keep the government's interest out of Rose Way. He must have knowledge that the men in power would not like revealed.

As she thought all of this she automatically wandered behind Hatcher, and that irritated her as well when she realized she did it. She should not follow him like a frightened dog (*but you have acted like a frightened dog, especially at the beginning*).

Altogether she was feeling very bothered and not at all scared, although she supposed she ought to be scared. They were trapped in a maze of magical rosebushes and had no way of knowing how long it might take to get out.

Her face was hot and gritty from the soot-stained fog they'd passed through in the night. The bright sun would have been a welcome relief from the dark warren of the Old City, but in this exposed maze it was another irritant. Though the roses' scent was not as thick and heavy as inside, there was no escaping the perfume. Alice was tired of roses, tired of walking.

She sat down in the middle of the maze, crossed her arms and legs and waited to see whether Hatcher would notice. Almost immediately he turned around and gave her a questioning look.

"What are you about, Alice? Are you hungry?"

"No," she said, and lifted her chin. "I've had enough. I'm not moving one step more."

"We have to get through this maze," Hatcher said, gesturing ahead of him. They were in a long tunnel with several turnings off the main thoroughfare ahead.

"We've no idea where to turn or how to get out. And Cheshire is likely sitting in his parlor laughing at us. I'm not an amusement for him. I'm not a toy," she said hotly, thinking of the term he'd used for her.

"No, you're not a toy," he said. "But I think I can find our way out of this if you let me try."

"Why?" Alice asked. "This isn't like the Old City, where you're retracing your steps from long ago. You're just guessing, same as anyone would."

Hatcher walked back and crouched on the ground in front of her. He stared hard into her eyes. "What happened to my quiet, trusting girl?"

"She was drugged," Alice said, thinking of the powders that the hospital had put in her food for ten years. "She's not anymore."

Hatcher's eyes lit up. "That's it, Alice. The powders!"

"What about them?" Alice asked. She was confused by the sudden change in his manner, and the way it undermined her rebellion.

"The powders kept your magic inside you," Hatcher said, grabbing her hands and pulling her to her feet. "If you hadn't been taking them all those years, you would have known you're a Magician long ago."

"Hatch, stop," Alice said, tugging her hands away and planting her feet. "I'm not a Magician. And—" She leaned close to his ear, a sudden flash of inspiration. "If I were a Magician you wouldn't want everyone to know about it, would you? You wouldn't want Cheshire to know about it. So you should stop talking about it so loud. We don't know who's listening. He could be watching us, hearing everything we say. He very likely is."

"He already thinks you are a Magician, whatever we say,"

Hatcher said. "Why do you think he was so interested that you knew the story of the Jabberwocky?"

"What's that to do with anything?" Alice asked, confused again. Every time she thought she'd caught up she fell behind again.

"It's not a well-known story he told. You could tell by the way he told it that he was certain we'd never heard it before," Hatcher said. "Who told you that story? Your mother?"

"Yes," Alice said.

"Where did she learn it from?"

Alice shrugged. "Her parents, I suppose."

Hatcher nodded. "Who learned it from their parents, and so on. Did your family always live in the New City?"

"I suppose so," Alice said. "I never learned otherwise."

"Alice," Hatcher said, his brows drawn together. "I can't feel the Jabberwocky in here."

Alice might be less befuddled than before, but Hatcher's brain was just as twisty as always. She sighed, and took his hand, and they walked along the path carved between the rosebushes. She thought that it was a good thing if Hatcher and the Jabberwocky were less connected, even if it were only temporary.

At the junction of every turning, Alice peeked into the opening, each time hoping for some clue to the exit. But the maze was always the same. They decided to stay on the main path.

"After all," Alice reasoned, "it must come to an end sometime. And when we reach that end you can simply cut through the bushes."

The leaves behind her rustled, and Alice spun around, for there was no wind.

Two vines exploded from the maze wall, and wrapped around her ankles. The vines tugged sharply and she fell hard to the ground on her back. Before she or Hatcher could do anything she was pulled along the grass and the roses closed around her.

Thorns pricked at her skin everywhere, poked at her face and hands and the top of her head and wormed through her jacket and pants. She thought Hatcher yelled her name but she couldn't tell, for roses were in her ears and her nose and under her eyelids, crawling inside her. She opened her mouth to scream and roses pushed their way inside, choking her.

Stop, stop, stop, stop, stop. She wished she were a Magician; she would make the roses go away, get them out of this maze, fly away from the Old City forever and forget about the Jabberwocky and the Rabbit and Cheshire and the Walrus and Mr. Carpenter and roses, everything that could make her scared or cry or bleed. She would make the roses burn to the ground so they could never hurt anyone again.

Her hands were hot, hot with her own blood running from the thorn pricks in her arms down over her palms, and suddenly there was smoke, and a sound like a million tiny creatures squealing. Then the thorns were yanked from her skin and the flowers crawled away from her throat and nose and ears and eyes and something pushed hard into her back, and she was out, flat on the grass and crying and spitting rose petals from her mouth.

"Alice, Alice." Hatcher's voice, and then Hatcher's hands all over her, patting and soothing, and then Hatcher's arms taking her into his lap and rocking her as she cried and cried and cried.

All the strength she thought she'd found was gone now, smashed beneath the roses' assault.

Hatcher rubbed his hand down her back and said, "Alice, my Alice, don't cry. I can't stand for you to cry."

"I w-want to go h-home," she said. Her tongue tasted like salt and roses.

"Where's home, my Alice?" Hatcher said. "Where's home? We don't have a home, you and I."

"Then I want to go back to the hospital," she said. "We were safe there. Nothing could hurt us. Nothing could grab us and take us away."

"Except the doctors," Hatcher said. "Or the medicine they gave us. Or our own memories. We weren't safe there, Alice. It was an illusion. And the hospital burned down. There's nowhere for us to go back to. We can go forward. We can find our way out."

She cried harder then, because she knew what he said was true. They had nowhere to go and no safe place to be, and they were trapped in this labyrinth by the whim of a madman.

"How do w-we even know there is a way out?" she said. "How do we know that Cheshire won't keep us here, running in circles forever?"

"We don't know," Hatcher said. "I do know this. You're a Magician, as sure as I'm mad."

"Not now, Hatch," she said. She was tired and scared and not up to fighting about this.

"Look," he said, taking her chin and turning her head toward the rosebushes.

There in the hedge was a hole—a smoking, charred, empty place where roses used to be.

"Did you set it on fire?" Alice asked. "Is that why they let me go?"

"You set it on fire," Hatcher said. "I don't think the roses will trouble us any longer."

At these words he stood, still holding her in his arms like a child. She never thought about how big and strong he was, but she was very tall and he could hold her like she was nothing, a little bit of a thing. He approached the wall of the maze, and Alice turned her head into his chest, her eyes closed.

"No," he said. "Look."

She opened her eyes just enough to see through the slits, and then opened them wider, astonished. The roses were curling back on themselves, rolling into tight little coils. Alice reached her hand toward the vines, her curiosity stronger than her fear.

The roses shrank away from her touch, emitting that high-pitched squeal, like they were afraid.

Afraid of her.

"A Magician?" she breathed.

"A Magician," Hatcher said.

"Perhaps," she said. It was wondrous if it were true, but also terrifying. She wasn't prepared for this.

"All right, then," Hatcher said, and put her down. "Can you walk now?"

Her legs were wobbly and her stomach heaved like she was seasick. Alice closed her eyes again and leaned on Hatcher's shoulder for a moment, breathing deep in through her nose. The reek of roses no longer pervaded the air. A fresh wind blew through the hedges, carrying with it the sweet, clean scent of grass.

They started forward again, periodically checking the turnings as they had before. Alice did not feel at all steady. Her heart thumped rapidly in her chest, and though every rose moved away from them as they passed, it was difficult not to feel frightened. The flowers were cautious for now. There was no guarantee they would be in the future.

She briefly considered trying to burn their way out of the maze. This plan was not practical for two reasons. First, Cheshire might resent the destruction of his plaything. He was not their friend, but it did not seem he was yet their enemy. Alice did not desire to make an enemy of him.

Then there was the question of how to burn the roses. Somehow she had performed magic—twice, according to Hatcher—but on neither occasion was she certain how she'd done it. She was afraid that if she tried to light the bushes on fire and nothing happened, then the roses would know they had nothing to fear from her, and attack.

They walked and the sun beat down, never changing position. There was no shadow cast by the maze, no place to hide from the continuous glare. They quickly drank all the water Hatcher carried in his bag, and it was nowhere near enough.

Alice removed her jacket and tied it around her waist, pushing the knife behind the belt of her pants. Hatcher followed suit, and Alice could now see how he kept all his weapons in place. He had rigged a sort of harness—it reminded her of mules pulling carts—with many sheaths and buckled it close to his body. The axe swung closest to his hand, near his waist, so he could grasp it at a moment's notice. Higher up there were knives big and small, and the gun that had frozen Cheshire's grin, if only for a moment. There was a line of grey sweat under the harness where it rubbed against Hatcher's shirt.

Her own face and neck and chest were soaked, though her throat was parched. Still the maze went on and on, with neither sight nor sound of water. After a while Hatcher started muttering.

"Rabbits and caterpillars and butterflies and carpenters," he said. "I'll cut through all of them like trees. Watch my axe swing wide and gleaming and they all fall down, knock down all the toy soldiers. Jenny. Who's Jenny? Cheshire thought I knew her. Jenny. Jenny. She had grey eyes."

Alice said, "You have grey eyes."

Her tongue was swollen in her mouth and the words didn't sound right in her ears.

"Jenny," Hatcher said again, and he clutched both sides of his head. Alice saw his knuckles whiten, as if he were trying to squeeze the knowledge from his skull. "Jenny. Cheshire thinks he's so smart. So smart, but he has to sleep sometime. Oh yes, he must sleep sometime."

Blood ran from Hatcher's left nostril as he spoke, over his lip and onto his chin, a torrent that made Alice still in alarm. She forgot how thirsty she was, how tired.

"Hatch," she said, pulling on his arm, trying to make him stop crushing his head. "Hatch, stop."

He tilted his head to one side, his eyes not recognizing her. "Are you Jenny? No, you're not Jenny. Your eyes are wrong."

"Hatcher," Alice said. "Come back to me."

"She had grey eyes," he said. "Grey eyes. You're too tall to be Jenny. Stop pretending to be her."

"I'm not Jenny," she said, trying to keep her voice firm and calm. "I'm Alice."

"Not Jenny," he said, and then his right hand was off his head and there was a knife in it.

Alice released his arm and stepped back. "All right, Hatch. All right."

She couldn't stop him from carving out her heart if he was so inclined. She knew she was no match for that blade or the hand that held it. So Alice moved away, walking backward, her eyes on Hatcher and her hands high. Fresh blood dripped on his shirt.

"Jenny," he said again, and his voice had gone crooning. "My little mermaid swimming in the sea, my Jenny."

He staggered to one side, caught his shirt on the thorns of the hedge. Alice's breath caught, but the roses did not twine around him. Hatcher tore loose from the thorns, stumbling forward.

Then Alice heard it. Someone was singing, singing in the most beautiful voice. Hatcher heard it too, for he stilled, turning his head in the direction of the voice.

"This way," he said, and ran for the nearest junction in the maze, a few feet behind them.

"Hatcher!" Alice called, running after him. She was astounded he had so much energy. His boot heels disappeared behind another turn, and she labored to catch up. "Hatcher!"

The voice still sang, too lovely to be real and somehow . . .

Not very nice, Alice thought. It was a little-girl thought, she knew, but it was also true. There was something cruel in that voice for all its beauty. She rounded the corner where she'd last seen Hatcher and came upon a four-way intersection like a cross.

"Hatcher!" she called again, running to each direction in turn and finding nothing. Hatcher was gone.

The voice stopped singing.

Now panic was in her stomach and her heart and her mouth. She'd never been without Hatcher, never all on her own, not since the day he spoke to her through the mouse hole. What would she do without Hatcher? How would she get by?

Find him, you silly nit, a firm voice said inside her head. That voice was disturbingly like Cheshire's. Alice did not like the notion that her mind would take on the identity of a person she disliked very much. *Use your wits and find him.*

"But how?" she said to herself as her eyes roamed all over, looking for evidence of Hatcher's passing.

The grass was not flattened to show his boot prints. There was nothing to show where he'd gone. The sun was brighter than ever, blinding her, making her see dark spots when she closed her eyes and bright yellow ones when her eyes were open. She rubbed at her face, blinking in the glare, and looked down at her boots for a moment to shake off the sun.

Next to her right heel was a tiny drop of red on a blade of grass, a little crimson jewel drying to brown in the never-ending heat.

Alice dropped to her hands and knees, her face very close to the grass. Her eyes searched ahead until she found another blade of grass carrying a red droplet, also rusting in the sun.

She tucked her head low, her nose just above the grass, and scurried forward (*like a puppy smelling something good*), following the intermittent stains of red in the grass to the right-hand turning. After a few moments she was certain Hatcher continued in that direction and stood again.

Alice tried to run, but she was far too tired and thirsty to keep up the pace for long. She sensed that Hatcher was in danger, but could not force her weary body to move any faster.

Hurry, Alice, hurry, hurry.

She reached another junction with two choices and put her nose to the ground again. This time the blood was fresher, still jewel-bright, and hope surged inside her. Perhaps he wasn't too far ahead. Perhaps she could still save him.

But the singing stopped.

That was worrisome, the lack of singing. To Alice's way of thinking the singing was meant to draw them to the singer. If she (Alice thought it sounded like a "she," although it could be a turtle for all she knew) wasn't singing anymore, then that meant she'd gotten the thing she wanted. Alice did not want that thing to be Hatcher.

The maze turned a corner ahead of her and Alice followed it. Then she stopped, and she stared.

Before her was a very large body of water. It was too large to be a pond, but too small to be a lake, and it was so blue it hurt the eyes. Alice could almost taste that water in her mouth. She wanted to dive into it, let the water cover her until she drowned.

In the center of the lake was a small island, and on the island was a tiny cottage painted up like pink-and-white-striped peppermint. There appeared to be no one on the island, and Hatcher was nowhere to be seen.

"Hatcher!" Alice shouted. "Hatcher!"

Then she saw it. There was a small pile of clothes close to the lapping water of the shore. More alarming was the stack of weapons on top of the dirty clothing. Hatcher's axe was there. Alice could not believe Hatcher would leave his axe behind.

She sat on the beach and pulled off her boots and pants and jacket, leaving only the oversized shirt. Her knife was in her hand as she dipped her feet in the water.

It was cold, but the cold was refreshing. Alice again felt an overwhelming urge to sink to the bottom of the lake and she shook her head from side to side to get that thought out of her mind.

She knew Hatcher was in trouble, or else he would have answered when she called. Still, she hesitated. Alice did not know how to swim. The only time she had been in water in the last ten years was when she and Hatcher had jumped into the fetid river to escape the burning hospital. She knew she should kick and move her arms, but how would she keep herself afloat? And the impulse to sink beneath the water was very strong. The lake was clearly enchanted, and Alice wasn't certain she would have the concentration for swimming and fighting off the urge to drown.

I need to get to Hatcher, she thought. She focused all of her will on this singular idea, and hoped it would be enough.

Alice waded into the water.

She half expected something terrifying to rise from the water, a green monster with long arms to grab or a silver-scaled dragon with razor-edged fangs. Her childhood picture books were full of creatures like these. Nothing disturbed the water save Alice herself.

There was only one thought in her mind—*Hatcher.* The water soon covered her knees, and her thighs, and then the bottom suddenly fell away and her head dipped below the surface.

The drop was so abrupt that she didn't have time to take a breath. The water closed over her, so light and refreshing after the sweltering heat of the maze. But she couldn't breathe. Her chest hurt from the strain of keeping air inside, and she sank very fast.

Alice opened her eyes underwater, found that it was clear and utterly calm. The floor of the lake was not far from her feet.

It was littered with skeletons.

She kicked hard then, up and away, not wanting to touch the abandoned bones at the bottom of the lake, not wanting to become another victim of whatever lived in that candy-striped cottage.

Her face broke the surface, her paddling just barely keeping her mouth and nose out of the water. The cottage was not far. She only needed to go a little way more. She gulped air, and sometimes water, and the water was sweet and delicious, like lemonade on a summer's day. She thought again that she might like to drift away to the bottom.

Hatcher, she thought again, and kept thinking it. *Hatcher, Hatcher, Hatcher.*

She struggled through the water, moving in tiny increments, and when her feet touched the sandy bottom near the cottage, she was surprised to discover she had made it there.

Alice crawled out of the water. The shirt she wore was heavy from the lake and it seemed to try to drag her back in, but her hands and knees moved forward and her lips spoke over and over, "Hatcher. Hatcher. Hatcher."

Then her fingers were in grass instead of sand, and she struggled to her feet, the shirt dripping puddles around her. The knife Bess had given her was gripped in her right hand.

The little house, white with red peppermint stripes slashed across it (*like blood,* Alice thought), was perfectly still. The door was the only entry. There were no windows, no indication that anyone was at home. Alice knew Hatcher was there, for he was not under the lake, rotting with the other bones. She opened the door, the red doorknob smooth beneath her touch.

Hatcher was there, naked on the floor, his eyes blank and far away. A woman with skin as luminescent as the moon crouched over him, her back to the door, all the bones of her spine showing through the skin. Alice did not stop to think. She took one step forward and plunged the knife into the woman's neck.

The woman arched her back, her face curling up toward Alice. She saw that that it was not a woman at all, but something from a nightmare, something with long teeth like needles that curved over the chin and eyes as blind as an earthworm. The point of Alice's knife protruded just a bit from the creature's throat.

Alice pulled the knife up hard and blood the color of milk spurted out of the creature's mouth. Its arms stiffened out like wings and it fell forward onto Hatcher, the white liquid pooling on his chest and stomach.

"Hatcher," Alice said, and pushed the creature off his body with her foot.

He sat up, rubbing the back of his head and looking sheepish. "I think she was going to eat me."

"I should say so," Alice said, averting her eyes. Hatcher had not intended to be naked before her.

Hatcher stood, seemingly unashamed of his lack of clothing, and stared down at the creature for a moment. "I wonder how long she's been here."

"Quite a while, if you consider all the bones in the bottom of the lake," Alice said.

Hatcher blinked. "Bones?"

"Many," Alice said. "Let's return to the other shore. We left all of our things there."

They exited the peppermint house—*an odd house for such a creature,* Alice thought; *there ought to have been a plump little witch inside*—and walked to the shore of the lake. Hatcher waded in immediately. Alice followed with more reluctance. She had not enjoyed the crossing the first time.

Hatcher turned around when he was waist deep. "What's the matter?"

"I can't really swim," Alice said.

"You made it here, didn't you?" Hatcher said, holding out his hand. "Let's go, silly girl."

Alice smiled a little, and put her hand in his.

The water rose up in a giant wave then, higher than any building in the City. Alice's mouth dropped open. Hatcher squeezed her hand tight and pulled her close just as the wave crashed over them.

A moment later all the world was rushing water and Hatcher's grip on her hand. Alice's head went under, bobbed up again, then repeated the process too many times to count.

She couldn't see anything except waves, and couldn't hear a thing save the pathetic splashing she made to stay afloat. Hatcher never let her go, not even for a moment, and she felt certain that at least they would be together whether or not they survived.

She thought, *I do not like Cheshire at all.*

The rushing river ended just as abruptly as it began. Alice and Hatcher slammed into hard cobblestone on their stomachs. Alice tasted blood in her mouth. She dropped her knife and wiped her eyes with her free hand (Hatcher had not loosed his grip on the other) and looked blearily around her.

They were in a dark alley, seemingly empty of people, with only a little light coming in at the far end. As her eyes adjusted, Alice saw a neat little pile of clothing in front of her, and several weapons stacked on top, including Hatcher's axe and gun.

Hatcher released her hand and knelt, inspecting the items as well as he could.

"Are they our things?" Alice asked. "Did Cheshire send them with us?"

"He just might be a Magician after all," Hatcher said, by way of answer. "Best to cover yourself before someone comes along."

They dressed quickly. Alice's pants and jacket and cap were dry, but the shirt was very damp. She wrung out the hem, pulling it away from her waist and watching water dribble onto the stone.

"You'll have to pull the jacket closed," Hatcher said.

Alice was thinking the same thing. The wet shirt made it much more apparent that she was not the boy she pretended to be. Her chest was small but noticeable when the fabric clung.

Hatcher rummaged through the bag of supplies. "There's food."

"Pies from Nell and apples and bread from Bess," Alice said.

Hatcher shook his head. "That food is gone. There's new food."

He pulled out a cake shaped like a rose. Alice waved her hands.

"I don't want any food from Cheshire," she said.

"Probably wise," Hatcher said. "I have my money still. We can get something else. I'm hungry."

Alice wasn't hungry at all. She supposed she ought to be, but everything that happened in Cheshire's house and maze crowded out thoughts of food. Was Cheshire really a Magician? Or had he simply learned to manipulate magic that was already there?

The question you ought to be asking is, are you *a Magician?*

She didn't feel like a Magician. Some strange things had occurred around her, but she was hardly a practitioner of magic. Above all she believed it was most important to make sure others did not think she was a Magician. She and Hatcher had enough trouble with the Jabberwocky.

(*and the Rabbit*)

Bess had told her to stay away from the Rabbit. Cheshire told her she'd taken out his eye, and that the Rabbit had never forgotten her. As they went deeper into the Old City the possibility increased that they would encounter the man who'd danced through her nightmares for years. He would know her for certain, for Cheshire had known her by the scar on her face, and the Rabbit was the one who put it there.

Hatcher snapped his fingers in front of Alice. "Did you hear me, Alice? We have to find out where we are."

"Yes," she said. She followed Hatcher, for she'd been standing still and staring into the distance, thinking about the Rabbit and Cheshire and the Jabberwocky.

And cakes. Only the day before she'd been dreaming of yellow cake iced with pink sugar and cream, but the thought of Cheshire's rose-shaped cakes made her shudder—and remember.

Four people around a table. Alice, Dor, the Rabbit, and a man in the shadows. They were laughing, all of them were laughing so much because everything was so funny, and the Rabbit told Alice she could have all the cake she liked. She couldn't stop eating it. The cake was so pretty and there was plenty of it, and it made everything seem funnier than before. No one else was eating cake. They drank tea and they smiled and laughed but only Alice ate the cake. Dor had some biscuits on her plate, little yellow biscuits she said tasted like lemons. Alice didn't want any biscuits. She could have biscuits at home.

After a while she felt sick and dizzy, her mother's voice in her head saying, "Too many sweets." She slumped in her chair, her eyes half-closed.

The man in the shadows took a slice of cake with purple frosting and put it on her plate, urging her to eat more. She didn't want any more but he cut a piece with his fork and pushed it in her mouth. Crumbs spilled over her lips and onto her chin and they all laughed again, all except Alice, who coughed and spluttered and took large gulps of tea. Who was that man? She couldn't see him. His hands were large, though, larger than both of her hands put together, and white as snow. No, not snow. Gloved. He had large hands and he wore white gloves.

Hatcher stopped at the end of the alley and Alice bumped her nose in his back. That brought her to the present again, and she peeked around his shoulder to see what made him pause.

He gestured with his hand. "Butterflies."

CHAPTER

10

Alice didn't know what he meant. She didn't see any butter-flies. There was a large building before them, directly across the alley. This building was strange, a construction of many different styles all jammed higgledy-piggledy on one another.

There were turrets and balconies and staircases that went up into nowhere, and tilted shacks that appeared to have been dropped on the roof of others, stacked up to the sky. Parts of the building crept into the structures on either side, like a bloated spider spreading its web all through the garden.

Alice wondered whether all the parts connected when you were inside. How would you climb up to that highest tower otherwise? It didn't appear that way, though. It looked like another maze to her, a different sort of maze, and she'd had quite enough of mazes.

Then she noticed the sign attached to the porch roof. It was made of tin and swung back and forth in the evening breeze.

BUTTERFLIES

Cheshire had delivered them right to the Caterpillar's doorstep. Only now they were there, Alice did not want to go up that doorstep. That mad building could only house a mad person.

Hatcher's mad, she thought.

Yes, but there is no evil in him, she thought back.

She didn't know why she thought "evil." The building was twisted and weird, but it didn't have to be evil. Except that she had that feeling, that same feeling of *wrongness* that she'd had in Nell and Harry's tavern, the feeling that something bad was before them and they ought to turn away while they still could.

She noticed Hatcher's hesitation also. "It's not right there, is it?"

"No," he said. "But we must go. He's the one Cheshire said would know about the blade."

"Cheshire also tried to kill us for his own amusement," Alice said. "Why should we trust anything Cheshire said?"

"Because it's all we have," Hatcher said.

Alice and Hatcher went to the door of Butterflies. Hatcher pushed it open and it creaked like the door of a haunted mansion in a story. Before them was a dusty, musty hallway with several doors. There was no one in the hall; nor was there any indication that anyone might be behind the doors.

Hatcher took his axe out of his jacket. Alice found the knife was already in her hand. They shuffled forward cautiously, and the door swung closed behind them with a decisive *thud*. Alice checked the knob and found what she'd already suspected.

"It won't open," she said. She should be frightened. Instead she was angry—angry at Cheshire for sending them here, angry with herself and Hatcher for listening.

Anger would not help them escape. Finding the Caterpillar would, although she doubted he would know anything about this blade that Cheshire spoke of. She did not believe that such a weapon existed at all, but that Cheshire had sent them here for some purpose of his own. "Let's try the doors. One of them must open, else how does the Caterpillar go about his business?"

She didn't like to think of his business, but there it was. He sold girls to men, and those men must have a way in and out. It was absurd to think that everyone who entered was unable to leave. How would the Caterpillar make money without men to spend it?

Hatcher tried the first door on their right. It was locked, as was the one Alice tried on the left. They moved steadily down the hall until they reached the very last one at the end. That was locked as well.

"What now?" she asked. She was not about to stand in the Caterpillar's dirty hallway forever.

A movement in the corner of her eye made her start. It was a large centipede—disgustingly large, in fact. The insect's length was easily half her forearm, and it was as thick as the little snakes that slithered between her mother's flowers in the garden. She cringed away from it, repulsed.

Hatcher followed her eyes. "It can't hurt you."

"How do you know?" Alice countered. "Roses aren't supposed to grab people and try to murder them, either."

Alice tracked the movement of the centipede as it moved away from her. It disappeared beneath a door she had not noticed before, and the reason she hadn't noticed it was because the top of the door was just below her knee. It was a very garish shade of red and had a tiny golden knob. Alice was just able to pinch it between her thumb and first finger.

"You don't suppose the Caterpillar really *is* a caterpillar?" Alice asked, glancing at Hatcher.

He shrugged. "There are Jabberwocks in the world. Why not?"

And that, Alice thought, *was very typical Hatcher logic.*

The door opened. Noise and smoke spilled out. Alice lowered her head to peer through the opening.

Someone's boots blocked the view. The boots were twined with a woman's bare feet, very dainty feet with shell-pink nails. Someone banged away at a piano, a discordant tune that made Alice's back teeth ache. Then the boots and feet moved away, clearing the view.

There was a very large room behind that little door, a room with many tables. Men sat at the tables, and they appeared to watch something that Alice could not see. Some of the men had women with them, and what they did to those women made Alice shudder and turn away. Decent folk should not do such things where others could see.

Hatcher nudged her aside so he could have a look. Alice gladly ceded the space to him. She had no wish to see any more.

He stood up. "There's nothing for it. We've got to get in there."

A hundred objections were on her tongue, but he shook his head before she could voice them.

"That's the only door that opened. I could break down the others. I got out of the hospital room. But I don't think that's what we're supposed to do."

"How do we know what we're supposed to do, Hatch?" Alice asked, slumping against the wall. "Every time we stop to talk to someone or catch our breath, a trader tries to take me or a street soldier tries to kill both of us. We came to this place because Cheshire told us to, but he hasn't exactly been helpful."

"He told us to come here, and he made sure we did," Hatcher said. "I only know how to go one way, Alice. Forward. I don't know how to turn back, retrace our steps, start over. I don't even know if we can. Our past was padded and drugged. At least out here we're free."

"We're not free. We're still dancing to someone else's tune," Alice said, but softly.

Hatcher rummaged in the bag and pulled out the cake that he'd presented to Alice earlier. The cake was as pristine as if it lay on a table, fresh from the cook's kitchen.

It should have crumbled, Alice thought. *It should have been smashed to bits in that bag.*

"This is what Cheshire gave us," Hatcher said. "He told us to come here, and he gave us this."

"Maybe we're supposed to give it to the Caterpillar," Alice said.

"No. You know that's not who it's for."

She didn't want to eat it, and she knew that was what Hatcher was saying they should do.

"What if it makes us sick?" Alice asked.

"Alice, my grandmother told you I was a Seer," Hatcher said.

She frowned at him. "You're claiming Seer powers want us to eat the cake that Cheshire gave you?"

"Well, no," Hatcher admitted. "I just wanted you to go along with me and stop arguing."

"Hatch, I was the one who knew something was going to happen at the tavern, not you," Alice said. "Why should we trust your instincts more than mine?"

She didn't have time to stop him. He lunged for her, and since Alice trusted him implicitly it did not occur to her that he might hurt her. By the time she realized what had happened the piece of cake was in her mouth and she'd swallowed it.

"You—" she began.

Then everything was spinning, spinning, spinning, like she was swirling down a drain. When the spinning stopped she was in front of the little red door, and Hatcher was next to her, grinning.

"If we see that centipede again I'm going to feed you to it," Alice said.

She opened the door—the knob fit perfectly in her hand now—and marched through it.

Hatcher jerked her out of the way just as a shiny pair of men's shoes nearly crushed her. They huddled close to the wall, so far unnoticed by the revelers in the room.

"Now what?" she hissed. "We're not going to get anywhere while we're the size of beetles."

He pulled a small bottle from his bag and presented it to her. There was a label with a pink rose on it. Pink liquid sloshed inside. Alice sighed. She would have liked to ask why Hatcher thought this would make them big again, or why he was so certain of their path. If she asked too many questions, though, he would find some other way to make her drink what was in that bottle. She knew that now.

She knew, also, that even though he loved her, he was not entirely trustworthy.

He's killed people, Alice. Why did you think he was trustworthy in the first place?

He waited, holding the bottle patiently.

She took it from him and unstopped the cork. The liquid tasted like rose petals, and she nearly spit it out. It didn't seem to want to go out, though, sliding down her throat and into her stomach before she could expel it.

Hatcher snatched the bottle back from her just as the room spun again. This time she could feel her arms and legs stretching, the muscle snapping back into place around her crackling bones.

No one seemed surprised by their sudden appearance. No one seemed to notice at all.

Now that they were taller, Alice could see what everyone stared at. There were several platforms set up around the room. Each of the platforms was boxed by glass walls, so it was almost as if you peered into a little room.

In these rooms were girls, naked girls with butterfly wings strapped to their shoulders. The girls posed in various positions, all of them suggestive and obviously pleasing to the crowd. The platforms were brightly lit, though Alice did not see how. The rest of the room was dim.

The air was thick with smoke, but it was not the comforting pipe-tobacco smoke that Alice remembered from her childhood. This smoke was spicy and somewhat sweet and made her nose wrinkle.

The few men who were not entranced by the posing butterflies had naked women with them. These women had elaborate tattoos of butterfly wings on their backs, and equally intricate paintings around their eyes and cheeks. The men fondled these girls while they sat in their laps. Some had pushed their girls to the table and pounded away between their legs, right out in public.

Alice didn't know where to look except the floor. Her legs shook and her hands were knotted in tight little fists. It was horrible, horrible what was happening. Those women made loud noises, as if they liked what the men were doing to them, but how could they? How could they like it when it hurt so much, when these men used them and left them here for another man to take?

(*she was screaming, and hot blood ran down the insides of her legs, and she was trying to keep him off her but he was stronger, so much stronger*)

Someone touched her shoulder, and she looked down to see a tiny girl whose head came to just the top of Alice's throat. The girl took Alice's hand in hers and guided that hand to her very large breast.

"You're shy, I can tell," the girl said, rubbing Alice's hand all over her chest. The swirls painted on her face sparkled in the low light. "Don't be shy. Come with me. I know what to do with shy boys like you."

Alice yanked her hand away as if the girl were on fire. The

girl pouted, looking insulted. Alice noticed her eyes were glazed and strange, and she wondered whether the girl really knew what she was doing.

"Am I not pretty enough for you? What about your friend?" the girl asked, sidling around to Hatcher.

Alice grabbed the girl's hair before she could do to Hatcher what she'd just done to Alice. Her hair was long and red and beautiful and knotted in a braid down her back so you could see the butterfly wing tattoos carved there.

And the tattoos *were* carved, Alice realized. It was not ink or paint but scarring. She touched the girl's back, felt the ridge built up there and the scab that meant the design had recently been retraced.

Horrible, Alice thought.

The girl interpreted Alice's tug on her braid and the touch on her back to mean something Alice had not intended. She snuggled into the curve of Alice's arm.

"Not so shy after all?" the girl asked, rubbing her body against Alice's side.

Alice looked at Hatcher helplessly, hoping for assistance. He stared at the girls under the glass with an odd, hungry look on his face.

He is *a man, Alice,* she thought. *And even the best of men might be lured by flesh dangled so willingly before them. Though you are not, whatever this poor confused creature might think.*

Alice carefully put her hands on the girl's shoulders and

pushed her away. She kept her eyes right on the other girl's eyes because there was nowhere else decent to look.

"You're very pretty," Alice said. "But I am not looking for a pretty girl tonight. I am looking for the Caterpillar."

"Are you sure?" the girl asked, and tried to grab at Alice again.

"Quite sure," Alice said firmly.

"The Caterpillar won't have any truck with you," the girl said, giving Alice an up-and-down look. "You don't look like you have any flash, and he only takes the ones with flash in his special room."

"Let me worry about that," Alice said. "Where is his 'special room'?"

The girl pointed to another red door on the far side of the long room. A large man who bore a distinct resemblance to Theodore, Cheshire's guard, stood there glowering at everyone who approached.

"I can suck you for twopence," the girl said as Alice tried to move away. "If you don't want a tumble."

Alice did not even know what "sucking" meant, though she was certain she didn't want it. "No, thank you."

The girl walked away, muttering under her breath about pocket money. Alice wondered where the girl would have put the twopence anyway.

She stood in front of Hatcher so that she blocked his view of the butterflies and waited for his eyes to see her again.

"Alice," he said, like he only just remembered who she was. His look sharpened, seemed to focus on her mouth. "Alice, I haven't had a woman in such a long time."

She feared then that he might give her away, that he might try to kiss her. Worse, he might try to kiss another girl, or take what was so freely offered throughout the room. She couldn't bear the thought of Hatcher acting like these other men, these animals so insensate of their own surroundings.

"It's not the time, Hatch," she said.

She didn't know what else to say. They needed to see the Caterpillar. They needed to leave before Hatcher did something he couldn't take back.

As they picked their way through the cheering, drinking, smoking crowd, another terrifying thought occurred to Alice. Had Cheshire sent them here to prove that she was nothing but a man's toy, as he said? Had he expected Hatcher to lose his mind, to treat her as the Rabbit had done?

If so, it was all the more reason to escape this place as soon as possible. Hatcher would regret anything that happened here. She was certain of that. But she was not confident she would be able to stop him.

The door to the Caterpillar's special room was just beside the last platform. As they reached it, the butterfly inside pressed herself against the glass and pushed one of her fingers inside her body. Alice resolutely turned her head away. She would never be able to sleep well again. Some might think this place full of wonder, but to her it was a house of horrors. Hatcher closed his hand around her elbow just for a moment, squeezing hard. She didn't know whether he was trying to reassure her or to keep himself under control.

The guard at the door gave Alice and Hatcher the same disdainful look as the naked girl who'd solicited Alice's attention. He was built on the same large scale as the guard at Cheshire's cottage. There was a resemblance in the face as well.

"Off with you," he said.

"You even sound like Theodore," Alice said, though she had not meant to say it. She hadn't really thought about what words she would use to convince him to let them in.

The guard's brows drew closer together, if that was possible. "Theodore? You know my brother?"

That explains many things, including how Cheshire knows so much about the Caterpillar, and perhaps how he knows of others as well. Anyone who enters this room is under this man's eye, Alice thought.

"Yes, we met him at Cheshire's cottage. What is your name?" Alice said, just as if she were in her parents' drawing room making a new acquaintance.

As long as she kept thinking like that, it was easier to ignore what went on behind her, to shake away the sight of girls on display like slabs of meat at the butcher's shop. She didn't look at Hatcher, but she hoped that he was not staring around like a wide-eyed child. She would prefer the dangerous

Hatcher, the one who killed a man because that man touched his shoulder.

The guard narrowed his eyes at her. "Theobald. Are you friends of Cheshire's?"

Alice wished she knew what the correct answer was. Did this man like or dislike Cheshire? Would he be more likely to allow them to enter if she said yes or no?

"I would not precisely call him a friend," Alice said. "We went to him for advice."

"He advised you to see the Caterpillar," Theobald said. He seemed smarter than his brother.

"Yes," Alice said. She sensed that the less she said, the better. Let Theobald draw his own conclusions about their business.

"The Caterpillar doesn't like to be disturbed when he's entertaining guests," Theobald said. "However, there is no one special with him this evening."

He did not immediately move aside, so Alice waited expectantly.

"Your names?" Theobald asked. He held his hands crossed together in front of him. As he said this, he opened one palm and held it flat.

Alice stared at his hand, confused for a moment. Fortunately Hatcher knew what to do. He drew a single piece of gold from his pocket and put it in Theobald's hand. The guard's eyes gleamed.

"Tell the Caterpillar my name is Nicholas," Hatcher said.

He didn't offer a name for Alice. The gold piece must have been sufficient not to warrant further pursuit, though, for Theobald nodded at them and slipped into the room. He moved so quickly and efficiently that Alice did not catch a glimpse of the room behind.

Now that the guard was out of sight she realized her heart pounded in her chest and her legs trembled. She was scared, scared that the Caterpillar would realize she was a girl and put her under glass like his other butterflies. Alice would never get away, not without Hatcher and the things Cheshire had sent in the sack. Her boy disguise had fooled only those who didn't look at her very closely.

"Don't be afraid," Hatcher said in a low voice.

She glanced at him. He seemed much more alert than before, more like the Hatcher he'd been since their escape. Hatcher always had changeable moods. Alice never realized when they were in the hospital how difficult those changes would be for her. In her own room she could let him rant or walk or pound the walls and it wouldn't really affect her, particularly since she took the powders, which made everything dull around the edges.

Out here the world was bright and sharp and full of hungry mouths waiting to eat her up. She couldn't afford Hatcher's instability, and she wouldn't leave him either.

They were bound together by love and need and other feelings she didn't entirely understand.

I've never been a woman, she thought. She didn't mean it like a woman who is a wife and performs wifely duties (like the ones the butterfly girls offered the men who entered the club), but a woman who sat in adult company, who saw the world through an adult's eyes. Her body had grown older but her mind was still trapped at sixteen, still unsure of how to act and how to be. She loved Hatcher, but it was a girl's love for her savior.

Would she have loved him if they'd met at a garden party, or at a ball? Would he have worn a high collar and starched cuffs, like her father, and told her about his work as a clerk in his father's law office? And would she have laughed at all of his attempts at humor, even when he wasn't very funny, and looked up at him with shining eyes when it was time for dancing? For a moment it was almost as if she could see them there, dressed like they belonged in the New City, spinning in circles together, like it was a memory of the past and not the ghost of a future that never was or could be.

Theobald returned then, and beckoned them inside. He returned to his post outside once they closed the door.

Like Cheshire's cottage, the Caterpillar's special room was extraordinary. It was long on two sides and short on the ends, and so stuffed with objects that Alice was surprised anyone could walk through the space.

The walls were lined with shelves from the floor right up to the ceiling. Every shelf teemed with *things*. There were boxes made of gold and silver and iron, encrusted with pearls or rubies or emeralds or sapphires or diamonds. There were chalices and cups and leather-bound books, fabrics that glittered and shone, tall glass jars filled with powders and unguents of various colors and consistencies. Caps of different shapes were stacked messily next to piles of exotic-looking feathers, taken from the tails of birds that never lived in the City. Every type of sword, dagger, axe, mace or hammer imaginable was there too, and brightly colored rugs were piled all around, strewn with fat, tasseled cushions.

It looks like the room of a sultan, Alice thought. Her mother had told her those stories when she was young, adventures in the faraway desert with magic lamps and flying carpets. At the opposite edge of the room lay a man in repose on several of the cushions, further adding to the impression that they were in the room of an eastern prince.

The man—who could only be the Caterpillar—inhaled from a long hookah, occasionally expelling smoke in thin clouds from his nostrils. There was something of the caterpillar about him, though Alice thought the name must have come from his use of "butterflies." He was long, very long and lean, and completely relaxed, his eyes drowsy. He stared at two large glass enclosures before him, and did not indicate he noticed their entrance at all.

Hatcher moved a little ahead of Alice. His hand was tucked inside his coat, though he did not take a weapon out. Alice patted her pocket, assured that her knife was still there. The Caterpillar did not appear threatening at all, but something had raised Hatcher's hackles, else he would not be so ready to swing the axe.

Alice could not clearly see what the Caterpillar was so interested in, though she imagined it must be more "butterflies." She heard a splash of water, and a fluttering noise like the beating of wings. Her curiosity was roused, and she peeked through the glass as they approached the Caterpillar, ready to look away quickly if she saw more of what she'd seen outside.

It was not more of the same. It was much, much worse.

Alice approached the glass, her stomach roiling though she was unable to look away. Behind the glass of one enclosure was a naked girl with iridescent pink butterfly wings. She was very thin, so thin Alice saw her ribs protruding through her white skin. Her eyes were violet, a startling color, but dull and ringed by black hollows. When she saw Alice she stretched her hands toward the glass in supplication, her eyes pleading.

The wings were not attached to her shoulders by straps. The girl's back had been cut from the top of her shoulder to the bottom of her rib cage on both sides of her spine. The beautiful butterfly wings were neatly sewn into the exposed muscle. As the girl flexed her shoulders, the wings would beat.

Alice pressed her hand against the cage—for that was what it was—and the butterfly matched her palm to Alice's. She moved her face close to the glass so the Caterpillar would not see her. Her lips moved slowly, mouthing two words to Alice.

Kill me.

Alice knew suddenly how Hatcher felt, why he showed his love for her by offering to shoot her instead of letting a criminal take her away. She wanted very much to end this woman's pain, to give her the release she desperately needed.

The girl turned her face away, and Alice then noticed that she moved with only her arms. Her legs were twisted at the knee, clearly broken by the hand of a human, so that she could do nothing except sit in a jar and flutter her wings for the Caterpillar's pleasure.

Alice was half-afraid to see what was in the next case, but she also wanted to know.

The second cage was a tank half-filled with water, and an angry mermaid swam in circles inside, occasionally surfacing to glare out at the assembly. Her lower half was comprised of silver scales and fins, and her upper body was that of a woman. Her hair was long and dark and rippled in the water. Alice leaned close to the glass, almost certain that there would be a row of stitches attaching the shiny scales to the woman's waist. But there was nothing that she could see. The mermaid seemed to be exactly that, but that was impossible. Everyone knew there were no such things as mermaids.

No such thing as magic either, or monsters that live in boxes beneath the hospital. No such thing as a cake that makes you small and a drink that makes you big.

She must start believing in impossible things, for impossible things kept appearing before her eyes.

"She's real," the Caterpillar said. His voice was lazy. "My friend and yours found her for me, in that maze of his."

"He's no friend," Alice said, and her voice was harsh.

She spun to face the Caterpillar, and the knife was in her hand. She wanted to leap upon him and stab out his eyes, make certain he'd never see his precious collection again.

The Caterpillar made a gentle tutting sound. He seemed wholly unconcerned by the knife.

"I think he would be disappointed to hear you say that. He delivered you to my door, did he not? And gave you the means to enter my private kingdom? For you would not have been able to enter without my permission otherwise." He took a long inhale from the hookah and continued. "It's quite extraordinary, is it not? The things that Magicians left lying about. The mermaid came from a lake in the center of a maze. She would seduce men and inspire them, give them dreams so they could go out into the world and inspire others. Now she belongs to me, and she does as I say, when I say it."

Alice glanced back at the mermaid, who was close to the glass now, her fingers curled like claws and her face white as death, but her eyes burned with hate. She knew that the mermaid did not seduce men by choice now. This beautiful, extraordinary creature was nothing but a tool for the Caterpillar, an oddity to be taken from her tank and presented to the highest bidder.

"Cheshire replaced her with another creature I found,

something very unique that was trapped in a bottle. She was very happy to be set free, and Cheshire ensures she is fed regularly."

"Not any longer," Alice said, and was pleased to see the surprise in the Caterpillar's eyes.

"You went through the maze? And survived the creature? Interesting. Interesting."

Alice felt she hated that word. "Interesting" meant that you attracted the notice of men who would hurt you to possess whatever they found "interesting" about you.

"She was not as lovely as my mermaid, I admit. I was happy to trade her to Cheshire. Mermaids and vorpal blades." The Caterpillar's voice drifted off, repeating the words over and over. "Mermaids and vorpal blades, mermaids and vorpal blades."

"A blade is why we are here," Hatcher said. Alice noticed he had his axe in his hand and his knuckles were white around the handle. He didn't care for this any better than she, and he was riding the edge of his temper.

"Oh, I know why you're here," the Caterpillar said.

"Cheshire told you," Hatcher said.

"No," the Caterpillar said. He sat forward suddenly, his eyes bright and sharp and much more aware than Alice had thought. "I knew as soon as I saw her. Pretty Alice."

(*A hand in her hair, pulling her head back. "Pretty little Alice, pretty little Alice."*)

Her heart seemed to fall away, her stomach pushed into her throat. She looked at the Caterpillar's hands, but they weren't right. They were not large like the man in the shadows, the man at the tea party from her nightmares. The Caterpillar wasn't that man. But how did he know? Why did he use those words?

The Caterpillar stood, unfolded himself to a giant height, towering over both Alice and Hatcher. "You want to know how I know, why your boy's disguise does not fool me. It is because of this. The Rabbit is a friend of mine. We share so many friends, you and I, little Alice."

He reached toward Alice's face, to touch the scar on her cheek. She was frozen by her fear, by the tangle of half-formed memory, by the growing terror that nothing would keep her safe from the Rabbit, for he had marked her so that everyone would know her.

His fingers never reached her. Hatcher's axe swung, and the Caterpillar's hand was gone. For a moment she was certain that Hatcher had taken that hand from the wrist, but the tall man stood before her, a terrible smile on his face and both hands folded in front of him.

Hatcher appeared bewildered, as though his blows had never missed their aim before, and Alice thought that was probably true.

"Yes, one must be quick around the Hatcher of Heathtown," the Caterpillar said, and gave Hatcher a nod of acknowledgment. "No one has ever used an axe so deliciously as you, Nicholas. She is yours, or so you think. I understand."

Alice did not wish to have another discussion about who owned her. It might be safer, she realized, to drop the boy disguise and let those they encountered think Hatcher was her caretaker. In the Old City there were very few ways for women to stay alive, and all of them involved a man. She did not, however, need to listen to the Caterpillar tell her what Cheshire had already said.

"Don't tell me that I belong to the Rabbit," she said. "He may have marked me, but I am not his."

The Caterpillar's smile widened. His face was extremely thin and so the smile was ghoulish. "It will be very amusing to see you tell him so—again. Will you take his other eye and leave him blind, as you wish to do to me?"

She must stop feeling surprised, or at least stop showing it on her face. How did he know what she was thinking? Then *she* knew, with complete certainty.

"You're a Magician," she said. "And Cheshire, as well."

The Caterpillar gave her a little bow, his eyes gleaming. "We recognize our own, do we not?"

It was a strange place and a strange time to recognize the truth of what Hatcher had tried to tell her. Yet in this house of horrors, with this hideous grinning monster before her, she knew it *was* true. She was a Magician. There should have been a sense of wonder or delight or even surprise. But the idea had been working away in the back of her mind ever since it was first presented to her. A Magician, and so the reason why Bess said she and Hatcher must find the Jabberwocky and defeat it, for no one else could.

Only that is not quite true, is it? There were other Magicians, so it was not a question of could, but would.

Alice was a Magician, but one who did not know how to find or use her magic, so she might as well not be at all. The Caterpillar and Cheshire, they used their magic to further their own aims. Nell had said, with tears in her eyes, that the return of the Magicians would mean the end of darkness and suffering. She did not know—nobody did—that some Magicians had never left, and they were the *cause* of that darkness and suffering.

Alice didn't know whether the Caterpillar could read her face or whether he used his magic to read her mind, so she pushed her busy thoughts away and tried to make her brain still. She thought of clouds on a summer's day, the way they drifted across the painfully blue sky, and made those clouds drift across her mind.

The Caterpillar watched her closely. He nodded. "Very nice, Alice."

Alice frowned. She did not want his approval.

The Caterpillar laughed. "I know you don't care for my approval. That one shot right out from between your eyes, you know. Like an arrow."

"So you can't really see all my thoughts," Alice said.

"Only those that are pointed in my direction," the Caterpillar said. "Including those you would try to hide, for hiding makes them shine all the brighter."

He gestured at the mermaid. "She wishes for my death hourly. When my friends come and lay between her thighs she thinks of how she will gut me with one of my many swords, how she will rip me open bit by bit, how I will scream and beg for mercy when she slices off my member or drives the sword through my asshole and out through my mouth."

Alice shuddered. She did not disagree with the sentiment, for she felt it was certainly deserved, but it made a horrible image.

"Yes, horrible," the Caterpillar agreed. He pointed at the butterfly. "This one also only thinks of death, but the death she wishes for is her own. Every day she hopes that I will break her neck as I broke her legs. I couldn't do it the same way, you know. I used hammers on her legs, and that would be a very inefficient way of breaking a neck. Much better to twist it, make it quick."

"Why don't you?" Alice asked, and tried not to think anything he might see. The clouds drifting in her mind became a thick batch of storm clouds, grey and protective.

"There are some men who like a girl who cannot get away," the Caterpillar said. "Not that any of them can get away, really, but I cater to all tastes. One paid extra to watch me break her in the first place."

A wrinkle appeared between his brows. "You're quite good at that. I shouldn't have told you how it worked. I can't see a thing now. And him—" He jerked his thumb at Hatcher. "His mind is like the New City square on Giving Day—all noise and lights and people running in every direction. It gives me a headache just to be near him."

Giving Day. Alice remembered going with her mother to the square to receive their gift from the leaders of the City. Everyone dressed in their very best, and there were fireworks and sweets and jugglers. All the children of the New City would be given a small wrapped box in return for good citizenship.

Inside there was always a silver coin, stamped with the year and the symbol the City leaders chose for that year. One coin had a wolf, another a tree, another a bear. All the symbols were meant to mean something about the path the City was taking that year, though Alice never really understood these.

She thought these things, but she was careful to keep the clouds in the forefront of her mind, so the Caterpillar could not have her memories. Cheshire must not be so adept at reading thoughts, else he would have plucked the fragmented memory of Alice taking the Rabbit's eye from her as she sat in his rose parlor.

"I am not interested in your *business*," Alice said, allowing her disgust to show. She'd had quite enough of listening to bad men speak. She wanted only to know where to find the blade so they could leave this place. "Do you have what we are seeking?"

The Caterpillar walked to the enclosure where the butterfly was kept. He stroked his fingers against the glass, musingly.

"I wish I did. Yet, in a way, I am glad I do not, for then *he* will not come seeking it here."

"Do you know where it is?" Hatcher asked. His voice was rough, and the skin of his face was pulled tight.

Alice felt a moment of alarm. The Jabberwocky must be working on him. It would be terrible if he had a fit now. She might be able to defend herself from the Caterpillar, but if he called Theobald in to help him . . .

She glanced at the girls in the cages. She would turn her knife on herself, chew out her own tongue, whatever was necessary. She would not allow the Caterpillar to put her in a tank for his own enjoyment, and then trade her to the Rabbit (for she knew that was what he would do) for someone more "interesting."

The Caterpillar continued to stroke his fingers over the glass, gazing at the girl he'd broken inside. "With the only one who could have it, since you are meant to find it."

It was always moving toward this. She knew that now, for how would she ever be free until she saw him again?

"The Rabbit," Alice said.

The Caterpillar nodded again. "How I will enjoy his face when he sees you again."

"It's nothing to do with you," Alice said. "Why would you be there?"

"The fastest way to the Rabbit's warren is underground," the Caterpillar said. "My paths can take you there. It will be so lovely for you to be reunited with your friend Dor, will it not?"

Dor? Alive? Alice realized she'd never contemplated the idea that Dor might not be dead. There was a blank hole in her memory—first Dor was there, at the tea party, and then she was gone. But if she was alive, then that could only mean her fate had been worse than death.

"Yes, little Dor," the Caterpillar said. "I hope you will forgive her now. She was supposed to take the money and leave you behind, but you took the Rabbit's eye and left her behind instead. Now she scurries like a little mouse, to and fro, at the Rabbit's bidding."

(*A small hand collecting gold from a larger one*)

It was too much, too much after finding out she was a Magician and that she was to see the Rabbit again. It was too much to discover that Dor, at the age of sixteen, had tried to sell her to a monster. Dor, who was supposed to have been her best friend, the friend she'd loved since she was a girl. The clouds parted, and the Caterpillar smiled.

"Ah, you did not know of her betrayal? Silly girl. How did you think you ended up in the Rabbit's den?"

"I—" Alice began, scrambling to collect her thoughts and hide them again. "I suppose I always thought he tricked her, that he cozened her with nice words so that she would come back."

"Why would a nice girl from the New City be in such a place to begin with? How would Dor have met the Rabbit so that he could charm her so thoroughly that she would take her innocent friends into a forbidden place?"

He was making her feel stupid, stupid and slow for not knowing. Why shouldn't she trust a friend, her most wonderful friend in the world? Why wouldn't she want just a little rebellion, just a taste of something dangerous? It wasn't supposed to hurt. It wasn't supposed to be scary. Dor had made it sound as though they were going on an adventure, an adventure she could hold close and remember that night when she snuggled under the covers, safe in her own bed.

"Of course she told you that, you nit," the Caterpillar said, and he was full of contempt now, peering down his long nose at her. "She wanted you to come along willingly. Still, her betrayal turned out all right for you. Not like Nicholas."

Alice looked at Hatcher. Sweat ran down the sides of his face. He was fighting hard, trying to stay here with her so he could keep her safe. She moved close to him, though she was afraid to put her arm around him or otherwise show the Caterpillar how much she cared. Every action, every word, could be used against them.

"What do you mean?" Hatcher asked.

"Why, Jenny, of course," the Caterpillar said.

There was that name again—*Jenny*. Just the thought of it had nearly driven Hatcher beyond the edge of reason in Cheshire's maze, and here was another who knew this name, knew that it was supposed to mean something to Hatcher.

"The Rabbit lied and said she would be safe, didn't he?" The Caterpillar tutted. "If you can't trust your employer, then who can you trust? Your child was supposed to be forbidden, was she not?"

"Employer?" Alice said. Hatcher had worked for the Rabbit? Was that why he'd always believed her when she'd spoken of him, because somewhere deep down, the memory of the Rabbit was buried? What had Hatcher done for this man, for this monster? Was he a guard dog like Theobald or Theodore? A snatcher of women, stuffing them into sacks? Her Hatcher, the one who had defended her, who kept her safe from those kinds of men?

"Child," Hatcher said. As he said that word he staggered back like he'd taken a blow to his stomach. "Child. Yes. My Jenny. My beautiful girl."

His eyes went wide, but not blank. A million memories ran across those grey eyes. Alice could see that they seized him, took his breath, pummeled his heart to pieces.

"What did he do?" Alice demanded.

"Nicholas? Or the Rabbit?" the Caterpillar asked.

He watched Hatcher fall to his knees, gasping for air, and the smirk on his face made Alice want to kill him right then, without question or mercy. She knew the hatred of the mermaid, the longing for not just blood but pain. The Caterpillar was hurting Hatcher, and Alice wanted to hurt the Caterpillar.

"Jenny," Hatcher said.

Alice had never seen him like this before, even when under the spell of the Jabberwocky. She'd never seen him laid low.

"He knows the story, for it's his own," the Caterpillar said. "But it's knotted in that snarl he calls a brain, and now he only thinks of one name—*Jenny*. I know the story too, for the Rabbit told me. I collect stories as well as things, you know."

Alice waited. He enjoyed the performance, and wanted her to ask for more. She would not give him what he wanted, as she had with Cheshire.

His eyes flickered with annoyance, but he continued. "Nicholas was a bad boy, once upon a time, though not as bad as he would become. He fought and he drank and caused trouble wherever he might. He was big and strong and handsome, and all the bad girls wanted to be on his arm. Don't you think he's handsome, Alice?"

Hatcher was handsome, she realized, not only to her eyes. He had the kind of bones and dramatic coloring that would attract attention, even now with the grizzled stubble on his chin and the madness in his eyes. And he was tall and strong, tall enough to make a tall girl like Alice feel small and protected. Girls in the Old City would like that.

The Caterpillar went on, seemingly satisfied by the expression on Alice's face. "He made his flash here and there, fighting for money in the pits while rich men laid their bets on him."

That's where his nose was broken, Alice thought.

"One day the Rabbit came to see Nicholas fight a man who was so large and unbeatable he was known only as the Grinder. The Grinder ground his opponents into meat, you see?"

The Caterpillar thought this was very funny, and laughed at his joke. Alice waited, practicing patience.

"Well, for a time it seemed that the Grinder would make a meal of Nicholas as he had with all the others. But your Hatcher can be unreasonable; have you noticed? He did not seem inclined to allow the Grinder to win. When it was over Nicholas' nose was pushed to one side and his eyes were nothing but puffed-up slits in his face, but his boot was on the Grinder's chest and the Grinder would not get up again.

"The Rabbit wanted a fighter of such spirit for himself. Nicholas was not inclined to agree. He knew what kind of man the Rabbit was, and what he did to women. Nicholas was better than men like the Rabbit and me, wasn't he?" The

Caterpillar's voice became harsh. "Thought he could climb out of the mud he'd been birthed in. So he said no.

"But the Rabbit, he does not hear 'no.' He thinks there is always a way, always a price. And do not fool yourself, Alice—there *is* always a way, always a price. Everyone can be bought. The Rabbit found Nicholas' price with Hattie.

"Hattie was one of the Rabbit's girls, and her eyes were sad and blue, just like yours, only there was no fight in them anymore. All the fight had gone out of her years ago. Nicholas saw her and he wanted that sadness to go away. He wanted to fix her. When the Rabbit came around with Hattie on his arm, Nicholas offered his service for her freedom."

Now, that was her Hatcher, Alice thought. That was exactly the sort of thing he would do.

"The Rabbit wanted a good fighter more than a used-up girl. He could get another girl anyplace, and considered that he'd gotten the better of the bargain. Nicholas married Hattie, and took her away and kept her safe. And when the Rabbit had a person who needed persuading, he would send Nicholas.

"Soon enough they had a bouncing baby girl with black hair and grey eyes, the image of her father, and they called her Jenny. And as the girl grew older, she grew prettier every day, and even as a young thing people would say she would grow up to be beautiful. When Nicholas heard that, he started to worry, for a beautiful girl in the Old City draws too much attention. He asked the Rabbit to send out word that she was not to be harmed, that she was under his protection. And the Rabbit promised he would.

"He promised, but the girl grew older, and at ten she was so pretty, too pretty to waste in Nicholas and Hattie's little hovel. A girl like that, so fresh and new and lovely, would fetch a glorious price. The Rabbit wanted to keep her for himself, but he didn't want to tempt fate. He had seen Nicholas when he was angry.

"One night, when Nicholas was out about the Rabbit's business, the Rabbit sent six men to his house. One of them took Jenny away. The other five kept themselves busy with Hattie, waiting for Nicholas. They were so rough in their play that she expired before Nicholas came home.

"When he returned he found his daughter gone, his wife raped and murdered. The neighbors heard the noise coming from inside the house, saw the blood running free under the door and into the street like a river. When the coppers came they had to send twenty men to pry the axe from his hand, and all that was left of the other men were unidentifiable bits.

"Nicholas was taken away, but he was not dead, and the Rabbit did not wish for the Hatcher of Heathtown to return for him one day. So he sold Jenny to a traveler from the East, who took her through the forest and over the mountains and far away, so that he would be safe. If Hatcher ever returned, the Rabbit would be safe, for only he knew the identity of the man who had taken her."

"Except he won't be safe," Hatcher said, his voice like a blade against a grindstone.

He rose to his feet, and his eyes burned. Even Alice, who loved him, who knew his heart, was afraid of him. This was the hunter, the hatcher, the butcher who slaughtered without fear of consequence.

"He won't be safe," Hatcher repeated. "For I will find him and I will strip the flesh from his bones piece by piece. There is no place the Rabbit can hide, no hole he can disappear into. I will not sleep again until I have heard him scream for mercy he will never receive."

The Caterpillar clapped his hands. "Wonderful, wonderful. Yes, there will be so much to see when the two of you meet the Rabbit again."

That was when Alice lunged.

CHAPTER

12

The Caterpillar had been so wrapped up in his own story, his own importance, his own sense of immunity from harm that he did not see her coming.

The knife was in her hand and she cut a necklace across his throat, felt the muscle give under the blade. The Caterpillar's blood spurted into her face as he fell to his knees, clutching at his neck, his mouth moving helplessly, trying to call Theobald. She stepped back as his arms flailed, reaching for her. She felt no remorse whatsoever as he fell to the floor, clawing at the rugs, desperately clinging to the hope of life.

The mermaid went wild in her tank, slamming her fin against the glass, surfacing to scream for joy. The noise drew Theobald, who threw open the door and rushed in, kicking it closed behind him.

He never had a chance. The axe was in Hatcher's hand, and Hatcher was already dreaming of blood.

It was the first time Alice had attacked someone on purpose, without defending her own or someone else's life. She ought to be worried, she supposed, that it was so easy to do.

Hatcher came to her side. "Why?"

There was no accusation in his question, just simple curiosity.

"Because of them," she said, and pointed to the girls behind the glass. "And because of you. He didn't have to hurt you, but he did."

"Now we go for the Rabbit," he said. "I have just as much reason as you to want to see him to his end."

"Yes," she said.

Perhaps Hatcher had even more reason than she to want revenge on the Rabbit. Alice had gotten her own self into trouble, doing something she wasn't supposed to do. Hatcher had taken a job with the Rabbit to protect somebody else, and the Rabbit had taken everyone he loved in exchange.

Hatcher frowned down at the flopping, grasping Caterpillar.

"I told you before, you have to make sure it's finished."

"I will," Alice said.

They waited. Hatcher took Alice's hand in his and they watched the Caterpillar bleed out, the knowledge of his own death in his eyes. It took longer than Alice thought it would. The Caterpillar wanted to live.

His breath exhaled finally in a long rattle, and he moved no more.

Alice and Hatcher went to the tanks. The butterfly was frozen in place, her eyes full of hope.

"How do we get you out?" Alice asked.

The butterfly and the mermaid pointed to a door nearly hidden by the Caterpillar's shelves. Alice found the latch and pushed it open, Hatcher close behind. Inside, there was a narrow dim hall that led to the rear of the enclosures. Two diaphanous robes that would reveal more than conceal hung on pegs by the doors.

Alice tried the doors, but neither would open. Hatcher pointed to the tiny opening under each knob.

"A key," he said. "The Caterpillar probably has it."

He pushed around Alice and went out to rummage through the body. After a few moments he returned, his hands covered in blood.

"It was around his neck," Hatcher said. "And that was the messiest bit."

Alice unlocked the first door, which held the butterfly, and handed the key to Hatcher so he could release the mermaid.

The girl had already crawled halfway to the door, but the effort of doing so had clearly exhausted her. She was so pale and thin and didn't look like she would survive for five minutes outside the Caterpillar's room, even if her legs weren't broken beyond use.

Alice knelt to pick her up. The butterfly wings beat at the girl's back as she held out a hand to stay Alice.

"Don't," the girl said. Her voice was as fluttery as her wings. "Don't try to take me from here. Kill me."

The ground beneath Alice suddenly shifted, and several items on the shelves crashed to the ground. Outside in the big room several of the girls screamed.

"What was that?" Alice asked.

"This place is held together by the Caterpillar's magic," the butterfly said. "Now there's nothing to keep it here."

The girl's lips turned faintly blue during this short speech. Alice realized she must struggle to breathe, always hunched over and with those horrible wings pulling on her muscles.

"Kill me," the girl said again, her eyes pleading. "You need to run before this building collapses on your head. You won't be able to drag me with you."

Alice knew she should do it, that it would be a mercy. But it was one thing to kill a bad man, and another to kill an innocent girl.

"She'll only be taken by some other man," said a voice behind Alice.

She glanced over her shoulder to see the mermaid and Hatcher standing there. The mermaid wore one of the robes, and her fin was replaced by human legs. Her wet hair dripped puddles around her feet. Her eyes softened as she looked at the butterfly.

"She's too exotic," the mermaid said. "And the Caterpillar made certain she wasn't good for anything else."

She crossed the room to the butterfly, and knelt beside her, and took her into her arms. She kissed the girl on the lips, very gently, then pushed the butterfly's head to her shoulder. The girl closed her eyes.

"We've only had each other for a long time, haven't we? Just you and me with this wall between us," the mermaid said.

Just like me and Hatcher, in the asylum, Alice thought.

The mermaid nodded at Alice. Alice hesitated. She didn't want the girl to suffer, not like the Caterpillar. She didn't know how to make it quick.

"I'll do it," Hatcher said, his axe in his hand. "You'd better lay her down and leave."

The ground beneath them shifted again, and this time Alice heard the walls cracking.

The mermaid frowned at Hatcher. "I want to be with her."

He shook his head. "You'd better go out."

Something in his face convinced her, though she was still reluctant. She lowered the butterfly to the ground, and Alice saw tears welling.

"It's what I want," the girl said. "Don't cry. This is what I want. I'll be free."

The mermaid nodded, brushing her hand through the girl's hair. Then she left.

Hatcher jerked his head at Alice, so that she would follow the mermaid out. Alice did so, her stomach roiling. The girl wanted this, she knew. But was it right? Were they saving her from the same fate elsewhere? Or would she have had a chance to find somewhere new, away from the Old City, where she could be happy?

How would she find that place, Alice? she thought. *Who would take her there, for she did not have the ability to take herself?*

Behind her she heard the wet *thwack* of Hatcher's axe. The girl never made a sound. Alice choked on her own cry. The mermaid stood outside the butterfly's enclosure, her back straight and rigid, her eyes dry. Hatcher closed the door behind him so neither of them would be tempted to look.

The floor moved then, tilted completely to one side, and they both tumbled into the wall, which crumbled under their touch. The paint peeled away in long strips like the grasping tentacles of a monster, swiping at their faces as they passed. The screaming continued in earnest outside, the cries of men joining the long, panicked screeches of the Caterpillar's butterflies.

"This way," the mermaid gasped. A chunk of the ceiling had landed on her forehead and she bled from a deep cut. She led them deeper through the narrow corridor. It zigged and zagged this way and that, but Alice thought they were going downward. It was hard to tell.

Alice was afraid, very afraid, that they would be buried in this tiny space. The sounds coming from other parts of the building made her think that others were already dying that way. There were many doors, tall and small, that emptied off this hallway but the mermaid passed all of them.

There was a tremendous crash behind them. They all turned to see the tunnel collapsing entirely behind them—the ceiling and the walls folding in, the floor falling away.

No one needed prompting. Alice, Hatcher and the mermaid ran. They ran, and ran, and everything went to pieces in their wake.

Alice did not know how long they ran, but the corridor came to an abrupt end at a large white door. Painted on it was a large smiling mouth, grotesque without a face attached.

"The key!" the mermaid shouted.

Alice had forgotten she held it. Frankly, she was surprised she had not dropped it. She put the key in the lock and pushed open the door. Hatcher and the mermaid tumbled in behind her, and Alice tasted dirt in her mouth. She twisted around to see the structure disintegrating right up to the edge of the doorframe. The weight of that mad, huge building settled on top of the hallway they had just run through, and kept falling.

Alice stared in astonishment as yet another impossible thing happened before her eyes—several impossible things, as a matter of fact.

The debris did not fall through the door. It slid down the frame as if there were glass in place blocking it. Alice saw wood and nails and doors and chairs and tables all tumbling, some in pieces and some whole.

There were also people tumbling, and they were also some in pieces and some whole.

The most incredible feature of all this was that all of these things continued to fall, like there was no end to the hole that had opened up. Alice wondered whether everything would keep going until it reached the center of the earth and then emerge on the other side, in the faraway East.

Hatcher seemed just as surprised as Alice, though the mermaid appeared indifferent. She stood, pulling the robe tight though it really covered nothing. "We go this way now. Unless you want to watch the Caterpillar's house fall into an abyss?"

"Why doesn't it stop?" Alice asked.

"Magic, of course," the mermaid said.

She seemed very scornful all of sudden, and not at all appreciative. That irritated Alice. She was tired and heartsick from the death of the butterfly, and her hands shook from their close escape in the collapsing building. She hadn't even taken a moment to properly look around, so now she did.

They were in what appeared to be a tunnel carved out of rock. The floor was packed dirt, and the passage began at the door they'd just entered. There were not any visible junctions that Alice could see. The cave was lit by lamps set at intervals. These lamps must have been lit by magic, for there was no flicker of candlelight, nor scent of gas.

"How do you know which way to go?" Alice asked. Hatcher helped her to her feet.

"Cheshire brought me this way when he traded me to the Caterpillar," she said. "And I am returning that way so I can have my vengeance on one of them, at least."

Alice hadn't imagined it. The mermaid *was* angry that Alice had killed the Caterpillar in her stead.

"If I hadn't done it," Alice said conversationally, "you and your friend would still be his prisoners."

The mermaid turned on Alice, eyes flashing. "He was mine to destroy. I would have made him kneel before me. I would have made him scream and cry."

As he did me. The words were not said, but they were there.

"He could read your thoughts," Alice said. "You would never have been able to keep him from seeing your intent. You would never have gone free."

"You did," the mermaid said. "I heard the Caterpillar say that you once belonged to the Rabbit. You escaped him. How?"

"I don't remember," Alice said.

Not remembering had never troubled her before. But now that it was clear she would have to face him—to get the blade to destroy the Jabberwock, to put her own mind at rest once and for all—it seemed a terrible disadvantage. Every person they had met thus far—at least, every person in a position of power—had known precisely who she was, had known more about her own story than she did. She did not want to remember, but she would have to.

"You must remember something," the mermaid persisted.

Alice shrugged, not liking the avidity in the mermaid's eyes. She wished to remember, but she had no desire to put her memories on display.

Hatcher watched the proceedings silently. Alice had the sense that his mind was only half-present, that he was thinking of something else.

Someone else, she thought. *Jenny.*

"Does this tunnel only take us to Cheshire?" Alice asked. "We need to get to the Rabbit, and soon, before the Jabberwock finds out he has the blade."

"Do you actually believe the Caterpillar told you the truth?" the mermaid asked. "What if he just wanted to see you captured by the Rabbit again?"

"She won't be," Hatcher said.

The mermaid frowned at him. "If he is anything like the Caterpillar, then you can't possibly guarantee that. Besides, I heard that story too. He took your daughter. How can you promise her that you'll keep her safe?"

"He will," Alice said before Hatcher could say anything else—or get angry. She didn't think he would hurt the mermaid on purpose, but the mention of Jenny had to be raw. "I will ask you again—does this path lead only to Cheshire, or can we reach the Rabbit?"

"There were other turnings," the mermaid said, indifferent. "I don't know precisely where they lead, but surely you were listening when the Caterpillar said the fastest track from his place to the Rabbit's was underground. You will find the Rabbit, as you want. And I will find Cheshire, as I want."

"Just how do you think you're going to make Cheshire pay?" Alice asked. "You've nothing to fight him with, and his roses . . . aren't nice."

The mermaid tossed her black hair. "I can still beguile a man, still give him dreams. I was never able to do it before, for the Caterpillar was always watching, always knowing. But I can give Cheshire dreams so horrible he'll claw his own eyes out, pull out his tongue, do whatever he must to make them cease. In the end he would carve out his own guts if I told him it would make the dreams go away. I don't think you can do that with your Rabbit, even if you are a Magician."

She said this in a doubtful way, like she could hardly believe the notion of Alice as a Magician. "You're hardly beguiling in those boys' clothes, with your hair so short."

"He's not *my* Rabbit," Alice said. "And I have other ways, as you well know."

She did not add that the thought of tempting any man, even to take vengeance upon him, made her shudder. She knew that it must not be all blood and pain and power exerted by one or another. She knew that married people did those things and that they enjoyed them—at least, they must, else the housemaids would not have giggled so every time a handsome man came to call.

Would Hatcher ask this of her one day? Would he ask her to open her body to him? She didn't know if she could, or if she would ever want to.

"The knife," the mermaid said, her contempt indicating what she thought of Alice's "ways." "So crude."

"Not as crude as sticking a sword in a man's bum," Alice said, thinking of what the Caterpillar had said of the mermaid's dreams.

"You killed him too quickly," the mermaid said.

Alice sighed, suddenly very tired. She was sorry for the mermaid, very sorry to see such a proud and beautiful creature laid low for so long. But she was not going to argue with this woman all day about the quality of a murder she'd committed. It was done. The Caterpillar and all his butterflies and all the men who'd used and abused them were falling into nothingness, perhaps forever. Alice was sorry for the girls, although she wasn't certain they would have escaped their fate even with the Caterpillar's death. She had learned very quickly that there was always another man waiting to scoop up a helpless girl and put her to his own use.

So instead of bandying with the mermaid further, she simply said, "You're welcome."

The mermaid did not have anything to say to that, so she stalked ahead of them, her pale body shimmering in the shadows. She didn't want to be grateful, Alice knew. She'd wanted to take her own fate in her own hands, not be rescued by someone else.

They walked along for a time, though they had no sense of how much time might have passed. The tunnel curved occasionally, but there were no junctions. They followed the mermaid because there was no other place to go.

Alice's feet began dragging on the ground, her boots leaving long trails behind her. Hatcher put his arm around her shoulder to lift her.

"I've got to take a break, Hatch," she said. "I'm so tired."

They had gone too many days without sleeping properly, and it was catching up to Alice. The lack of rest didn't seem to bother Hatcher, which made her feel irritated. For some reason it disturbed her to think that the mermaid might find her weak.

Alice realized that she'd expected not only gratitude from the mermaid, but sympathy. They had both survived evil men. The mermaid ought to have shown some fellow feeling for Alice. But the only time the creature had appeared human was when she'd held the butterfly in her arms.

"We have to stop," Hatcher called to the mermaid, who'd gotten far ahead of them. He lowered Alice to the ground, where she slumped against the cave wall.

"Then stop," the mermaid said. "I am not tired."

"But what about the Rabbit?" Alice asked.

"I'm certain he will find you if you do not find him," the mermaid said, and laughed.

Then she was gone.

"I hate to say it, but I am relieved to see her go," Alice said.

"Yes, it's easier without another obligation," Hatcher said. "It will be difficult enough to get close to the Rabbit as it is."

"I didn't mean because she was an obligation," Alice said. "I only meant that she was unpleasant. Though she is correct. It won't be difficult to get close to the Rabbit. He obviously wishes to see me again, if he has mentioned my name so often that everyone knows it."

"It won't be difficult to see him if you walk to his door and announce yourself," Hatcher said. "But I don't want him to keep you. We must at least attempt stealth."

"I don't suppose there is any food in that pack other than Cheshire's magic cake?" Alice asked hopefully.

Hatcher rummaged in the bag and placed all the remaining items on the dirt floor. The cloaks were still there, and the rope, and Hatcher's extra weapons. The bread and apples that Bess had given them were gone, and so were Nell's pies and the cake and drink from Cheshire. In their place was a pile of sandwiches wrapped in sacking, and a tall green glass bottle stoppered with a cork. Hatcher removed the cork and sniffed the contents.

"Cider," he said, offering it to Alice.

"Should we trust it?" Alice asked. "The last drink Cheshire gave us made us large. It would not be a good thing to grow so large that we're trapped in this tunnel."

"This is all we have," Hatcher said. "It's this or we starve until we can leave this tunnel, and when we leave it, we will likely be on the Rabbit's doorstep."

"Cheshire has played some sort of game with us ever since we arrived at his cottage," Alice said.

"You believe he sent us into the maze to be eaten by the creature?" Hatcher asked.

Alice nodded. "And when that failed, he ensured we arrived at the Caterpillar's."

"Do you think the sandwiches are poisoned?" Hatcher asked.

"I don't know," Alice said. "But I don't think Cheshire means us any good. And how is he doing this? Yes, he's a Magician. I comprehend that. Is he watching us? Does he know what's happening? Or is he guessing? Has he actually expected we would survive all along? Did he plan for us to rid him of his monster?"

Hatcher shook his head. "I don't know, Alice. I'm hungry. I'll risk it."

"And what if they are poisoned?" Alice asked, watching in alarm as Hatcher raise one of the sandwiches to his lips. "Who will find Jenny then? Who will help me destroy the Jabberwock?"

Hatcher's mouth twisted in a grimace. "I suppose it's not worth the risk."

"No," Alice said. "Let's . . . let's just take a nap. Maybe when we wake we won't feel so hungry."

Hatcher repacked all the items in the bag. Then he leaned against the cave wall with his legs straight and put the axe in his lap, his hand loosely clasping the weapon. He held his other arm out for Alice to crawl into, and she did. His body was warm and safe, and he smelled clean, like the water of the lake that had washed them to the Caterpillar's door.

Alice expected only to doze, for she was in a strange place, and though they had not seen any folk besides the mermaid, others surely used this path. But she dropped into a deep sleep almost immediately, and she was not troubled by dreams.

She woke to a sound like a cork leaving a bottle, and there was a faint scent of sulfur.

Alice opened her eyes as Hatcher sat up straight, wakened by the same noise that disturbed her.

There was a plate in the middle of the path, just beyond the soles of their boots. On that plate were the same sandwiches that Hatcher had reluctantly rewrapped and placed inside his sack again.

Leaning against the plate was a white card with a picture of a smiling cat on it. Alice picked the card up and turned it over as Hatcher jumped to his feet, looking in both directions, the axe ready.

There were several words printed in large block letters on the back of the card. Alice held the card closer so she could see it in the dim light.

NOT POISONED.

EAT NOW.

LATER THERE WILL NOT BE TIME.

THE FUN IS ONLY BEGINNING!

Alice handed the card to Hatcher, who read it aloud.

"Could he have been here?" Alice asked. "I don't see any footprints."

"Nor I," he said. "He must be watching us somehow."

Alice felt the back of her neck prickle. It was not a very nice feeling, to think that someone was watching you from afar, to feel that you had no private moments.

"If he is watching us," Alice said, "then he knows the mermaid was released, and that she is coming for him."

"Yes," Hatcher said. "And he will also know that I killed Theobald."

"Theodore won't like that," Alice said, thinking of the big guard who had scowled at them.

"I'm not concerned with Theodore," Hatcher said with the ease of a man who has killed many and survived much.

"Hatch," Alice said. She picked up one of the sandwiches, considering. She didn't think Cheshire would lie to them outright. His way seemed to be concealment, trickery. So if he said the sandwiches were not poisoned, then they probably were not. Probably.

"Mmm?" he said. He had walked a little way down the tunnel in the direction the mermaid had gone.

Alice took a bite of the sandwich. It tasted very good, like the cucumber sandwiches her mother liked to have for tea.

"Do you remember what you did for the Rabbit?" Alice asked.

This wasn't precisely what she'd wanted to ask. She'd wanted to ask whether he'd remembered *before* the Caterpillar told him of Jenny, whether he had deliberately concealed his connection with the man who had tried to buy her and keep her as his prize.

He walked back to her and crouched before the plate of sandwiches, picked one up and shoved half in his mouth in one bite. "I didn't remember the Rabbit at all until the Caterpillar told that tale. Then I could see the faces of men I'd fought, feel their flesh give under my hands. I can see Hattie's eyes, so sad and blue, and Jenny's, bright and grey. I can see all of us together, having our tea at a tiny table that Hattie polished until it gleamed, and my knuckles scabbed from the day's work. But the Rabbit . . . I can't really see his face. I should be able to. It's blocked out, somehow, by the idea of him that you put in my head. The fellow with the long ears and the blue-green eyes."

"That's not what you remember?" Alice asked.

"I don't think he had long ears," Hatcher said, and his face had that squashed-trying-to-remember look that he got sometimes. "It doesn't seem right, your Rabbit and my Rabbit."

"Maybe the ears came later," Alice said. "He is a Magician, or so the Caterpillar said."

"All these Magicians," Hatcher said, his voice musing. "They must have the ministers in their pockets, else why were they not chased from the City like the others?"

"Do you think that the ministers know?" Alice asked. "Maybe the Rabbit and the Caterpillar and Cheshire and any others hid themselves so well that they weren't suspected."

"Rose Way isn't exactly hiding," Hatcher said. "And even the Caterpillar's place was not of this world, and looked it from the outside. No, I think that Cheshire and the Caterpillar just had something to offer the men in power, and so were allowed to stay."

"Or the Magicians who stayed knew something about the ministers, something they could use against the City," Alice said. "Cheshire, in particular, probably holds more secrets than a wishing well."

Hatcher dropped the sandwich suddenly, gripping both sides of his head. Alice spit out the last bit of her sandwich, terrified that the food was poisoned after all.

"Alice," Hatcher said. "Everything is breaking apart inside."

"Was it the sandwich?" she asked, scrambling to his side. Why had she thought Cheshire trustworthy? "Do you feel sick?"

"No," he said. "Not like that. It's my head. All the things I couldn't remember are leaking through now, dribbling through the cracks. Hattie and Jenny. The Rabbit. Bess. I remember being small, and Bess making bread in the kitchen, singing a song about a butterfly."

"No," Alice said, rubbing his back, trying to soothe. His muscles jumped, as if sparking with lightning underneath the skin. "That was me. That is the song I sang to you in the hospital."

"It's all mixed up," he said. "It was all right before, when I didn't remember anything except the blood and the axe slicing through them. I didn't know about Jenny. Now it hurts inside my head and my heart is going to crack open, crack and shatter into a million pieces because I can't bear it, Alice. I can't bear to know what might be happening to her, somewhere far away from me."

He stood and paced, his head twitching. Alice hadn't seen him this agitated since they'd escaped the asylum. While they'd been out and free, his madness had receded, mitigated by the lack of walls around him. The Caterpillar's knowledge might have broken open Hatcher's memory, but the walls around them couldn't be helping.

It was close in this tunnel, and there was no sense of freedom, only a forced march on a singular path.

Hatcher strode back and forth, back and forth, taking no more space than he would if he were in his cell, even though that space was available.

When they'd been locked in their own rooms, Alice had just let Hatcher's fits run their course. She didn't have many options when they were in separate rooms. Many nights she'd fallen asleep to the sound of him ranting and pacing on the other side of the mouse hole.

Now she wasn't certain what to do. He might lash out at her if she tried to stop him. But he might be lost to her if she didn't.

She deliberately placed her body in his path. He plowed into her but she kept her feet, putting her hands on his shoulders and forcing him to look at her. His eyes rolled in his head, the whites showing like a frightened horse.

"Hatcher," she said. "We will find her. First we'll find the Rabbit. Then we'll find the Jabberwock. And then we'll find Jenny. We'll find her."

Alice wondered whether this meant they would be doomed to wander forever like Gilgamesh in the old story, seeking something they couldn't find. They didn't know where Jenny was, only that she was far away. And the little girl Hatcher remembered was grown now. She might not recall her father. She might even hate him.

Hatcher's body vibrated under her hands. He was a taut bowstring, ready to shoot.

"Be with me now," Alice said, putting her face close to his. "Be here with me. Everything else is the past or the future. Don't think about them. Be here with me, right now."

She took his hand and placed it over her heart and breathed slow and easy, hoping he would follow her. A few moments later he was following the rhythm of her breath so that their inhales and exhales matched. His gaze sharpened, focused, recognized that she was Alice.

She smiled at him, but it was a tired smile. They had slept a little. They had eaten a little. There was so far to go still, and Alice was weary, and there was more fighting to come. She wished for a safe place to rest her head, a sanctuary for them to return to after their task was done. But there was no such place for them, and after the Jabberwock, there was Jenny.

Hatcher nodded, letting her know he was all right, and her hands fell away. He had kicked over the plate of sandwiches while rushing back and forth in his fit. Another white card was revealed, previously hidden beneath the food. Alice picked it up.

THERE WILL BE THREE
P.S. DON'T WORRY ABOUT THE MERMAID

"'There will be three'?" Alice asked. "Three of what?"

Hatcher stilled, waving a hand to silence her. Alice cocked her head, listening close. There was a sound of claws scraping in the dirt from the tunnel ahead, and something else—a kind of clicking, chittering sound.

"It sounds like—" Alice began.

"Rats," Hatcher finished.

"Rats," Alice said. "I don't like rats."

"Cheshire said there would only be three," Hatcher said.

He collected their sack of supplies, slung it over his shoulder, took out the axe and started in the direction of the noise.

"Why are you walking *toward* the noise?" Alice asked, panic settling into her chest. "And why are we trusting Cheshire?"

She didn't know why the thought of rats scared her more than the Caterpillar or the creature that had tried to eat Hatcher in Cheshire's maze. Perhaps because the Caterpillar was a man, and thus could be distracted or reasoned with. As for the creature in the maze, Alice had seen it so briefly and acted so quickly she hadn't had an opportunity to be frightened. She scurried along behind Hatcher, the knife in her right hand.

"I'm walking toward the noise because we will meet the cause whether we stand or move. Cheshire . . . Well, the sandwiches weren't poisoned, were they?" Hatcher said.

"There are such things as slow-acting poisons," Alice said.

"If Cheshire wanted us dead, he would have let the roses strangle us," Hatcher said. "I think he wants us to prove we're worthy of his help."

"A few moments ago you couldn't even think in a straight line," Alice muttered. "Now you know what Cheshire's intentions are?"

Hatcher grinned. "Just because I'm mad doesn't mean I'm not right. And you were mad not so long ago yourself."

The chittering grew louder, faster than Alice wished. Why was Hatcher rushing toward their fate? Why not wait and hope the creatures turned around, went in another direction?

Because Hatcher, whatever his flaws, would always pick a headfirst fight.

And Alice, because she had chosen him, would always be dragged with him.

Alice saw their eyes first, burning red out of the darkness. Then the teeth flashed, sharp and vicious. Hatcher paused, set his feet apart, blocking the tunnel. Alice resisted the very strong urge to cower behind him.

These were very large rats. Very, very large rats. Rats the size of horses. The lead rat would be able to touch its nose to Hatcher's chest. Their horrible furless tails dragged along behind their enormous bodies. Alice hated rats' tails most of all. There was something primal and repulsive about them, serpentine and yet not.

"There are more than three," Alice said. There was something like a dozen or more, all moving steadily in their direction. She would never believe another thing Cheshire told her. In fact, she heartily hoped she would never encounter that strange little Magician ever again.

"Yes," Hatcher said, and raised his axe as they approached.

"You can hardly kill them all," Alice said.

He smiled again, and Alice saw the longing inside him for blood and mayhem. "I'll enjoy trying."

The lead rat stopped when it was a few feet from Alice and Hatcher. Alice wasn't accustomed to crediting animals with emotion, but something about the rat seemed frightened. It shuffled its feet in the dirt restlessly, shaking its head to and fro. Alice noted the rat had a long white patch next to its mouth, almost like a scar from a knife.

"Will you let us pass?" the rat said.

Alice's mouth dropped open. She couldn't help it. She'd seen many strange things already, but never had an animal spoken to her before.

"There's nowhere to go," Alice said, remembering her manners. "That tunnel ends at the Caterpillar's house."

Hatcher's hand dropped a little, and he stared at Alice, then at the rat. "Are you speaking to that creature?"

"Yes," Alice said.

"And the Caterpillar's house has fallen," the rat said. "We know. Everyone knows. You must have been the one to do it, else you would not be leaving the wreckage."

"Who is 'everyone'?" Alice asked.

"All the creatures who live undertown, all of the men who use these tunnels for their own purpose," the rat said.

"Why are you running toward the Caterpillar's?" Alice said. "Why go to a dead end?"

The rat shifted again, its red eyes glancing behind. It moved forward, and Alice resisted the urge to flinch as it approached her. It would not do to show fear to something with teeth so large.

"The Walrus is rampaging," the rat whispered, looking over its hump as if it expected to see the man behind him. "The Walrus and Mr. Carpenter are at war. The Caterpillar and the Walrus were allied against their enemies, so the Walrus was able to hold his own streets and those he stole from Mr. Carpenter. Now that the Caterpillar is dead, the Walrus finds none to stand with him, for he has poached on their territories for too long. Those who did not intervene before, like the Rabbit, will now side with Mr. Carpenter, and the Walrus will be destroyed."

"Why did the Rabbit stay out of it before?"

"Because the Rabbit was allied with the Caterpillar as well, so he agreed to be a neutral party. There is no more Caterpillar, and therefore no need to be neutral."

"But why do you run from a war in the streets?" Alice asked. "What does it have to do with you?"

"The Walrus is rampaging," the rat repeated.

"I'm sorry; I don't understand what that means," Alice said.

"The Walrus uses some of us to fight in his ring. He likes to watch fighting, rats and humans and whatever other animal he can find. But he is so angry now he is killing anyone he sees, even those who served him loyally." The rat whispered again. "He's sworn to eat and murder whoever removed the Caterpillar."

"You mean murder and eat," Alice said.

"No, I mean eat and murder," the rat said. "I'd rather it the other way around, wouldn't you?"

"I'd rather it not at all," Alice said.

"So we are running and hiding where the Walrus will not find us, the place he would least suspect," the rat said. "We have eight children in our nest, and I want them to live to bear my grandchildren."

Alice peered at the other rats huddled behind the leader. Several of them were smaller than he.

"What is your name?" Alice asked.

"Nicodemus," the rat replied. "And this is my nest-mate, Asora."

He nudged one of the rats with his tail, and she came forward, bowing her head at Alice.

"And I am Alice," she said. "This is Hatcher."

Nicodemus looked at Hatcher's axe and then at his face. "*The* Hatcher?"

Hatcher didn't reply, which Alice thought was very rude. She had never imagined she would be having a conversation with a rat, much less one so large, but there they were. She answered for him, giving him a little frown.

"I suppose," she said. "I only know one Hatcher."

"The Walrus is looking for him, and you," Nicodemus said.

"Because of the Caterpillar?" Alice asked. She couldn't conceal her surprise. How would the Walrus know they had anything to do with the Caterpillar's death?

"Because Hatcher—if it's the same Hatcher—was once called Nicholas, and he fought a man called the Grinder in the ring," the rat said. His eyes willed Alice to understand.

Alice pointed at Hatcher. "He fought the Grinder."

"The Grinder never fought again after that day," Nicodemus said. "The Grinder is now the Walrus."

"He wants revenge," Alice said.

"What's it saying about the Grinder?" Hatcher asked.

"You heard him," Alice said.

"I heard him, but I didn't understand him," Hatcher said. "Only you."

This must have something to do with magic, Alice thought, but there wasn't time to think about the whys and hows. Besides, there was a more important question.

"I'll explain later," she said to Hatcher. Then, to Nicodemus, "What is the Walrus' interest in me?"

"Do you know a girl called Dolly?" Nicodemus asked.

"Dolly?" Alice asked, her face blank.

"Dolly?" Hatcher said. "That silly serving girl? The one you made me give money to?"

"Oh, Dolly," Alice said, and remembered the flash of cunning she'd seen on the girl's face. "She went straight to the Walrus and told him I was a Magician, didn't she?"

"Yes," the rat said. "Although it didn't do her any good. The Walrus took a liking to her right away."

Alice shuddered, for she knew what that meant. Dolly had met the fate she had so feared.

"The Walrus very much desires the flesh of a Magician. He knows so many but has no such power himself." Nicodemus gave Alice a meaningful stare.

Alice decided then and there that she would ask Hatcher to take her head from her neck before she would be brought before the Walrus.

"How is it that you know so much?" Alice asked.

"The Walrus speaks freely before us, for to him we are only dumb creatures, exotics for his ring," the rat said. "Most humans do, so we hear many things. Our smaller kin know every secret, for they live inside the walls and under the streets and men do not hide their worst actions from us."

"May I ask . . . if it's not impolite, may I know how it is that you are so much larger than others of your kind?" Alice didn't like to say "rats." They might prefer to be called something else.

"Magic, of course. An elixir sold to the Walrus by the Caterpillar."

But not, I think, made by the Caterpillar, Alice thought. That was Cheshire's magic, a cake to make you small and a drink to make you tall.

"What would you have done if I were not a Magician and could not speak to you?" Alice wondered aloud.

Nicodemus flashed his teeth at her, and it was not a smile. "If you did not speak, we would have fed you to our children."

Alice was very glad that Hatcher could not understand the rat, for she was certain he would have taken the rat's words as a threat.

"Thank you," Alice said, nudging Hatcher to one side. He went, but very reluctantly. "Thank you for warning us of the Walrus' intentions. I wish you and your family well."

The rat bowed his head at Alice. "I hope you do not cross paths with him. He is not so kindly as the Caterpillar."

The Caterpillar was not kindly at all, so Alice took the remark in the spirit it was meant. The Walrus was worse.

Alice and Hatcher pressed against the cave wall to allow the rats to pass by. The passage was so narrow that several animals brushed against them. Alice held her breath, trying not to smell the musky animal scent of them, trying not to shudder at the swipe of their fur and their tails.

Finally, they were gone, their chittering and claw scrapes fading in the distance. Hatcher gave her a questioning look.

Alice sighed, and started walking in the direction the rats

had come from. As she walked, she explained what she had heard.

"The Grinder is the Walrus," Hatcher said. "That's not good for us at all. I made certain, the night I fought him, that he would never grind anybody ever again."

"What did you do to him?" asked Alice.

"I broke his hands," Hatcher said. "And his wrists. Someone—the Rabbit, I think—told me later that they never healed right, that the bones are knotted and twisted under his skin. You can talk to animals."

"I suppose I can," Alice said, not in the least surprised by the sudden change in subject.

"That's a useful gift," Hatcher said. "Without it we would have had to fight those rats."

"And we might not have survived."

"We would have survived," Hatcher said. It was not arrogance, just assurance. Hatcher knew he would always find a way out.

"I wonder if they would have liked to return to their normal size," Alice said. "We could have given them some of Cheshire's cake."

"We could have except that the cake is no longer in my pack," Hatcher said.

"Oh, that's right," Alice said. "Still, the Walrus must be very frightening in his current state to scare creatures like that so badly that they would hide in a dead-ended tunnel."

"He was not a pleasant fighter," Hatcher said. "He would cheat if he could get away with it, carry things like nails and pincers in his palm to use when nobody was looking. He had no honor."

"And now he eats people. Girls," Alice amended.

"And Magicians."

"Can it be that all the territories are controlled by Magicians?" Alice asked. "All except the Walrus'?"

"I don't know that all of them would be," Hatcher said doubtfully. "Bosses rise and fall. Anyone with magic would rise without falling, unless another Magician removed him. And the Old City is large, larger than the New City. Most of the streets are controlled by petty criminals, men who own a few streets and have a few thugs to enforce their will. No, they can't all be Magicians. But the ones who have a lot of power, a lot of territory—they are Magicians."

"I wonder if Mr. Carpenter is a Magician," Alice said.

"Even if he is, he won't like us. We killed two of his sentries," Hatcher said.

"He doesn't know that," Alice said. "And he's the Walrus' enemy."

"We're not going to get involved in a war between the Walrus and Mr. Carpenter," Hatcher said.

"I think we may already be involved," Alice said. "I would rather take my chances with Mr. Carpenter than face the Walrus. Hatcher, don't you think it's strange that everyone we've met has known who we were before—before the hospital, I mean."

Hatcher appeared unconcerned. "We drew the attention of important men, before and after. Our paths keep intersecting with theirs. And, though I know you dislike to hear it—that scar on your face was put there for a reason."

"So that anyone who saw me would know what the Rabbit had done. So that I would never be able to hide from him," Alice said, touching the long ridge that ran down one side of her face. She'd hated the scar at first because it made her ugly. Now she hated it because it revealed her story to everyone she met, everyone who knew of Alice and the Rabbit. Even after the Rabbit was dead and gone she would still have his mark. She would never be able to forget him.

But he was never able to forget you either. You marked him too.

She wished she could remember all of it, remember sinking the knife into that blue-green eye. She wished she could remember the pain she'd given him and not only the pain he'd given her.

Alice was thinking hard on that memory, trying to recall, so she wasn't really paying attention to where she was going. She stopped when her nose struck wood.

She blinked, stepping back. Hatcher was frowning.

"Well, Cheshire did say there would be three," he said.

CHAPTER

14

Before them were three wooden doors, all painted in pink and white candy stripes like the creature's house on the island in the maze. There was no indication where the doors might lead.

"One goes to the Rabbit," Alice said. "The Caterpillar told us that. One must go to Cheshire, because the mermaid said she was taken this way when she was first traded to the Caterpillar. What about the third?"

"The Walrus?" Hatcher guessed. "The rats had to come from somewhere."

"The rats. Right," Alice said.

She peered at the ground, looking for signs that the extra-sized rodents had entered through one particular door. But the dirt was scratched and mashed by the passage of many feet, and there was no way to tell from which door they might have come.

"I'm not comfortable with guessing," Alice said. "The wrong door would take us straight into the Walrus' arms."

"Perhaps. Perhaps not," Hatcher said. "We don't know exactly where these passages lead. They may lead to underground entrances to the Rabbit's and the Walrus' and Cheshire's lairs. Or the tunnels may lead us to the streets, close to them but not directly to them."

"I'd still rather not take a chance," Alice said. "As long as the Walrus knows he is looking for a tall girl with a scar on her face, I'm at risk."

"I told you, I won't let him take you," Hatcher said.

Alice sighed. "Even you can be taken by surprise, Hatch."

She reached for the knob of the middle door. Hatcher positioned himself next to the doorframe with his axe in his hand, flattened against the cavern wall. If anyone tried to rush through when Alice opened the door they would not have an opportunity to regret it.

The entrance swung open to reveal . . . nothing. On the other side there was simply a continuation of the same kind of cave they'd passed through already. Alice was disappointed. She'd hoped for some indication of the passage's destination.

Her nose twitched as she reached for the handle to pull the door shut again. "Roses," she said. "Cheshire is this way."

Hatcher sniffed the air. "Yes. Roses."

"I never want to smell another rose again," Alice said, closing it hastily.

They checked behind the other doors, but there was no sign to tell where they might lead.

"Use your magic," Hatcher urged.

Alice stared at him. "I've no idea how. What am I supposed to do, hold my finger out like a divining rod and hope it sends us in the direction of the Rabbit?"

"You've got magic inside you," Hatcher said. "You talked to the rats. You set the roses on fire."

"I did those things without thinking."

"Then don't think now," he said.

That might be logical to Hatcher, but it didn't make much sense to Alice. Still, she walked in front of the left-hand passage and did the only thing she could think of to do. She put her hand on the door, and thought of the Rabbit, the picture of him that she had in her head. The long white ears, the blue-green eyes (*eye*, she corrected), the tall hat.

"A hat!" Alice exclaimed. "He always wore a tall hat."

"Who?" Hatcher said.

"The Rabbit," Alice said, narrowing her eyes, trying to picture his face. "I remembered. He was tall too. Tall like you."

"We're a lot of giants," Hatcher said. "You are the tallest girl I've ever known. The Caterpillar was bigger than both of us. And the Walrus, well—if he is the Grinder, then he's bigger than you and me and the Rabbit all put together."

"Hatcher," she said, realizing something. "You're a Seer. Why don't you try?"

"Seeing's not like that," he said. "Visions just come to me without my thinking about them."

"Then don't think now," Alice said tartly.

She hadn't gotten anything from touching the door. The image of the Rabbit had emerged from concentration on the past. Still, she tried the same method on the other door, with no results. She sat cross-legged in the dirt before the three choices and looked at each in turn. Hatcher joined her, tracing patterns in the ground with the handle of his axe.

"What's that?" Alice asked, pointing at a coiled symbol he had carved in the ground. It looked like the pattern of a snail shell, spiraling inward.

He drew four stars around the spiral, one at each point of the compass. Something about the symbol was familiar to Alice, though she couldn't remember where she'd seen it. She touched the center of the spiral with one finger.

And suddenly she was not there in that cavern with Hatcher. She was in the top of a high tower, and all around her potions bubbled and dusty books sang with knowledge. Her hands were not her own anymore, but the hands of a man much, much older than she. He held a blade as long as Alice's forearm, and just as wide. It shone silver in the firelight, and the handle was glittering and black. Just under the hilt was the coil with four stars around it. She stared at the blade, and her heart was heavy, for she did not want to do that which she must. She did not wish to destroy her friend. But he was no longer her friend. He was the Jabberwock now, keeper of dark magic, and dark magic had no place in this world.

"Alice?"

Hatcher's voice, coming from far away, like he spoke to her through a tube. She'd played that game when she was young, talking to her friend (*Dor, but Dor wasn't her friend anymore*) through a long hollow piece of wood they'd found after a violent storm. It made their voices strange, gave them heft that their girl-chirps didn't ordinarily have.

"Alice?" His hands were at her shoulders, shaking.

"I saw the blade," she said, and opened her eyes. Hatcher's face was before her, and behind that, the cave ceiling. "What happened?"

"You touched that coil, and there was a spark," Hatcher said, helping her sit up. "And then you went white and fell backward."

"I saw the blade," she repeated. "The one we have to find, the one the Rabbit has. We have to get to it before the Jabberwock does. All these other things happening made me half forget. We're here underground, and the Walrus might be rampaging but the Jabberwock is stalking, stalking, stalking. Once he finds the blade he will destroy it, and take his lost magic, and then we won't be able to stop him."

Hatcher nodded. "Yes. We need to think of the Jabberwock and not our own troubles."

"Though our own troubles seem to mesh with our quest for the Jabberwock, at least a little," Alice said. "Still, the blade is the important thing."

"Then which way to go?" Hatcher asked.

"I still don't know for certain," Alice admitted. "Let's try the left. And go cautiously."

"And if we catch a whiff of the Walrus, then I finish the job I should have finished long ago," Hatcher said.

They entered the left-hand door. As with the middle door, Alice was disappointed to find there was no guard. A guard could be persuaded to give up information. It was almost as if all those who used the passages completely trusted the other three.

That may have been so, Alice considered. The Caterpillar and Cheshire were friends, as were the Caterpillar and the Rabbit. The Rabbit tolerated the Walrus for the sake of the Caterpillar.

But the rats had said that now that the Caterpillar was gone, the Rabbit would side with Mr. Carpenter against the Walrus. If that was so, then a direct passage to the Walrus' place seemed like an easy way to rid yourself of an enemy.

After another long walk (*all we do is walk and fight to break up the walking,* Alice thought) they came upon another door. This door *was* guarded, though on the other side. Alice and Hatcher heard voices through the wood, though they couldn't make out what was said.

"Which?" Alice whispered in Hatcher's ear. "The Walrus or the Rabbit?"

"We'll have to take a chance," Hatcher said. "It sounds like there are two of them. You silence yours, and I'll question the other one."

What a terribly civilized way of putting it, Alice thought. *"Silence" him. Not "cut his throat open with your knife," which is what Hatcher is actually asking me to do.*

They opened the door quickly, surprising the guards. Both men were at their ease, eating a meal from pails. Alice was upon her man before he was able to reach the spear that lay at his side. She silenced him, as Hatcher had asked her to do.

The second man was quicker off the mark, and gave Hatcher a moment of trouble. The result was that Hatcher lost his temper and the guard lost his head, and they had no one to question.

Alice wrinkled her nose at Hatcher. "I thought you wanted to question him."

"I saw—"

"Red. I know," Alice said. She pushed the first man's legs out of the way with the toe of her boot. That was when she noticed the way the guards were dressed—exactly like the men who'd attacked in the tavern. "These are the Walrus' men."

Hatcher swore. "Damn. It's a long walk back to the other doors."

Alice hurried back to the door and pulled on it. It wouldn't budge. She turned the knob again, tried pushing. It still would not move. She stared at Hatcher, her eyes wide.

"We can't get out," she said.

The first thrumming of panic had started in her chest. She did not want to meet the Walrus. He frightened her much more than the Rabbit, whom she felt, somehow, she was able to best. She had beaten him once, escaped him once, and she had survived much on this journey already. The Rabbit was a bogeyman, but an old bogeyman, familiar and comforting in the predictability of his evil. The Walrus was a horror not yet seen, a nightmare that she did not want to experience.

She did not want to be eaten alive.

Hatcher nudged her to one side, put some force into the door. Nothing.

"If I break it down it will make noise. That might attract others," he said.

Alice nodded. The tunnel curved almost immediately to the left after the small entryway where the guards had been eating. She cautiously approached the curve and peeked around the corner.

There was a set of steps that led upward a few feet from the turn. She tiptoed along, wincing each time her boots scraped the dirt or knocked tiny pebbles against the cave wall. At the top of the steps was a trapdoor.

She returned to Hatcher and described the situation.

"You'd best stand just past the bottom of the stairs, where nobody can see you," Hatcher said. "You might be able to take one or two by surprise."

"Just how many soldiers do you think I can fight on my own?" Alice asked.

"As many as necessary," Hatcher said. "I believe in you, Alice."

She felt for the first time that she wanted to kiss him, that she wanted to know what it was like when she chose it. So she did.

His lips were soft and she could taste his surprise, and then his pleasure. He did not put his arms around her, or try to hold her to him. She put her hands on his shoulders to steady herself as she pulled away, for she felt dizzy from her toes to her eyelashes.

Hatcher smiled at her, and she smiled back. It was nice, Alice mused, to remember that there was a purpose to living besides madness and death. Then she took up her place at the bottom of the stairs, and Hatcher set himself to work.

There was a great deal of noise as Hatcher threw his body against the door with increasing amounts of force. With every blow Alice was certain that a dozen men would stream down the steps with murder in their eyes, but no one came.

After a time it became clear that Hatcher was not going to break the door down. Alice went to him, put a hand out to stop him.

Hatcher next took his axe from his jacket. The first blow left no mark on the door but took a chip from the blade. Hatcher tucked the axe away without a word. Alice knew he wouldn't risk any more harm to his favorite weapon. "We can't get out that way," she said.

She saw that he had come to this conclusion already but that he still tried, perhaps driven by the thought of what might occur if the Walrus discovered their presence.

"We have to go up, Hatch," Alice said. "We have no choice. We can't stay down here and wait for the changing guard to discover us."

"How did the rats get out?" Hatcher said, panting from the exertion. "They couldn't have come this way. But this way is the only way that we saw."

"We must have missed something," Alice said. "A secret turning."

"Rats that size did not crawl from any tunnel that we missed," Hatcher said.

Alice was inclined to agree. Still, the mystery of the rats' escape hardly mattered. Their own escape was paramount.

Hatcher took the lead up the stairs. When he reached the trapdoor he listened hard for any sound of movement above. Alice didn't hear anything, and after a moment Hatcher slowly opened the trap.

The smell hit them first, so overwhelming that Alice coughed, bile rising in her throat. She hastily covered her mouth with her arm. Hatcher's lips pressed together as he slowly eased the door up and climbed out. He hurried away from the exit, waving his hand to show that Alice should stay.

She presumed he was checking the room for people who might object to their sudden appearance. As always, his boots made hardly a sound. For such a large man he walked very light.

Soon enough he returned and gestured for her to follow him.

"I'm not certain you want to see this," he said. He looked as though he wished to unsee it himself.

"I can hardly walk about with my eyes closed," Alice said as her head cleared the trap and she saw what was in the room.

The stench hit her harder then, and she ducked her head under so she was sick on the stairs.

Well, if Cheshire did poison the sandwiches, then they're out of me now, Alice thought. She was trying desperately to think about anything other than what she could see.

Alice had killed four times now. Always it was in defense of herself or someone else——to save Hatcher, to save Nell and Dolly, to stop a guard from sounding the alarm. She did not think she would ever enjoy it, as Hatcher seemed to, but she'd quickly grasped the necessity of it in the Old City. Here, you made someone else suffer before they did you.

What was in this place was not done in defense of a life. It was carnage, pure and simple.

They were in some kind of storage room, and everywhere they looked, there were bodies of girls. Alice could tell they were girls only because they were naked. All of their faces had been gnawed off, ragged bits of skin remaining where the

Walrus' teeth had missed. There were bite marks elsewhere too, but Alice did not want to look too closely. She did not want to look at all.

"What kind of a man does this?" she said. She fought the impulse to hide her face. The time for hiding was over, she realized. She must see the monster for what it was.

"He's not a man," Hatcher said. "No man would do this."

Hatcher was angry, Alice realized. Much angrier than he'd been on any occasion before, and that did not bode well. When Hatcher was angry he tended to be more . . . spontaneous.

"There's Dolly," he said, and pointed to a body at the top of one of the piles. "That stupid girl. That stupid, stupid girl."

Alice wasn't certain how he could identify the thing as Dolly, but she would take Hatcher's word for it.

"Yes, she was foolish," Alice said. "She thought she would be rewarded for telling him about me. And you."

There was one exit other than the trapdoor. Hatcher went to the door and listened.

"There are people out there," he said. "Sounds like quite a lot of people, actually."

Alice joined him. It did sound as though there was a great deal of activity on the other side of the door. She heard that buzzing murmur that happens when a large group has gathered in one place—the shuffling of feet, the ebb and flow of small conversation, the occasional shout to a friend or the jostle that results in an indignant cry.

"What do you think?" Alice asked.

It didn't seem wise to rush in with the intention of hacking their way through a crowd of people. They might be the Walrus' soldiers, in which case Alice and Hatcher might remove a few while surprise was on their side before they were overwhelmed. Or they might not be soldiers, but innocent people, and Alice did not want to harm any innocents.

Though really, she thought, *anyone who is near the Walrus can't possibly be innocent. He's a criminal. At best they are men come to use the girls that the Walrus didn't eat. At worst they work for him, stealing those girls from their lives, keeping them here when they would try to escape.*

"Wait," Hatcher said. "Listen."

Alice concentrated on the noise through the door. The crowd had quieted, and an announcement was being made. She couldn't quite make it out, but the crowd roared in response, cheering and clapping. A moment later they quieted again, and the same procedure repeated.

"It's a fight ring," Hatcher said, pulling his ear away from the door. "Alice, this is perfect. We only need to slip into the crowd and then follow when they leave. There must be an exit nearby for such a large group to be present."

Alice hesitated. "What if they are simply those who work for the Walrus, not men from outside? There's no assurance of an exit then."

"We know there is no exit from here," Hatcher said. "And we'd best leave this room before the guard changes and we're discovered."

"What happened to your cap?" Hatcher asked.

Alice rubbed the short hair on top of her head, surprised to find the hat missing. "I must have lost it somewhere. I didn't notice. There have been so many strange things happening."

"Your face is so distinctive," Hatcher said. "Take mine. It's easier to cover your scar with it. If we are fortunate, the room will be hidden in shadow."

Alice pulled the cap low over her eyes. The plan was very risky, but it did seem they had no other option available. They must leave this room before they were cornered.

The crowd roared on the other side of the door, and Hatcher judged it time to slip inside. His choice was a good one, as the men standing just on the other side of the door were preoccupied with the action below in the ring. Hatcher immediately scuttled along the edge of the horde, distancing them from the door to the underground tunnel. Alice's scarred cheek faced the wall, which was lucky, because anyone who glanced at her would not be able to see the distinctive mark.

The room was arranged like a round arena, with wooden benches stacked on risers above an open center. It reeked of sweat and tobacco and desperation as men shouted themselves hoarse in favor of the fighter they'd bet on. Girls in various states of undress roamed through the crowd offering trays of refreshment for sale. *And a peek of the other merchandise on offer,* Alice thought angrily as several of the girls were groped by drunken men.

In the fight ring was a skinny man, ropy with muscle and wearing only an eye patch and a pair of ragged pants. His opponent was—

Alice stopped and stared. Hatcher realized she was no longer behind him and went back to her side.

"What is it?" he asked.

"A rabbit," she said, and pointed.

The skinny man's opponent was, indeed, a rabbit—a large white rabbit with pink eyes. His fur, probably once fluffy and soft, was matted and covered in copper stains like faded blood.

Hatcher frowned. "Not *the* Rabbit. The one we're looking for."

"No," Alice said, shaking her head. "He must be another poor creature given Cheshire's growing potion, like the rats."

The man danced and spun and struck the rabbit, who returned the blows only halfheartedly. Even from this distance Alice could see the sad, broken expression in his eyes.

Then the whip came out of the darkness, striking the white rabbit on the back, and she saw the man who held it.

He was, indeed, monstrous, though not in the way Alice expected. Dolly's description had given her an impression of someone so enormous he could not move, a massive bloated blob without form or feature. The Walrus was not like that.

The Walrus was very tall and powerfully built, a mass of muscle slightly gone to seed. His belly was large, reflecting his appetites, but his arms were twice the size of Alice's legs put together, and his legs were twice his arms. His face was partially hidden in shadow, though Alice thought his eyes glinted in cruel amusement as the rabbit fell to the ground.

Now she could see the striped marks of blows old and new on the rabbit's back, and her heart ached. The throng of men shouted for the rabbit to rise again, and as he did the skinny man punched his pink, twitching nose. The rabbit's whiskers, Alice noted, were broken to many different lengths and his front right tooth was cracked down to a very small nub.

"We can't leave him here," Alice said, as Hatcher put his hand on her elbow and pulled her along again.

"We can't sneak a giant white rabbit from the ring directly under the Walrus' nose," Hatcher said. "Besides, what will we do with him after? Take him with us to meet the other Rabbit?"

Alice wrenched her arm free. "We can't leave him here," she repeated, mulishly. "He's an innocent creature."

"The world is full of innocent creatures," Hatcher snapped, drawing close to her ear so no one would overhear them. "You were one yourself once, and no one saved you."

"You saved Hattie," Alice said.

"She wasn't innocent by the time I found her."

"Yet you still saved her."

"What about all the girls we left behind in the Caterpillar's? What about the other screaming inmates of the asylum that we let burn?" Hatcher asked. "There was a reason we didn't save them. We can't save everybody."

"No," Alice said. "We can't save everybody. But we can save somebody. And I don't want to leave the rabbit behind."

"Why?" Hatcher asked. "Why now?"

"He's helpless," Alice said. She felt she couldn't fully explain what the rabbit represented to her, the way the sight of him made her heart ache. "He doesn't belong here. He belongs in a field, nibbling dandelion greens. I don't know, Hatch. I just can't leave him. I can't bring myself to leave him."

Hatcher sighed, his grey eyes full of some unidentifiable expression—something like amusement and frustration and love and anger all mixed together.

"I knew one day you would find your line, Alice," Hatcher said. "I just didn't think it would be right now."

"My line?" Alice asked.

"The line that you won't cross. You won't leave the rabbit. You won't cross that line."

Hatcher folded his fingers together and cracked the knuckles. "I suppose this has been coming for some time. I didn't follow my own advice."

"What advice?" Alice asked.

"To finish him off," Hatcher said. "That was my mistake, and I should fix it. Stay here."

He pushed his way through the mob until he was almost to the bottom bench. Then he kicked a man in the back so that he fell forward on his chin, knocking into the man in front of him. Hatcher climbed on the bench as his victim struggled to get to his feet, tangling with the other drunks around him. Everyone's eyes went to the scuffle in the crowd, including the Walrus'.

Hatcher took his axe from his coat and raised his voice loud above the murmuring crowd.

"GRINDER!"

CHAPTER
15

Alice's heart was in her mouth. She had not intended this, that he would declare himself before the Walrus and all the gathered throng. Her mind had been concocting plans of secrecy, spiriting away the poor rabbit in the dark of night.

The Walrus stepped from the shadow into the light of the ring. His face was wide, with long whiskers that ran down his jaw, and the eyes were small and cruel. The whip dragged on the floor beside him, loosely clutched in one huge hand.

A huge, *gloved* hand.

(*Huge hands in white gloves, slicing a large piece of cake and urging her to eat, eat more. A heavy, frightening laugh as Alice shoveled the cake into her mouth, not knowing how to stop even though she wanted to, even though her stomach hurt and her head spun in circles.*

The same dark voice speaking. Alice wasn't supposed to hear.

"You told me I could have her, that you bought her for me."

"And I did." The second voice soothing. "But it is my right to break her first."

"She's no good to me if you break her magic," the first voice growled.

And then Alice knew that harm was coming to her, and she tried to run, but the man with the gloved hands caught her, held her with in his giant grip, and the Rabbit smiled, stroking his hand over her hair, pulling her braid until it hurt.

"Pretty little Alice," he crooned. "Why do you want to leave the party so soon?")

The Walrus, the Grinder, whatever he was called—he was the other man at the party. Dor had sold Alice to the Rabbit, and the Rabbit had intended to give her to the Walrus to be—

(eaten)

It was even more horrible than being the Rabbit's toy. The Walrus had meant to eat her, to take her magic away, to become a Magician himself and so stand as an equal with the Caterpillar and the Rabbit and Cheshire.

Now Hatcher taunted the Walrus, and might be killed, all because she felt sorry for the poor rabbit forced to fight in the ring for the Walrus' amusement.

"Nicholas," the Walrus said.

His voice sent shudders of fear down Alice's spine. It was a voice that had forgotten how to be human, how to love and care and fear the darkness. It was *part* of the darkness now, his heart mired in greed and desire and pain.

"So you do remember me," Hatcher said.

The Walrus clenched his jaw. "How could I forget? Though I understand they don't call you Nicholas anymore."

He gestured at the axe in Hatcher's hand, and Hatcher nodded in acknowledgment. Everyone was silent and still, watching the Walrus and Hatcher.

"Recently I sent some men across town to do some business for me," the Walrus continued. "Some of those men did not return. They were found in a tavern, with axe marks all over their bodies."

Hatcher said nothing. Alice wished she could see his face. His body was relaxed, completely unconcerned.

"A girl came to me. Just a little serving wench with only half a brain, telling me a story about a madman who killed all the men in one blow, a madman who was accompanied by a girl dressed as a boy."

The Walrus scanned the crowd behind Hatcher. Alice did not breathe. If the Walrus saw her, he would recognize her in a second.

"There was something special about this girl who accompanied the madman, according to this little tale-telling fool," he said. "Something I could hardly countenance, as a matter of fact. But then some of my men also spoke of a shadow, a monster that drank the blood of the dead. Do you know that some of my best soldiers wake up at night screaming now, scared that this creature will come for them? I knew then that the stories the serving wench told must be true, for only a Magician could raise such a creature."

Alice nearly laughed aloud. The Walrus thought she had raised the Jabberwocky, that she controlled it. As if she would ever want to do such a thing. As if such a monster *could* be controlled.

The Walrus paced slowly in Hatcher's direction. The men on the benches in front of Hatcher rapidly dispersed at his approach, causing a sudden stampede toward the exits. Alice was pushed against the wall, elbowed in the stomach and neck and face as men fought to escape before something terrible happened. There was a definite sense in the air that something terrible *would* happen, and that you did not want to be in its path.

The skinny fighter slipped out of the ring, following the jostling crowd. The rabbit tried to crawl away from the Walrus, his paws inching across the dirty floor, his back bleeding from the strike of the whip.

The Walrus kicked him, and the rabbit cried out.

"Leave him alone," Alice said.

The last of the gamblers trickled out, though the sound of their passage—shouting voices, trampling feet—echoed back into the nearly empty room. All that remained was Alice and Hatcher, the Walrus and the rabbit.

"Ah, there you are, my Alice. I've been expecting you for so long. I could hardly believe it when that stupid serving girl told me you were alive," the Walrus said. He gave her a long look up and down as she went to Hatcher's side. "You've gotten quite skinny. Hardly enough meat on you to bother with."

He showed her his teeth, small and dirty and copper-stained.

Alice gave him a cool appraisal in return. Inside she was trembling, her heart hammering away, but she would not show it. She would not give this monster what he wanted. "You've gotten quite fat. I doubt you're fast enough to catch me, in any case. 'The Walrus' is quite an apt name for you."

The Walrus lashed out with the whip then. It might have struck Alice's face, given her a mark on her other cheek to match the one from the Rabbit, but for Hatcher. He sliced the end of the whip cleanly away before it could reach her, the blade so close she felt the breeze made by its passing.

The tip fell to the ground with a loud clatter, and Alice saw that the leather was edged in silver, so that it would hurt more when it struck. She gave the Walrus a look of disgust.

"You think you're quite a man, don't you?" she said. "Torturing creatures weaker than you because you're afraid of a fair fight."

"I fear nothing," the Walrus said.

A sudden thought occurred to Alice. "What about me?"

His lips twisted in a smile of disbelief. "Afraid of a skinny girl? You're nothing without your guard dog."

"Now, you know that's not true, Walrus," Alice said in a schoolteacher tone. "You said yourself your men returned telling tales of a monster made of darkness, and that some of them wake up screaming."

"Ruined, they are," Walrus said, his voice bitter. Alice noticed he had been speaking very deliberately before, that his accent had been well-bred, and now it slipped away a little. "What am I to do with a bunch of mewling babies? I sent my best men out, and Carpenter's soldiers were nothing but a lark to them. But you were there, with your illusions."

Alice couldn't help it. She laughed. Hatcher gave her an odd look. The Walrus' face registered surprise at her total lack of fear.

"He thinks the Jabberwocky is an illusion," she said, giggling.

Hatcher laughed too, then, long and loud. The Walrus stared at the two of them.

"You're not telling me that it's real?" the Walrus scoffed. "You don't frighten me. It's all talk, a show you put on to drive my men off."

"Well, you can think that if you like," Alice said. "You'll know better when he comes this way. He's quite real, and he's not attached to a leash."

Alice hoped the Walrus would think the Jabberwocky was her pet, but that she had loosed him for reasons of her own. She'd like it very much if he were afraid of her, she realized. She wanted him to quake and cry, as so many girls no doubt had before he'd finished with them.

"I'll believe it when I see it," the Walrus said, but Alice thought she saw concern that hadn't been there before.

She stepped off the bench then and into the ring. Hatcher stayed where he was. Alice knew he would make certain the Walrus would not touch her.

The big man shuffled his feet a little, not backing away from her, but unable to conceal his uncertainty at her behavior. She was not acting like girls usually acted in his presence, she knew.

But she was not interested in the Walrus. The rabbit had continued its slow progress toward the edge of the ring, panting with the effort. Alice veered away from the Walrus, deliberately turning her back to him.

She had to trust Hatcher now. Without him the Walrus would try to take her, would have tried already. He was off balance from her behavior but he would soon remember that he considered her nothing more than a thing to be used and thrown away.

The rabbit paused as it heard her approach, its eyes wide with fear. She held her hands up to show she meant no harm.

"Shh," she said. "Shh, I won't hurt you."

"It's only a dumb beast," the Walrus jeered. "He thinks

you'll kick him like all the rest. He can't understand you."

"Yes, he can," Alice said, and smiled encouragingly at the rabbit as she knelt beside him. "What are you called?"

She could see the disbelief mixed with hope in his expression. His mouth moved, at first making no sound. Then a surprising baritone emerged.

"Pipkin," he said.

"That's a lovely name, like the name a mother gives its littlest one," Alice said, stroking the rabbit's paw. The fur was matted and grey.

"I was the smallest of my litter," he said. "Not that you would know it now."

"Do you think you could try and sit up, Pipkin?"

The rabbit shook his head. "My legs are broken."

"In this fight?" Alice asked. She had not seen the skinny man strike such a blow; nor had the Walrus' whip touched Pipkin's legs.

"Before this," he said. "They have been broken for three days, but the Walrus has forced me to fight for him anyway, and whipped me when I was unable to stand. He was angry that the rats escaped, so angry."

"Why didn't they take you with them?"

"I was already broken," Pipkin said. "I couldn't run, and they had their children to think of."

"What's he saying?" the Walrus demanded. "You understand all that squeaking?"

Alice ignored him. "I wish I could do something for you, Pipkin. I wish I could help you stand again."

A little breeze whistled past her ear, and she thought it sounded like, *Wish granted.*

And then, even softer, so soft she was almost entirely sure she imagined it: *Remember, a wish has power.*

A small violet bottle appeared in her left hand. On the label was the face of a smiling cat. A tag attached to the neck read, "For Pipkin."

She could only hope it would not harm the rabbit further. Cheshire clearly watched over them, but Alice was unsure why. His help wasn't always helpful either. She was still irritated about the maze and the creature that had nearly eaten Hatcher.

She uncorked the bottle and told the rabbit, "Drink this. It will make you better."

"Where'd you get that?" the Walrus said, then caught a glimpse of the label. "That damned Cheshire. Damned interfering little pipsqueak."

Wind rustled through the room again, and it sounded like laughter. Cheshire was the one who'd given the Walrus the potion to make rabbits and rats large in the first place, and so it was only right, in Alice's mind, that he provide the cure.

Pipkin opened his mouth so Alice could pour the mixture in. He swallowed, closing his eyes and placing his head back on the ground.

Alice waited. Pipkin groaned, his body contorting. Still

she waited. The rabbit's body went stiff and straight as a board, his face a rictus of pain. Then Alice saw his tooth, the broken tooth, grow to its proper size again and match its mate.

All of Pipkin's fur fell off his body suddenly, as though someone had sheared him, and fresh new white fur grew in just as fast, covering the scars on his back. His left foot tapped the ground in a rapid tattoo, and then he burst up in a tremendous leap, soaring high above Alice and landing before the Walrus. He rested on all fours like a proper rabbit instead of one playing at being human. He was suddenly very beautiful and, Alice thought, very fierce. She had never noticed before that rabbits had such very sharp claws.

Alice stood and went to his side. It was like standing beside an enormous polar bear (she'd heard a story about polar bears once, though she couldn't remember where), glossy and dangerous.

The Walrus did not appear very much like a monster now. He looked like a child who'd been caught doing wrong and knew his punishment loomed.

"How long have you been here?" Alice asked, rubbing her hand into Pipkin's ruff. The fur was so soft she wanted to bury her face in it, but that probably was not polite. She'd only just met this rabbit, after all.

"I don't know how long in human time, and I couldn't see the moon to show the passing of the seasons, but I am much older than I was when I first arrived," Pipkin growled. "The Walrus took me from my mate and children, from a place in the country, far away from all the filth and stink of this City. He brought me here, and fed me potions, and made me large so he could use me to fight. Some people were, apparently, getting tired of watching rats and wanted more exotic creatures. There was a cat too, and a horse and three dogs."

"What happened to them?" Alice asked. She was watching the Walrus very closely. He was cornered now, and cornered animals will behave unpredictably.

"They died," Pipkin said, and snarled in the Walrus' face.

The big man took a step back, then two; then his legs knocked against the first row of benches around the ring. The Walrus glanced from Alice to Hatcher to Pipkin, and his face said he did not like his chances.

"I thank you for helping me," Pipkin said. "And it seems as though you have some history with this man, and came seeking revenge."

"Not on purpose," Alice said. "We hadn't intended to come here at all, but since it happened, Hatcher thought it best to finish the job he started so long ago."

Alice knew the Walrus could not understand the rabbit, but he certainly could understand her.

"Hatcher, as you call him, hasn't a chance of finishing me," the Walrus said, but his voice was not as steady as it should have been.

"I don't think I'll have to now," Hatcher said softly, exchanging a look with the rabbit.

Pipkin nodded at him. "I thank you for your consideration. I have witnessed too many atrocities here to leave without avenging them."

Alice did not translate this for Hatcher. He seemed to understand.

"Before you do that, I wish the Walrus to tell me something," Alice said. "Where is the Rabbit?"

The Walrus' eyebrows raised. "Going to do him in, are you? Knock us all down one by one like a falling house of cards? First the Caterpillar, then me, then the Rabbit?"

"My business is no concern of yours," Alice said. "You can tell me where to find him, though it will not redeem what you would have done to me."

"You were supposed to be mine," the Walrus said through his teeth. "The Rabbit promised. And somehow you got away, and I haven't been able to find another Magician since, though I've eaten all the girls I could find, hoping I might stumble on another who didn't know her own power."

For a moment she felt sick, sicker than when she'd seen all the stacked girls in the storage room. All these years, all these lives lost because the Walrus was searching for someone like Alice. All those girls died because Alice had not. She wanted to weep, but the time for weeping had passed.

Something hardened inside Alice then, a piece of her heart that would forever be cold and untouchable. One day, long ago, she'd gone seeking an adventure and found terror instead. That day had changed the course of her life, and left her hands awash in blood. It was not her fault, but this was how it must be. She understood that now.

"Tell me where the Rabbit is," Alice said.

The Walrus laughed, and it was not a pleasant laugh. "I should. I should send you right to his doorstep, and let you both take what's coming to you. In this deck of cards he is the King, and even with your butcher at your side you'll find you won't knock him down so easily."

"I did before," Alice said. "I was drugged, and he raped me, and I was terrified. But I still took out his eye. I still got away."

"You surprised him," the Walrus said. "That won't happen again."

"You needn't worry about it," Alice said. "You'll be dead in any case."

"Yes," the Walrus said. "I will. So there's no reason for me to make your job easier. Find the Rabbit yourself."

Alice glanced at Hatcher, wondering whether it would be worth trying to force the information from the Walrus. Hatcher shook his head. She went to Hatcher then, and they turned to leave.

"He's yours, Pipkin," Alice said.

She did not hear the rabbit lunge, but she heard the

Walrus scream. Alice did not look back. It was enough to know the monster was dying, and would soon join the ranks of women he had destroyed.

Alice did not know what happened to the soul after death, but if there were any justice in the world, then all those dead girls would haunt the Walrus until the stars exploded and time came to an end.

She and Hatcher exited the ring and entered the passageway at the top of the arena. It was nothing but plain wooden walls and a dirt floor, and it showed the passing of many feet. There was a staircase at the end, and Alice presumed it led into the street. She imagined the Walrus would not have wanted common gamblers to see the rest of his operations.

Hatcher started for the stairs, but Alice stayed him. Something had occurred to her.

"What if there are other girls here?"

"Alive ones?" Hatcher asked.

She nodded. "We ought to ask Pipkin if he knows."

They returned to the ring, where the Walrus was now many small and unrecognizable pieces. The stench was horrific, though it did not seem to bother Pipkin. He turned toward them as they returned, with a quizzical look on his face. His muzzle was coated in fresh blood, very red against his white fur.

"Pipkin, are there any others imprisoned here?" Alice

asked. She removed her coat, placing the knife in the rope that held up her pants. "May I?"

Pipkin nodded, and Alice wiped the blood from his face with her jacket. "Very handsome," she said.

"There are many girls sold to men," Pipkin said. "I could hear them screaming from my cage. There are also some that the Walrus saved for his own use."

Hatcher sighed. "We're crusaders, are we now? We're going to free all these girls and send them into the streets, helpless?"

"They won't be helpless," Pipkin said. "I will stay with them."

Alice translated this. Hatcher appeared doubtful that an oversized rabbit could defend a pack of crying girls from the men who would prey on them. Alice narrowed her eyes at him so these doubts were not voiced aloud.

"And a wonderful champion you will be too," Alice said. "Do you know where they are?"

Pipkin nodded, and gestured with his head toward the opposite side of the ring. There was an entryway Alice had not noticed before, carved in between the rows of benches.

"What about the Walrus' soldiers?" Alice asked.

Pipkin considered. "Some of them are loyal to him, though most of them came back broken after the raid on Carpenter. The ones remaining are frightened by the tales they've heard, and only keep working because the Walrus frightens them."

Alice quickly told Hatcher what Pipkin said. Hatcher considered. "It shouldn't be so difficult, then, to get the girls out."

"Yes," Alice said.

"Lead the way," Hatcher said.

Pipkin nudged open the door with his nose. There was a smoldering cigarette just inside the passage. Hatcher rubbed it out with his boot.

"Someone watching," he said. "No doubt he's gone to tell the others that the Walrus is dead and their fighting rabbit killed him."

There was a stair that led down just to the left of the entry, and then a hallway before them that slanted up.

"That was the way to my cage," Pipkin said, his head gesturing toward the downward stair. "The girls are kept upstairs, though I am not certain where. I only know what I hear the guards saying."

"It's very helpful," Alice said. "This way, Hatch."

Hatcher took the lead, his axe in his hand. The passage led up to a very large room, a kind of oversized parlor, decked out in red velvets and carved wood. It looked, Alice thought, precisely as a bordello should look, if you thought of such things. There appeared to be no one in the room.

The windows were open, letting in the night air. It always seemed to be night in the Old City.

In the center of the room was a wide set of velvet-covered steps, sweeping up to the left and right. As they reached the steps Hatcher suddenly broke away and kicked over a heavy chair in the corner of the room.

The girl who hid behind it screamed bloody murder when she saw Hatcher standing over her with the axe. Alice frowned at him and went to soothe the girl, who scuttled away as Alice approached. Hatcher backed away, tucking the axe out of sight.

"It's all right," Alice said. "We're not going to hurt you."

The girl kept screaming, and Alice had to slap her to make her stop. She was sorry for it, but they had things to get on with. The girl had very pale skin and the imprint of Alice's hand was red against her cheek.

"What's your name?" Alice asked.

"Rose," the girl said. "Tom came back yelling that the Walrus was butchered and that we'd all get it too. Everyone cleared out of here in a hurry, but I was afraid to go out in the street on my own in the dark."

Alice gave her an approving nod. "Very wise. Now, Rose, can you help us? Do you know if there is anyone left here?"

"Is he the butcher? The one who killed the Walrus?" Rose asked, her eyes wide as she looked at Hatcher. "Will he kill me too?"

"He won't kill you," Alice said firmly. "And he didn't kill the Walrus. That was Pipkin."

A furrow appeared between Rose's brows. "Pipkin?"

"The rabbit," Alice said.

"I thought I was imagining him," Rose said. "I've never seen a rabbit so big."

"It's not usual," Alice said.

Rose slid around Alice and approached Pipkin, her hand out. "Can I touch him?"

Pipkin nodded regally.

"He understands me?" Rose asked, looking back at Alice. "Yes."

She seemed like a little child at a petting zoo, cautious and excited at the same time. Her attitude clashed with her dress, which was nothing more than a lacy slip with a thin red robe covering her shoulders. Her eyes were ringed with smeared black paint.

Rose patted Pipkin on the head between his long ears, and the rabbit bumped against her hand. The girl giggled, and she seemed so young that Alice's heart ached.

"Thank you," she said to Pipkin. "Thank you for killing him."

Alice had been raised to think violence was wrong, that a person should never take another's life. She was learning that there were times when it was necessary, and even right. The gratitude shining on Rose's face only confirmed that notion.

"Do you have somewhere you can go, Rose?" Alice asked. "A family?"

Rose shook her head. "My mam had her neck broken when the Walrus' soldiers came for me and my sister. She fought them like a demon, and they killed her for it. My sister died the first year here. She wouldn't eat."

She was very matter-of-fact about it. There wasn't really any other way to be, Alice thought. *If you let the grief in, it might consume you.*

"Is there anyone left upstairs?" Alice asked.

"Probably," Rose said, leaning against Pipkin's side and resting her head there. "I didn't see anyone come down, and if the men are at their business they won't be out until they've gotten their money's worth."

"What about the girls the Walrus kept for himself?" Alice asked.

"They're in his room at the end of the hall, locked in. You'll need his key."

"Where is his key?" Alice asked.

"He always keeps it with him," Rose said.

Alice was not about to return to the Walrus' remains and sift through the pieces to search for the missing key. "We'll find another way. Pipkin, would you stay with Rose until we return? We'll send the girls down to you as we discover them."

"Yes," he said. "What shall I do with the men?"

Alice repeated this question to Hatcher, who smiled his grim hatcher's smile.

"There won't be any. But if one slips away, you can feel free to do what you think is right."

Hatcher and Alice climbed the steps. When they reached the junction Hatcher shook his head at the look on Alice's face, cutting off the suggestion in her eyes. "We're not splitting. We'll do one side and then the other."

"It's not efficient," Alice argued. "And if the men on the left side hear noise from the right, they may get away."

"Pipkin will do his duty," Hatcher said. "He's listened to the girls screaming upstairs for years."

"You seem very confident in him all of a sudden," Alice said.

"He was very gentle with that girl," he said.

That, Alice realized, carried more weight with Hatcher than the rabbit's brutal disassembly of the Walrus. And that was why she loved him—even though he was mad and would probably never be sane, even though he was a dangerous murderer—

(*You are too, though. You killed the Caterpillar without thinking about it. You saw red, just like Hatcher.*)

—and even though their future was hardly assured. Alice had not allowed herself to think on it too deeply, but there was certainly a possibility that they might not survive the encounter with the Jabberwocky—or, for that matter, the Rabbit.

There were five doors on this side of the landing. Now that they were closer Alice and Hatcher heard the expected noises coming from the rooms. And when Hatcher opened the door they saw the expected tableau. Hatcher dispatched the man before he could shout in alarm—indeed, before he even realized they had entered the room.

Alice rushed to the girl's side before she could scream, hastily explained that they were there to help and sent her downstairs to stay with Rose and Pipkin. And then they moved to the next room, and the next, and all through the balcony on both sides until all the men were dead and all the girls were gathered in a weeping, exhausted cluster around Pipkin.

Finally, only the Walrus' room remained. It was tucked at the end of a small corridor, separate from the other rooms. Hatcher peered at the lock, the door, the frame, and then snorted in contempt.

"It's just for show," he said. "So no curious birds flutter in here and see the Walrus' merchandise."

He kicked the door twice, hard, and it broke open.

Inside there were five girls, naked and stuffed inside tiny little cages that had them hunched and twisted. They began to sob when they saw Alice, crying out for help. A silver key hung on a peg near the cages, and in a short while all the girls were free. They all struggled to stand after their time in the confined space, leaning against the walls or the doorframe. One girl, tiny and red-haired, kept collapsing to the floor.

Hatcher finally scooped her up in his arms, where she promptly gave him a smile of thanks and fell asleep.

"She's not slept since she got here," one of the others said. "She's cried for twelve days straight."

Alice searched the room for clothes and found only the Walrus' oversized shirts. She handed them to each girl with an apologetic look. It could not be pleasant to wear the clothing of your tormentor.

And he had tormented them. All of the girls had bite marks on their bodies and bruising at their hips where he'd held them down.

Alice allowed two particularly hobbled girls to use her for support, and the whole party limped downstairs. The other women were gathered around Pipkin, all of them with a hand or a finger on the great rabbit, like he was a lodestone attracting their touch. All eyes turned to Alice, waiting for her to tell them what to do.

She realized it was a terrible responsibility to free them, and that Hatcher had tried to tell her this many times. They belonged to her now, all these little lost lambs, and if they were hurt, it would be her fault.

"Do any of you have families to return to?" Alice asked.

Not one girl assented. They all had stories like Rose—a parent or brother killed in their taking, a sister who expired or was traded away to another house. There was nothing for these girls in the Old City except more suffering.

Alice wasn't certain what to do then, but Pipkin spoke.

"I will take them with me, out of the City, and return to my place in the country," he said. "They may find their own way then, or stay with me, as they choose."

"How?" Alice asked. "You would have to pass through the New City, and the soldiers will hardly let such a large group out of the Old City. Not to mention that you are, well, conspicuous."

If a rabbit could grin, then that was what Pipkin did just then. "There are places. Aboveground is not the only way to travel. I remember the path they took when the Walrus first brought me here. I can find it again."

"Tunnels that the Walrus and the Rabbit and Cheshire and the Caterpillar use for their own purpose," Alice warned.

"But the Caterpillar is dead, and so is the Walrus, and you will soon do the same for the Rabbit. Cheshire, I think, is not interested in us," Pipkin said.

Alice explained Pipkin's suggestion to the women. To her great surprise, all consented to accompany him. She would not have thought that City girls would go to the country willingly, even with all of the dangers in the City.

"We've nothing to stay here for," Rose said. "At least out there we'd have a chance."

Alice worried that they would not be able to eat without supplies or money, or that the Walrus' victims would be unable to walk. Pipkin took three of the weakest girls on his back, and assured Alice they could forage.

"It might be nice," said one of the girls. "Picking berries and all that. I had some strawberries once when I was young. My brother nicked them off a seller's cart. Never tasted anything so sweet."

So it was settled, and Alice could see Hatcher's relief. He'd sympathized with their lot, and once committed, he'd freed them with his usual efficiency. But Alice knew he feared dragging the crowd around behind them like a long rat's tail.

Pipkin explained that the entry to the underground tunnel out of the City was near. Alice thought she and Hatcher should accompany them to the place. She hoped their own quest succeeded, that they would take the blade from the Rabbit and destroy the Jabberwocky. That completed, they could use the passage Pipkin spoke of to escape the Old City and begin their search for Jenny.

We've come so far and there is still so much ahead, Alice thought as she led the group out the front doors of the Walrus' establishment.

The silence in the street outside should have warned her.

Alice stopped just past the threshold, turned to send the girls back inside, but it was too late. They'd been tempted by the promise of freedom, far away from the cruelty of the Walrus and his ilk. They crowded around and past her, speaking hopefully of their futures.

Then they stopped, and gasped, and covered their mouths with their hands. Some of them started to cry softly.

The street was littered with the dead. Everywhere Alice looked she saw bodies of men and women and children. There were dead dogs and horses and cats too, and so much blood that a river of it flowed down the middle of the street.

"How can this be?" Pipkin asked.

"The Jabberwocky," Hatcher said.

"Hatcher, how is it that you didn't feel him pass?" asked Alice.

"I haven't felt him since you sent him away," Hatcher said. "I thought at first it was Cheshire's maze, and then that the Jabberwock wasn't near. But he was near. He just didn't want you to know, Alice."

"Do you think he knows about the Rabbit?" Alice asked. "That the Rabbit has the blade, I mean."

"I think he's angry," Hatcher said, looking at all the destruction before them. "He must not know, not yet. He's getting frustrated that he cannot find it."

"What will we do now?" one of the girls cried, and several of them raised their voices, repeating the same question.

"We'll do just as we intended to do," Alice said. "Pipkin will take you out of the City."

"How?" Rose said. "Whatever did this will come for us too."

"An angel of death," one of the girls said. Others murmured their agreement.

"An angel of death will find you whether you hide in the house or not," Alice said. "Pipkin, show us the way."

The rabbit moved into the street, carefully picking his way over the bodies as best he could. His white paws were soon stained red, as were the bare feet of the women. Not one of them had shoes—"shoes mean we can run away," one girl told Alice—and several wept so hard they could barely see in front of them. Alice and Hatcher brought up the rear of the group, ensuring the stragglers did not fall behind. Alice tried not to think about what squished beneath her boots.

Their progress was so slow that Alice feared they would be caught out in the open by the Jabberwock. Hatcher pointed out in a low whisper that the Jabberwock had no reason to think he'd left anyone alive behind. It seemed to take hours, though in truth it was only a few blocks away, just as Pipkin said.

There was a little shack crammed between two larger buildings. On one side was a tavern very much like the one Nell and Harry had. On the other was a shop that sold medicines for healing.

"In there," Pipkin said, indicating the shack. His memory was very clear for a rabbit who'd used the path only once, and Alice told him so.

"Rabbits don't forget," he said.

It sounded like a promise to Alice, and a warning about the other Rabbit.

There must have been guards posted once; otherwise curious folk might wander in, and that didn't seem the sort of thing the

Walrus would approve. Any watchers were likely mixed in with the Jabberwocky's other victims. Just inside the door was a slanting hill dug into the dirt, and below a cave like the one Alice and Hatcher had taken from the Caterpillar's to the Walrus'. The girls rushed down the ramp, whooping with joy.

Pipkin sniffed, and beat the ground with his back legs. "Can't you smell it?"

Alice copied him. There was the damp mustiness that she associated with being underground, and the stale wood of the shack. "The cave?"

Pipkin shook his head. "Open fields, and flowers and trees and butterflies and rain."

Alice remembered the dream she'd once had, of a cottage by the lake and someone bringing her tea, and thought that might be a home for her and Hatcher. She longed suddenly to go with Pipkin too.

"I'd best follow them before they get off too far on their own," Pipkin said. He nudged Alice with his nose, and she smiled, and he disappeared down the tunnel.

Hatcher took Alice's hand. "We can't go."

"I know," she said. Her future didn't have butterflies and flowers and rain followed by sunshine. Her future slogged through a river of blood to find the well from which it sprung.

She buried her head in Hatcher's shoulder, ashamed of the tears pricking in her eyes. She couldn't run away now, and let everyone in the Old City fall beneath the Jabberwock's wrath. And if the monster found the blade, its rage would only spread until there was no safe place, not even in a cottage by a clear blue lake.

So she and Hatcher left the tunnel behind, and followed not the white rabbit but the red river. There were no other crumbs for them, as they had to find Alice's Rabbit but had no notion of how to do it. Anyone who might have told them about the Rabbit's place was dead.

"Hatcher," Alice said. "Everyone calls you the Hatcher of Heathtown."

"Yes," he said. "That's where I lived before, with Hattie and Jenny."

"Could you find it again?" Alice asked. "You said before you followed a map in your head from Bess' place."

Hatcher glanced about. "I don't see anything familiar. I don't think I've ever been here before. Though it's not easy to tell with all this."

He gestured at the massacre around them, which only increased in number as they followed in the Jabberwocky's wake. Alice noticed that several of the buildings had holes torn in the front, as if the creature had broken through the walls to get at those cowering inside.

"But if you do see something familiar," Alice persisted. "You could find Heathtown."

"And then find my way to the Rabbit's from there," Hatcher said, understanding.

"Yes," she said, and then put her hand on his shoulder. "Though I'm sorry to have to take you back to that place."

A muscle flexed in his jaw. "You'll have to go back to the Rabbit's, won't you? If you can face that, then I can face this."

It wasn't quite the same, Alice thought. She still didn't remember all of what happened and she suspected that, thanks to the Caterpillar, Hatcher remembered everything. It was broken and mixed with other things in his mind, but it was all there. It was easier for Alice, or at least it would be until her memory returned completely.

Perhaps then she would be afraid. A strange thing had happened in the presence of the Walrus, though. She'd felt very frightened, especially after she remembered what he'd intended to do to her, after she saw his gloved hands and remembered those hands forcing her to eat cake that made her sick and dizzy.

When she'd seen Pipkin being whipped, her fear had disappeared, and it had never properly returned. She was not stronger than the Walrus. He could overpower her easily. She didn't even know what to do with the magic she possessed. But she had not been afraid.

In not being afraid she had frightened *him*, because a girl who was not afraid was a girl who might harm him. And Alice was the girl who had escaped the Rabbit. She must remember that when she saw him again. Alice had escaped. Cheshire and the Caterpillar had talked of the Rabbit's mark on her, but she had marked him too. She had made sure he wouldn't forget her.

(*Rabbits don't forget*)

The night seemed to go on and on, and Alice thought the sun might never rise again now that the Jabberwock raged through the Old City. Rats emerged from the dark places, feasting on those in the street. After meeting Nicodemus she did not begrudge them the meal. They needed to survive too.

She was not tired from the walk, as she expected she might be, but her stomach growled.

"I heard that," Hatcher said. "Why didn't you say something before?"

"I'm ashamed to be hungry," she admitted. "It doesn't seem right."

"They're dead, Alice," Hatcher said. "We are still living, and we wish to remain so."

They found the remains of a greengrocer's, food scattered out into the street. Inside there were some fruits and breads on the shelves that appeared untouched. Alice hungrily wolfed down half a loaf of bread, facing the wall the entire time so the sight of the dead did not stop her from eating. Hatcher was right. They were alive, and they needed to do what they must.

All around them were not only bodies but also the crushed remains of lives. The furniture lovingly owned, smashed to bits. The dress saved for, pennies put aside until a girl could triumphantly walk into a shop and point to the one in the window, ripped to shreds on her broken body. The shop windows shattered, the carts overturned. It made Alice realize how much of life was full of empty stuff, objects longed for because the hope of them made your small life seem bigger, better, brighter.

Alice had that once—the happy home, the pretty dresses, all the good things to eat that she wanted. But it wasn't enough. She'd wanted danger and darkness, just a taste, and in an instant everything she had was swept away forever. She thought that any of these girls, these sad dead girls, would have been happy to have Alice's life before the Rabbit.

They reached a place where four large streets intersected like a cross, and there was a square in the center. The trail of bodies continued ahead of them, but the streets to the right and left were clear. There was no movement in either direction, though, and Alice assumed that anyone with sense had gone inside and bolted their doors.

"Which way?" Alice asked.

Hatcher spun in a circle, concentrating hard. "It seems like I've been here. The square. Something about it."

"Did you bring Jenny here on Giving Day?" Alice asked.

"There's no Giving Day in the Old City," Hatcher said. "The ministers wouldn't waste pennies on the rabble."

Alice fell silent, chastened yet again by the differences between them. Their lives had been so different before the hospital. Without tragedy they would never have crossed paths at all. Should she be happy that they had found each other, or sad at the choices that led them there?

"That way," Hatcher said finally, his face triumphant. "Heathtown is that way."

Alice was relieved that their path diverged from the trail of bodies. Their boots left bloody marks behind for some time, their passage apparent to anyone. They could only hope that no one was following them.

Everyone who might have reason to is dead, Alice reasoned. *Or is ahead, not behind.*

The empty street was nearly as eerie as the one filled with the remains of the dead. This was a creature worse than any criminal, gang or boss. There were accepted norms of behavior for those types. Unrestrained massacre was not one of them.

The sky lightened to a light violet color, not committing to blue. Alice could not see the sun, which hovered just below the line of one-story shanties that comprised Heathtown. Hatcher was silent, lost in his memories, and Alice was afraid to speak, to break the hush that blanketed the City.

Hatcher stopped walking. "We're here."

He pointed to one of the shanties. It looked no different from the others to Alice, except perhaps a bit more run-down. The single window was boarded. No smoke emitted from the small chimney in back as it did from some of the others.

Hatcher walked to the door.

"What if somebody lives there now?" Alice said.

She didn't like the look on his face. He was like a man in a trance, gone to some time far away from the one they were in, seeing things that weren't there anymore.

"Nobody would live here," he said softly. "It's a haunted place. Can't you feel it? Her ghost always waits for me."

He pushed the door open and went inside. Alice quickly glanced up and down the street, then followed.

Inside were a few broken sticks of furniture, and the evidence of fires recently set in the small fireplace—likely young boys using the shanty as a place to smoke cigarettes and drink stolen ale and tell each other stories of the murderer who used to live here.

Hatcher paused in the center of the room, turning in a slow circle. The wood floor under his feet had a few rusty stains on it, stains that might have been the last remains of one bloody night.

"She used to spin cloth there. She was terrible at it. She wasn't a very good cook either, but we managed. I ate burnt toast every day and told her it was delicious. She kept the house very clean, took pride in the way things shone and gleamed because she'd never had anything of her own before. And our bed was there, behind a curtain. I liked to watch her in the early morning, watching her breath rise and fall, and know that she was mine. Then she would open those blue eyes and smile, soft and sleepy, and she would love me. She loved me. She loved me, and I failed her."

He fell to his knees then, and wept. Alice didn't know what to do. She felt she shouldn't intrude here, where Hattie's ghost lingered, where he stopped being Nicholas and became Hatcher instead.

She realized that part of her was a bit envious of Hatcher. Yes, he had lost his love and his child in the most terrible way possible. But he had known happiness too. He had lived as an adult in the adult world, and Alice had never had that.

You might have it someday, with him, she thought.

Yes, she might. They might someday live in a cottage by a lake, away from the fog and the blood and all the Magicians. They might, but there was a long road before them.

Alice waited, and after a time Hatcher stood.

"I'm ready now," he said.

When he faced her again she knew Nicholas was gone forever. He'd said good-bye to that man here, and to Hattie, and to the last threads that tethered him to his old life. He was Hatcher, now and forever.

"I know where to find the Rabbit," he said.

They left the shanty and returned to the street. Alice might have imagined it, but she thought there was a cool breeze around her neck as they departed. She felt a pulse of warmth on her chest, and realized the rose pendant that Bess had given her was glowing.

"I forgot about this," Alice said.

"Bess gave you that for a reason."

"I think it must have to do with magic," Alice said. "I don't feel any different, though, now that I know I'm a Magician. I don't feel as though I have lots of powers that could come out of my fingertips."

She thought of the wish-granting jinni in the stories of the desert, and all the wonders he could create. Could she do something like that? *A wish has power.*

According to Hatcher she had set the roses on fire in Cheshire's maze. She'd been terrified, had only wanted to escape the strangling roses. Could she do such a thing again?

"I wonder if Cheshire would teach you how to use your magic," Hatcher said.

"I don't want lessons from Cheshire," Alice said firmly. She did not want anything from Cheshire. Despite his occasional assistance, she did not like him.

"You need a guide, someone who can help you with your power, and the only Magicians we know are the Caterpillar, Cheshire and the Rabbit."

"There are more out there, somewhere," Alice said. "They were driven from the City, but they live. The Caterpillar said we recognize our own. When we leave the City we're sure to encounter some."

She did not say that she was a little afraid of being a Magician, and what she might discover inside. The two most difficult tasks were before them now, and she did not wish to be distracted.

Though magic might be helpful, she thought.

It might be, but then, it might not be. The Jabberwocky was the essence of the most evil Magician who had ever lived. The other Magicians in the City were horrible men. Perhaps magic only corrupted. Alice did not want that. She was only just discovering who she was, and she wished to stay Alice.

The shanties of Heathtown gradually gave way to the taller buildings they'd seen in the rest of the City. Hatcher moved like a hunter now, a creature on the scent of prey. He did not hesitate. He knew where the Rabbit was, and Hatcher would drive him into the ground.

Alice was not afraid. She felt she ought to be, that it might keep her alive. She simply couldn't feel afraid. They had seen so much already. All the horror and blood and monsters and fear crystallized to a fine thin shard inside her, harder than diamonds. What was one more monster in the face of so many?

"Hatcher," Alice said. "Had you thought about what we've done? Killing the Caterpillar and the Walrus?"

"We didn't kill the Walrus," Hatcher said.

"We helped. At any rate, that is not the point. The point is that we've made empty places where men of power used to be. What will happen now?"

"Someone will take their place," Hatcher said. "Likely more than one person for each territory. The Caterpillar and the Walrus were strong men with large chunks of the City in their pockets."

"Will it be better under someone new?" Alice asked.

She hoped so. She hoped that she had not killed the Caterpillar only to have an identical man spring from the same place, like in the story where the hero kept cutting the heads off a monster only to have more emerge.

"Maybe," Hatcher said. "No matter who is in charge, the people of the City will go on living as best they can. They have no other choice."

This was true, Alice reflected. People like Nell and Harry, and even poor stupid Dolly. They built something in the City—a tavern, a bookshop, a potato cart—and they worked at it day after day because they hoped. They saw all the misery around them. They knew the risks they took just in climbing from their beds each day. But they still hoped—hoped for success, happiness, a better future. There was no other choice. If they tried to escape the Old City, they would be caught by the soldiers who patrolled the New City and sent back. No one was allowed to leave. No one.

"Why can't we leave the City, Hatcher?" Alice asked.

"Because the ministers and the bosses need someone to use, to keep down," Hatcher said. "Do you think anyone would choose to stay here?"

"No," Alice said. "I don't think they would."

"So all the big men would be sitting in their houses, with no money to count and no one to kick," Hatcher said. "Do you know what they'd do then? They'd go out and find another city, and this time they'd make sure everyone stayed. They would find a way. Men like that need someone's neck under their boot or they don't feel right about themselves."

"I hope it's beautiful outside," Alice said. "Outside the City, I mean."

She was thinking of the girls who'd escaped with Pipkin, and hoped that they ran in the grass with bare feet, laughing in the sun. She wanted a promise of joy for someone, even if she could not have it for herself.

There was some activity on the streets now, not like it would be on a normal day (*a no-Jabberwocky day*) but Alice and Hatcher did pass the occasional person going about furtive business. No one respectable would be about. Alice wondered where the Jabberwocky was now, and what the City leaders would do if the monster slaughtered every living soul.

"Escape in their airship, most likely," Alice muttered.

When she was a child she'd thought the ministers the most wonderful people in the world. Giving Day proved that. They gave these lovely gifts to all the children of the City, and patted those children on the head and told them they would grow up to be good citizens. Alice had not realized that they were only interested in clean, wealthy children from the New City. She had not realized that men in power were only interested in power and not good deeds. She'd learned much since escaping from the hospital. Sometimes she wished she could unlearn it. There was comfort in ignorance, in thinking the world a certain way and not knowing any different.

Hatcher did not hear her speak, or didn't care to find out what that statement meant. He was driven by purpose, and that purpose did not include Alice's meandering thoughts.

Then, suddenly, they were there.

After all the years of dreaming of him, of waking to escape the memories, of hoping that he was only something she imagined, she had returned to the place where it all began.

It was not very impressive.

There was not even a structure aboveground, only a flat, dirt-covered lot. Before it was a stone staircase that led down from the street to a door flanked by two men with no nonsense in their eyes. They made no movement indicating they cared about the presence of Alice and Hatcher near the top of the steps, but Alice was certain they had been noted.

"Of course. A rabbit would want a warren underground," Alice said.

"It is a warren, if I remember it right," Hatcher said. "Lots of hallways, little rooms, places to get lost in."

"Yes, it is like that," Alice said, and her eyes widened. "I remembered. Hatcher, I remember running though the hallways, bumping into people, men who tried to grab me, but I kept going because they couldn't hold me. They were so surprised."

"Why were they surprised?" Hatcher said.

Alice closed her eyes tight. She felt her old body again, that sixteen-year-old girl. Her legs hurt, and in between her legs, and she could hardly hold a breath in her lungs. Her cheek bled. She felt the hot wet fall of it on her neck and shoulder and breast. Her dress was torn and flapped against her legs, and her feet were bare but in her hand she gripped a knife, the knife he had so carelessly left to one side. On the end of the knife was a blue-green eye.

"I had his eye," she said, opening her own eyes again. "It shocked people, even the hard soldiers, and I had so much blood on me they weren't to know that it was almost all mine. He has men loyal to him. Not like the Walrus. Not men who only want money or the chance to do violence. Men who love him, though I don't understand why."

"They loved him, so they ran to him. That saved you," Hatcher said. "They wanted to know if he lived."

"There was a lot of blood on my hand, and on the knife," Alice said slowly. "The knife was his. He always carried it. As soon as they saw it, they thought he was dead."

His neck was arched back in his pleasure, and his eyes were closed. Her fingers closed around the hilt of the knife and arched around and she stabbed him in the back, over and over, and something hard and tough ripped under the blade. He opened his eyes, screaming, and she plunged the knife into the left one and pulled hard. There was blood all over, and he was still on top of her. She kicked and bucked until he was off, rolling on the mattress and holding his hand over his eye. He had another knife in his boot—he still wore his boots—and he slashed at her face as she rolled away onto the floor. She scrambled to her feet, holding the knife in her hand, afraid to let it go, and he was screaming after her. Everyone was running toward him, and she ran away. Hands tried to hold her but there was blood everywhere and she was slippery with it. She kept running and running, turning and ducking and twisting, and then somehow she was out in the street and they weren't following. She ran and ran and ran, and anyone who saw her turned away, for her face was wild and she was coated with blood and she was holding a knife with an eye on the end of it. She ran until she couldn't run anymore, until she was almost to the edge of the New City, and she dropped the Rabbit's knife into the river. The water curdled and steamed around it, so poisonous that it melted the blade and the hilt and the eye, and then it was gone, and Alice lay down by the river and slept.

"You remember it all now," Hatcher said, and it wasn't a question.

"Yes," she said. She was beyond weeping for the child she once was. "It is, more or less, what you would expect. Except for the part where I escaped. Nobody expected that."

The door at the bottom of the steps opened and a woman emerged. She spoke quietly to the soldiers, who disappeared inside. She was not the sort of woman Alice imagined seeing in a place like this. The girls who danced for hooting patrons in the Caterpillar's lair—that was the kind of woman she expected.

This woman was hunched with age or care, and her hair was the color of Hatcher's eyes, grey like iron. She wore a grey shawl over a grey dress, and walked in tiny steps. Altogether she gave the impression of an oversized mouse, and when she lifted her gaze to Alice, her eyes glittered out of a narrow lined face.

"Dor?" Alice said.

Of all the things she'd seen, this shocked her the most. Her friend, her young and pretty friend, was gone forever. They were both twenty-six, but Dor looked like a careworn grandmother. Her hands were knotted with protruding blue veins.

"He said you would come back. He's been waiting. This morning he woke and he told me that today was the day his Alice would return," Dor said. Her voice was just as ancient as the rest of her, and bitter. "Always his Alice, you are, despite what you did to him."

Alice walked slowly down the steps. She'd lost her cap and her jacket, and the little knife she carried was visible in the rope looped around her waist. She looked like what she was—a very tall girl with a scar on her face and short hair, not disguised as a boy anymore. She towered above Dor, whose eyes flashed as she glared up at her old friend.

"What right have you to be angry with me?" Alice asked. "You, who tried to sell me as though I belonged to you? You, who would have seen me eaten alive by a monster who wanted my magic?"

"You left me here," Dor said. "You escaped, but you left me here."

"As you would have done to me," Alice said.

She wished she could feel sorrow. She remembered playing with Dor from the time she was small, hiding behind her mother's rosebushes and giggling with secrets. This girl had been her constant companion, but she changed, and Alice had not seen it. Dor's reward had been the same fate she would have wished on Alice. There was only one thing she wished to know.

"Why?"

"After all this time, that is what you say?" Dor said. "Where is your anger?"

"I am not angry with you," Alice said. "I just wish to know why."

It was true. She wasn't angry. Dor had been punished. There was nothing Alice could do to make it worse.

"'Why' is a girl's question, and we are no longer girls," Dor said, and turned away. "He's waiting."

Just inside the door was a long wide hallway. On each side were the Rabbit's soldiers, standing at attention. Each held a weapon—a knife or a sword or an axe—and all of them watched Alice with eager, cruel eyes. They hated her, she realized, hated her for what she had done to their master.

Dor had ensured that they knew who Alice was, and Alice was certain that they would also make sure she did not escape the Rabbit's warren twice.

Hatcher smiled when he saw the men waiting to cut them down.

Dor shuffled ahead, her footsteps slow. Alice expected to be taken deep inside the Rabbit's lair, into the maze that had nearly trapped her once before. But Dor led them to the end of the main hall, to a large carved entry fit for a king, and inside they found the Rabbit.

Again, he was not as Alice expected.

*

In her memory he was strong and vital, his hands hard and bruising. This man could not have hurt her if he wanted.

His left eye was covered with a gaudy gold patch, decorated with emeralds and rubies. His body was shriveled, a memory of what it once was, and the large silk robe he wore could not hide this. He sat in a chair (*just like a throne*) in the center of the room. Alice was certain he could not move from it without help, and that it must have been her doing that made him so. When the knife plunged into his back, she had broken something, something that could not be repaired.

His ears were, in fact, long and white, as was the hair on his head. The backs of his hands were also coated in white fluff.

"Alice, my Alice," he said.

(*Pretty Alice*)

It wasn't even the same voice coming out of the same mouth. His face was heavily powdered, white as the hair and the ears. His one blue-green eye shone out of that pale face. This broken, shrunken creature was her nightmare?

They were the only four in the room, and the door was shut. There was nothing but the chair and bare walls and floor, the color of fresh snow.

"You've come back to me at last," he said. "And who is this you've brought with you? Nicholas?"

"What happened to your ears?" Hatcher said. He couldn't seem to stop staring at them. "They weren't like that before."

"One of Cheshire's potions," the Rabbit said. "He thought it would be amusing if I more closely resembled my name."

The Rabbit's tone told Alice that he did not find this as amusing as Cheshire.

"Where's Jenny?" Hatcher said.

"I thought you might want to discuss her," the Rabbit said, looking crafty.

"You broke your promise to me," Hatcher said.

"I made no promise," the Rabbit said.

"You did," Hatcher said, and there was no room for argument. "Now tell me where you sent her."

"Her beauty is legendary," the Rabbit said dreamily. "I have heard, often, from my friend in the East, and she has legions of admirers."

"Tell me his name," Hatcher said.

"No, I don't think so," the Rabbit said. "But I will tell you hers. They call her Sahar, and he tells me it means the time just before dawn, for her hair is like the night before the sunrise, and her eyes as cool as the moon."

"Her name is Jenny," Hatcher said.

"Not anymore. I wish we had some tea and cakes. Wouldn't that be lovely, Alice? So we could all have a tea party, like we did so long ago."

The Rabbit was behaving like a grandfather meeting his wayward grandchildren for the first time in many years. He held out his hands to Alice, who frowned at him.

"I think you're confused about why we have come," she said.

"Why, you've come to finish me off, have you not?" the Rabbit said, and his eye flashed. "Come to take vengeance for what was done to you. And Nicholas, I am certain, will ensure the job is done correctly. He has a way with axes."

Alice stared at the Rabbit, and then at Dor, who'd knelt at his side with her head bowed like a supplicant.

"You *want* me to kill you," she said slowly. "No one else will do it, and you've been waiting for me to return."

"I expected you to come blazing in with a sword and a halo of golden hair, like an avenging angel," the Rabbit admitted. "Instead you look rather underfed, and all your beautiful hair is gone, and you don't even have a sword with you at all."

"Where would I get a sword?" Alice asked.

"You're an enterprising girl," the Rabbit said. "If you want one, you would have it. Still, that knife you have will do the job nicely."

He tilted his head back and showed his throat, which was powdered like his face. Alice approached him then, though she did not take the knife from her waist. He watched her, his remaining eye slitted.

She reached her hand out and swiped her fingers down the side of his cheek, brushing away the powder.

All of his veins showed black underneath the skin, like cracking marble. Alice stepped back, staring. Her fingers felt burnt where they had touched him.

"Yes," he snarled, his face suddenly contorted with anger. "Do you see what you have done to me? Do you see what you have wrought? You left me a half-alive thing, magicless and broken. And now it is only right that you finish it."

"Magicless?" Alice asked. "I took your magic?"

"Of course you did, you stupid girl," he snapped. "That knife you stole was made by a Magician, and it draws power from those like us. I've hidden my weakness from the others all these years, but now it can be over. No one else has the courage to free me."

"You deserve no such courtesy from me," Alice said faintly, though she hardly heard her own voice coming out of her mouth. All she could hear was, *That knife you stole was made by a Magician*. "The knife. Hatcher, the knife."

Hatcher had his axe in his hand, ready to throw it if the Rabbit had moved when Alice approached him. "Which knife?"

"The knife for the Jabberwocky," she said. "The Magician's knife."

Hatcher looked from Alice to the Rabbit. "That was the knife you used on his eye."

She nodded.

"What happened to it?"

"I threw it in the river," she said. "It melted."

The Rabbit stared at her. "You threw a priceless Magician's artifact into the stinking river?"

"Yes," Alice said. "And now the Jabberwocky rampages through the City, and only the blade could stop him."

The Rabbit threw his head back again, and mirthless laughter poured forth. "Then it matters not if you will have mercy on me, for we are all dead."

Fear returned then, sweeping over her like the Jabberwocky's shadow. They'd had nothing to be afraid of as long as there was the hope of the blade. But that hope was gone, disappeared in the river ten years before, and none of them had known it. Not even the Jabberwocky.

"Why didn't he feel that his magic was destroyed?" Alice asked.

"For that matter, why didn't I?" the Rabbit asked. "My own power was inside that blade, and I never felt its loss."

His remaining eye narrowed, considering Alice.

"Perhaps the magic wasn't in the blade," he said, and his smile went very wide and dangerous. "Perhaps it went into the one who used it."

She saw his hope flare, a dangerous hope, the chance to recover what she had taken from him.

"Dor," the Rabbit said. "Go and fetch Samuel and Gideon for me."

Dor stood slowly, and it seemed to Alice that she was lost in a dream. She tilted her head at the Rabbit, moved close to them so that their faces nearly touched.

"Do you think you'll get your magic back from her?" Dor asked.

"Yes," the Rabbit said.

Alice thought the Rabbit assumed much. Hatcher would bury his axe in Dor's head before she crossed half the length of the room.

"If you do, what use would you have for me?" Her voice was flat, expressionless.

"I would still need you, of course, my little Dor-mouse," the Rabbit said. "You have cared for me all these years, kept my secret. If my power returns, you will be rewarded."

He was salivating now, the taste of his magic practically on his tongue. He would promise anything, say anything, Alice knew.

And Dor knew too.

She kissed him, and her arms went around his neck. No, Alice thought. Not her arms. Her hands.

Once upon a time it would have been impossible for Dor's little hands to surround his throat. Now they just fit, and she was stronger than the Rabbit. Much stronger.

His eyes bulged, and his hands drummed against the chair. Alice could not see Dor's face, only her hands, white with exertion.

When she was done, she turned to Hatcher and Alice. There was no sadness or relief, only expectation.

"Good-bye, Dor," Alice said.

"Good-bye, Alice," Dor said.

Hatcher swung his axe.

18

Dor's head rolled away across the floor. Fractures appeared in the walls, and the ground trembled. The men in the hall outside cried out in alarm.

"Is it like the Caterpillar?" Alice asked. "Now that the Rabbit is dead, his place will fall to pieces?"

Hatcher shook his head. "He had no magic left, remember? I think it's something else."

"The Jabberwocky," Alice said. "Hatcher, we don't have the blade. It's gone forever."

"But we don't need it," Hatcher said, and grabbed her hand, pulling her toward the door.

"What do you mean?" she said.

The trembling ceased, as if a giant creature had paused in its pursuit, and was perhaps devouring its prey.

"The magic we need is in you. The Rabbit said so," Hatcher said.

"The Rabbit said a lot of things," Alice said. "He didn't

tell you how to find Jenny, though."

This Alice regretted almost as much as the fatal accident of throwing away the magic blade. The Rabbit was the only person who knew Jenny's fate, and now he was gone.

"He told us enough," Hatcher said. "She's gone to the East, and her beauty is legendary, and she is called Sahar. It is enough to go on."

The East, the mysterious land of deserts and jinnis and magic lamps and rugs that flew through the air. It seemed like a dream, a dream that they would never fulfill because the shadow of the Jabberwock stood in their path as it always had.

"And how will we get there?" Alice asked. She did not say that Jenny was no longer a child, and that even if they found her she might not wish to see him again.

"You have no faith, Alice," Hatcher said. "You never have."

This was true. Hatcher always believed they would escape the hospital. He had prepared for that day. Alice never thought about what was around the bend, only what was before her. Perhaps that was how Dor had led her so easily to the Rabbit in the first place.

"You say you know you're a Magician, but you've never really believed it," Hatcher said. "I told you, and Bess told you, and Nell told you. The Caterpillar said it was true and the Walrus said he was going to eat your flesh ten years ago to take your power. But you still did not believe, not entirely.

"You knew Cheshire's story of the good Magician and his

lost friend. You set the roses afire, and you frightened the Jabberwocky away. The only reason you met me in the first place, through that mouse hole, was because Dor knew you were a Magician when you were a child, and sold you to the Rabbit. You must have shown something even then, though you don't recall it."

"Don't you think my parents would have noticed if I were a Magician?" Alice cried. "Don't you think I would have?"

Her mother's eyes, wide and frightened, twisting Alice's wrist.

She was five or six, playing in the garden on the first warm spring day, and she'd wanted some butterflies, but it was too early for butterflies. She danced in a circle, thinking of pretty butterflies, pink and yellow and blue and green and purple; she wished all the little buds of spring on the trees were butterflies, and suddenly there were butterflies everywhere. Their wings brushed her ears and her eyelashes and she laughed and laughed and laughed, until her mother came out of the house and grabbed her.

"What did you do, Alice?"

"Nothing!" She hadn't. She was dancing, and then there were butterflies.

"What did you do?" She'd never heard her mother like this before, desperate and afraid.

"I only wished," Alice said. "I wished for butterflies, and then there were. My wish came true."

"Alice," her mother said, and she turned her face from the butterflies as though the sight made her ill. "You must be careful when you wish. You never know who might be watching."

"Because a wish is a secret," Alice said. "It won't come true if you say it aloud."

"Yes, darling," her mother said, and pulled her tight in her arms. "You must never say your wishes aloud, or even think them out in the sunlight. Only at night, before you fall asleep. That's when you wish."

"Why didn't she tell me?" Alice said. "Why? Why did she let me go on thinking I was normal, that I was just like everyone else?"

"She wanted you to be," Hatcher said. "You said she was the one who told you the story when you were young. Your mother was likely a Magician too, but she learned to hide it."

It was hard to think of her beautiful, proper mother as a Magician. It was hard to think that if her mother had magic, she had denied that magic in herself; she had tried to crush it in her child.

The ground shook again, and an unearthly roar echoed through the hall. It was the sound Alice imagined a dragon would make, the sound of death on wings.

"How will we survive this?" she said. "Cheshire said only the blade could defeat the Jabberwock. Even if I have that magic inside me, I don't know what I would do with it. Wave my hands about? Say a spell? I don't know what to do. I don't know the words."

A wish has power.

Alice didn't know whether she heard the word inside her head, or whether it floated on the air. Hatcher's face twitched, so she suspected he might have heard it too.

"Cheshire?" Alice asked.

Wish.

"When I was a little girl my mother told me to only make my wishes in the night, when no one could see them," Alice said. "The night we escaped from the hospital I dreamed of fire. Hatch, I think I set the Jabberwocky free."

"You set us free as well," Hatcher said.

A red river running through the middle of the street, and bodies beyond counting lying still and silent.

"Is all the blood he spilled on my hands?" Alice asked. "Am I responsible?"

"He would have escaped sooner or later," Hatcher said. "I felt him rising. Alice, you cannot be responsible for what he is, or the choices he made when he was human."

"I can be responsible for my own," she said.

"Yes," Hatcher said. "You can. You can do what you were made for. You can destroy the Jabberwocky. Alice, you won't be alone."

Alice nodded, and tried not to think panicking thoughts. Cheshire said to wish. What should she wish? What could she wish? Wish to turn the Jabberwocky into a butterfly like she did those first tightly curled buds of spring? If she wished the Jabberwocky would disappear into a puff of smoke, would that happen?

She didn't think so. The Jabberwocky was a Magician, even if part of his magic was missing. He might just snatch them up and devour them before Alice had a chance to do anything.

They opened the door to see the rows of loyal soldiers still in place, and Alice sighed. She'd forgotten about them. There was only the Jabberwocky for her now, and they had no time for this nonsense.

Hatcher raised his axe, ready to slice his way through all of the Rabbit's pawns, but Alice shook her head. She wanted to try something first.

"I wish you would all go to sleep," she said.

Each man slumped in his place, eyes closed, and soon they were all dozing.

"I think we should kill them anyway," Hatcher said. "They were loyal to the Rabbit. When they wake up and find out what we've done they'll come after us."

"We didn't do it. Dor did."

"They won't know that. There will be a dead king and a dead queen, and we the last ones who saw them alive."

"We won't be in the City anymore," Alice said. *Or we might be in the Jabberwock's belly.* "It won't matter."

Hatcher shuffled in place. "I don't like leaving them unfinished."

"There will be plenty of blood for you outside," Alice said, recognizing his mood. "The Jabberwock, remember?"

"Can't I just . . . ?" Hatcher began.

"No."

She paused at the exit, clearing her mind. He was outside.

"Can you feel him, Hatch? I can," she said. "Like a great bird that fills up the sky with its wings."

"No," he said. "He's hidden from me now."

She opened the door, and climbed the steps.

A man stood in the middle of the street, an average-sized man wearing a black suit and a black cape and very shiny black shoes.

Alice turned to Hatcher then, and put her hand on his cheek, and let him see the love in her eyes.

"You're not alone, Alice," he repeated.

"Sleep until it's over," she said. "Sleep, little butterfly."

She caught him as he fell, and lowered him gently to the ground, his axe clutched in his hand.

Then she walked out to face the Jabberwocky. Her heart did not pound. Her breath did not pant. She felt apart from her body, lighter than air, as if she were in a dream and only watching it all.

His face was bright and curious. Something about it reminded Alice of Cheshire, and his eagerness to learn everything about them. His eyes were very black, though, black like a night without candles or stars.

She stopped when she was within arm's length of him, and cocked her head to one side.

"You aren't what I expected," she said.

"What did you expect?" he asked.

Alice gestured with her hands, holding them above her head. "Something bigger."

"More like a monster, then? I can do that if you like," he said.

She shook her head. "I don't prefer it. This is fine."

"You touched the blade that cut me," he said. "I can smell it upon you. I felt it when you drove me out."

"I didn't mean to do that," Alice said. "I only wanted you to leave Hatcher alone."

"Hatcher? The one who dreams of blood?" the Jabberwocky asked. "Yes, I liked him very much. His dreams kept me alive, made me stronger. I couldn't risk keeping the connection open with you about. Once you're gone he'll feed me for a good long while, and protect me when I'm at rest. We are kin, Hatcher and I, in our hearts."

"No," Alice said, and it was a "no" to all he had just spoken.

"You think you will stop me?" The Jabberwock laughed softly.

"You are not kin, you and Hatcher," Alice said. "He dreams of blood, yes, but not the blood of the innocent. He is more human than you or I will ever be."

"You're just like him, you know. Your grandfather of many greats past. You even look like him." He waved his hand around the shape of Alice's face. "Here, in the bones. It shows. And in the contempt you have for me in your eyes, those same cold blue eyes that he had."

His voice never changed but something underneath it became deep and dark, the warning growl of an animal.

"What else could I have?" Alice asked. Her eyes were wide and innocent. "You are a terrible creature, a thing that should not be."

"And who are you to decide what should and should not be?" the Jabberwocky said, and now Alice saw his shadow on the ground, stretching back over all the paths walked by her and Hatcher, covering the whole City in its blanket. "You are nothing but a child to the universe, a mote of dust drifting in an ocean of galaxies. Your magic is a small and puny thing compared to mine. I know the deepest secrets of the earth, and I know a power you could never understand."

"That is true," Alice said. "I could never understand you."

She would never comprehend the need to hurt those who never hurt her, the need to hate for the sake of hating. She never wanted to rule over others in fear. No, she would never understand the Jabberwocky.

Nor, it suddenly occurred to her, would he understand *her*. That was a power too—the power to be incomprehensible to great beings, beings that would expect her to behave just like them.

Wish.

"Give me your hand," she said, and held out her own.

The Jabberwocky narrowed his eyes in suspicion. "You will not be able to trick me thus; nor will you put me to sleep like your friend."

"I don't wish to trick you, or put you to sleep," Alice said, and it sounded true because it was true.

"You cannot force me out of existence," the Jabberwocky said. "My magic is stronger than yours."

"If you are so much more powerful than I, then you have nothing to fear," Alice said.

She knew then that he was frightened of her, deep in the well of his soul, for he did not understand her. She faced him with clear eyes and a clear heart, without trembling or crying. She was nothing like anyone he had met before.

She waited. He placed his hand in hers. His hands were cold, colder than snow in January, and Alice thought she could feel all the evil in the world trapped just under the surface of his skin.

"Now what will you do, little girl?" the Jabberwocky said.

She was dancing in her mind now, dancing through the garden on the first warm day of spring, wings brushing against her ears and landing in her hair, fluttering beauties just out of reach.

The rose pendant on her chest glowed, and the Jabberwocky squinted against its light.

"I wish you were a little purple butterfly in a jar," Alice said, her voice high and clear. "A very little jar without holes."

The Jabberwocky's eyes widened, and for one moment his hand squeezed convulsively on hers. She felt a tug deep in her chest, as though the bit of him that had accidentally been trapped inside her was trying to get out.

Then there was a scream, a scream not from the Jabberwocky's mouth but his shadow, a primal roar of pain and fury and disbelief, disbelief that such a simple child could have defeated him.

The wind blew Alice's hair and streamed dust in her eyes. It whipped into a vast dark cloud that started in the sky and ended a few inches from her feet.

Then the cloud was gone, and the shadow was gone, and all was silent.

A little green jar, just the size to fit in her pocket, rested near the toe of her boot. The top was sealed shut. Inside it a purple butterfly the size of her thumb beat its wings angrily against the glass.

Alice picked up the jar and held it at eye level. The Jabberwocky fluttered faster, throwing its body in her direction. She imagined his angry little eyes cursing her, though he was so small she could not see them.

"I'm going to put this jar in my pocket now," Alice said, and the Jabberwocky stilled. "I'm going to put it in my pocket and I am going to forget you. It will be a very long time before I recall that you are there. When I next take this from my pocket, your wings will no longer beat. And when I pass by a river or a lake, one with very deep water, I will throw this out into the middle and watch it sink, and never think on you again. One day I will have a daughter of my own, and I will not tell her the story of the good Magician who trapped the Jabberwocky. I will not tell her so that the world forgets your name, forgets you ever existed. It will be as if you never were in the first place."

At this the butterfly frantically resumed its activity. Alice closed her hand around the jar and pushed it deep inside the pocket of her pants. It felt heavier than a jar that size ought to, like it concealed something larger than a fluttering insect.

Alice sighed. Somehow things had not quite turned out as she expected. In her mind she would find the blade that defeated the Jabberwocky, and use it to vanquish him like that girl in the story who led all the soldiers. She'd thought Hatcher would be at her side, her white knight, defending her from the Jabberwocky's armies.

Life is not much like stories, Alice thought. Still, her life had a giant talking rabbit in it, and she didn't think that was very common.

She had lived. Hatcher had lived, and all of their enemies were vanquished.

And she was a Magician.

Applause broke out behind her, obscene in the silence. Alice knew who it was before she turned to face him.

Hatcher had woken, and was rubbing his head and frowning at the little man who stood a few feet from him. Alice could read the thoughts that ran across his face, and saw when he decided that chopping off Cheshire's head wasn't worth the trouble.

"Cheshire," Alice said. "I suppose I ought to thank you."

"No need for thanks, no need," Cheshire said.

"I said I ought to thank you. I didn't say I would."

Cheshire was not moved in the least by her rudeness. "That was just magnificent, my dear. Magnificent. And not at all what he expected, was it? Such an interesting solution."

There was that word again—"interesting." Alice hated being interesting.

"Just what was your stake in all this?" Hatcher asked. He joined Alice, giving her a sideways glance that told her she would pay later for putting him to sleep.

Cheshire patted his hands together, softly now. It was as if he couldn't stop clapping, couldn't contain his excitement.

"Why, you've given me the whole City on a platter," Cheshire said, spreading his arms wider than the grin plastered on his face. "What wonderful, wonderful children you are."

Hatcher stared. "You mean all the territories? You're taking them now?"

"Yes, yes," he said, and his eyes gleamed. "The Caterpillar and the Walrus and the Rabbit all fell down, like lovely little dominoes before the flick of her hand. Mr. Carpenter is nothing, nothing but a human, and he'll be gone soon too. Theodore is seeing to that. Oh, speaking of Theodore—he was not very happy with you about Theobald, Hatcher. But I convinced him it was all for the best. Yes, all for the best."

"Why did you send us into the maze?" Alice asked.

"Oh, just a little test. If you could survive the creature, then I was certain you'd be up to the task ahead," Cheshire said.

"What about the mermaid?" Alice said.

"Back swimming in her lake, as she ought to be," Cheshire said. "Her magic does not work on me, you know. It's how I was able to take her out and deliver her to the Caterpillar in the first place. She should have remembered that."

Alice wanted to be angry at Cheshire, but she was too tired. He'd always been interested in something besides their success; she'd known that. And he had helped—in his own strange way. Hatcher said Cheshire didn't deal in girls, so hopefully all those girls taken would be set free to better lives.

Still, enough was enough, and Cheshire was hardly a hero. If Alice and Hatcher died it would have made little difference to him. He would have found some way to benefit.

"I wish you would stop watching us from afar," Alice said, putting the emphasis on the first two words.

She heard a little popping noise then, like something had broken in the space between them.

Cheshire frowned. "That was not very fun of you at all, Alice. I've so enjoyed your adventures."

"Yes, but they are *my* adventures," Alice said. "And I think we will get along just fine without your assistance from now on."

"But so many exciting things to come! The quest for Hatcher's daughter!" Cheshire said. He sounded a little whiny now, like a child who'd been denied sweets.

"You'll have plenty to do," Alice said. "You won't have time to watch us."

She deliberately turned her back then, and started walking away. Hatcher joined her, tucking his axe away underneath his jacket.

Cheshire laughed softly behind them.

Alice couldn't help herself. She looked over her shoulder, and saw him fading away bit by bit, until all that remained was his wide, white smile, and then that was gone too.

Hatcher didn't speak for a long while. Alice waited for him, feeling she shouldn't try to explain her actions unless forced to do so.

"I suppose you thought I would distract you," Hatcher finally said.

"No," she answered. "I was afraid the Jabberwocky would take you."

He considered this, and then took her hand in his, squeezing it tight. "That I can understand."

She told him then of what happened while he slept. He asked to see the jar with the Jabberwocky inside, and Alice shook her head.

"I said I wouldn't take it out again until I'd forgotten about it, and then he would be dead. So I think it's like a promise, or a wish, or a magic spell. He has to stay there until I forget and remember again."

The City slowly woke up as they walked, people emerging from their homes and blinking as if seeing the sun for the first time. When they passed the square and crossed to the path where the Jabberwocky had wreaked death, they saw survivors loading bodies on carts.

"There will be a terrible burning," Alice said. "It will draw the attention of the ministers. They will have to help people here."

"They don't have to do anything, Alice, if they don't wish it," Hatcher said.

"*I* wish it," Alice said. "I wish the ministers would help clean up the Old City, give money and food and shelter to those that have lost theirs."

"You're getting quite dangerous with those wishes," Hatcher said. "I'd best not cross you, or you'll wish me right out of existence."

"No," Alice said. "I have only one wish, but it's a secret

wish, and I cannot speak it aloud."

I wish that you will love me forever, forever and always, until the end of time.

It was not a thing to say aloud, for a wish like that shouldn't be forced on the other. Alice was grown-up enough to know that. If he loved her, she wanted it to be because he wished it too.

He smiled then. "I have the same wish, and I'll keep it in my secret heart, just like you."

They reached the place where the tunnel led out of the City and slipped into the shack. Once inside, Alice hesitated.

"Should we lock the door? Block it somehow? Keep others from leaving the City?"

Hatcher considered. "It's Cheshire's territory now, so it's his problem. He's sure to plug up the hole soon. We should get away while we still can, and good luck to anyone else who stumbles onto the tunnels."

Yes, Alice thought. *Let as many escape as they can, if they can find this place.*

She could smell the promise of green grass and sunshine, and butterflies dancing in the wind as they entered the cave.

The footprints of the girls who'd passed before them were in the dirt, and the giant paw prints of Pipkin. Alice thought she heard their laughter far ahead. She smiled at Hatcher, and started to run, her laughter chasing theirs.

"Alice!" he called, and she heard him laugh too, and the pounding of his feet, nearly upon her. "What are you doing?"

She couldn't stop laughing, the happiness she had never hoped for overflowing in her heart. "Following the white rabbit, of course."

ABOUT THE AUTHOR

Christina Henry is a horror and dark fantasy author whose works include *The House that Horror Built*, *Good Girls Don't Die*, *Horseman*, *Near the Bone*, *The Ghost Tree*, *Looking Glass*, *The Girl in Red*, *The Mermaid*, *Lost Boy*, *Red Queen*, *Alice* and the seven- book urban fantasy Black Wings series.

She enjoys running long distances, reading anything she can get her hands on and watching movies with samurai, zombies and/ or subtitles in her spare time. She lives in Chicago with her husband and son. Follow her on Threads, Facebook and Instagram @authorchristinahenry, and on her website www.christinahenry.net.

ALSO AVAILABLE FROM TITAN BOOKS

RED QUEEN
CHRISTINA HENRY

The land outside of the Old City was supposed to be green, lush, hopeful. A place where Alice could finally rest, no longer the plaything of the Rabbit, the pawn of Cheshire, or the prey of the Jabberwocky. But the verdant fields are nothing but ash—and hope is nowhere to be found.

Still, Alice and Hatcher are on a mission to find his daughter, a quest they will not forsake even as it takes them deep into the clutches of the mad White Queen and her goblin or into the realm of the twisted and cruel Black King.

The pieces are set and the game has already begun. Each move brings Alice closer to her destiny. But, to win, she will need to harness her newfound abilities and ally herself with someone even more powerful—the mysterious and vengeful Red Queen...

PRAISE FOR THE SERIES
"A dark and deeply disturbing revisit of *Alice's Adventures in Wonderland*. Who *wouldn't* like it?" *Kirkus Reviews*

TITANBOOKS.COM

ALSO AVAILABLE FROM TITAN BOOKS

LOST BOY
CHRISTINA HENRY

There is one version of my story that everyone knows. And then there is the truth. Once I loved a boy called Peter Pan.

Peter brought me to his island because there were no rules and no grownups to make us mind. He brought boys from the Other Place to join in the fun, but Peter's idea of fun is sharper than a pirate's sword. He wants always to be that shining sun that we all revolve around. He'll do anything to be that sun. Peter promised we would all be young and happy forever.

Peter will say I'm a villain, that I wronged him, that I never was his friend.

Peter Lies.

"You'll never look at Peter Pan in the same way again"
The Guardian

TITANBOOKS.COM

ALSO AVAILABLE FROM TITAN BOOKS

THE HOUSE THAT HORROR BUILT

CHRISTINA HENRY

Single mom Harry Adams has always loved horror movies, so when she's offered a job cleaning for revered horror director Javier Castillo, she leaps at the chance. His forbidding Chicago mansion, Bright Horses, is filled from top to bottom with terrifying props and costumes, as well as glittering awards from his decades-long career making films that thrilled audiences and dominated the box office—until family tragedy and scandal forced him to vanish from the industry.

Javier values discretion, so Harry tries to clean the house immaculately and keep her head down—she needs the money from this job to support her son. But then she starts hearing noises from behind a locked door. Noises that sound remarkably like a human voice calling for help, though Javier lives alone and never has visitors. Harry knows that not asking questions is a vital part of keeping her job, but she soon finds that the house—and her enigmatic boss— have secrets she can't ignore…

"Henry's spooky tale has a scary face, but it has a heart of gold."
Gabino Iglesias for the *New York Times*

TITANBOOKS.COM

For more fantastic fiction, author events, competitions,
limited editions and more

VISIT OUR WEBSITE
titanbooks.com

LIKE US ON FACEBOOK
facebook.com/titanbooks

FOLLOW US ON TWITTER
@TitanBooks

EMAIL US
readerfeedback@titanemail.com